ACCLAIM FOR
JAMES PATTERSON'S HOTTEST SERIES!

PRIVATE GAMES

"EVEN IF YOU ARE NOT INTERESTED IN THE SUMMER GAMES, YOU WILL WANT TO READ THE BOOK, NOT ONLY FOR ITS THRILL-A-PAGE PLOTTING BUT ALSO FOR THE OPENING DAY SPECTACLE THAT'S ON DISPLAY...*PRIVATE GAMES* SHOWS BOTH PATTERSON AND SULLIVAN TO BE AT THE TOP OF THEIRS."

—BookReporter.com

"ANOTHER FAST-PACED, ACTION-PACKED THRILLER THAT WILL HAVE YOU NOT WANTING TO PUT IT DOWN UNTIL THE VERY LAST PAGE."

—ThePhantomParagrapher.blogspot.com

"[AN] EXCELLENT READ...THE WRITING IS BETTER, THE CHARACTERS MORE DEVELOPED, AND THE STORY MORE SUSPENSEFUL THAN MOST OF THE RECENT JAMES PATTERSON NOVELS...LOOK FOR *PRIVATE BERLIN*."

—TheMysteryReader.com

"PATTERSON, HE OF SIX DOZEN NOVELS AND COUNTING, HAS AN UNCANNY KNACK FOR THE TIMELY THRILLER, AND THIS ONE IS NO EXCEPTION...A PLEASANT ROMP."

—*Kirkus Reviews*

"THIS ONE IS SET UP WITH SHORT CHAPTERS THAT YOU CAN'T HELP FLY THROUGH...I REALLY HAVE COME TO ENJOY THE PRIVATE SERIES AND HOPE THIS SERIES CONTINUES FOR A LONG TIME."

—AlwayswithaBook.blogspot.com

PRIVATE: #1 SUSPECT

"BETWEEN THE COVERS OF THE FIRST TWO BOOKS (*PRIVATE* AND *#1 SUSPECT*) IS SOME OF JAMES PATTERSON'S BEST WORK TO DATE...A PLOT THAT CONTAINS SUBSTANCE WITHOUT SACRIFICING READABILITY AND IS INHABITED BY CHARACTERS WHO ARE SYMPATHETIC AND MULTI-DIMENSIONAL. PATTERSON AND PAE-TRO'S CONCEPT AND EXECUTION IS FLAW-LESS...And if someone doesn't latch on to these novels for a television drama, they should find employment in another industry. Jump on now."

—BookReporter.com

PRIVATE

"A QUICK READ WITH SHORT CHAPTERS AND LOADS OF ACTION...DESTINED TO BECOME ANOTHER SUCCESSFUL SERIES IN THE JAMES PATTERSON ARSENAL...If you are a Patterson fan, you will not be disappointed...Jack Morgan is a great protagonist...Bring on even more PRIVATE."

—TheMysteryReader.com

"A FUN AND ENJOYABLE READ...PATTERSON LETS THE READER FEEL LIKE THEY ARE RIGHT THERE IN THE ACTION...It's such a treat knowing there is so much more to explore about [these] characters...He certainly set things up for some explosive action in future novels."

—CurlingUpbytheFire.blogspot.com

"*PRIVATE* MIXES ACTION, MYSTERY, AND PERSONAL DRAMA TO CREATE A HIGHLY READABLE AND ENTERTAINING EXPERIENCE. If this first volume is any indication, Patterson and Paetro may well be on their way to rivaling—and possibly surpassing—the popularity of their Women's Murder Club series."

—BookReporter.com

THE PRIVATE NOVELS

Private Games (with Mark Sullivan)

Private: #1 Suspect (with Maxine Paetro)

Private (with Maxine Paetro)

A complete list of books by James Patterson is at the back of this book. For previews of upcoming books and more information about James Patterson, please visit his website or find him on Facebook or at your app store.

Private London

James Patterson
AND
Mark Pearson

GRAND CENTRAL
PUBLISHING

LARGE PRINT

Grand Central Publishing Edition

This Grand Central Publishing edition is published by arrangement with Random House UK, 20 Vauxhall Bridge Road, London SW1V 2SA.

Grand Central Publishing
Hachette Book Group
237 Park Avenue
New York, NY 10017

www.HachetteBookGroup.com

Printed in the United States of America

RRD-C

First Grand Central Publishing Edition: December 2012
10 9 8 7 6 5 4 3 2 1

Grand Central Publishing is a division of Hachette Book Group, Inc. The Grand Central Publishing name and logo is a trademark of Hachette Book Group, Inc.

The Hachette Speakers Bureau provides a wide range of authors for speaking events. To find out more, go to www.hachettespeakersbu reau.com or call (866) 376-6591.

LCCN: 2012944629
ISBN 978-1-4555-2815-8 (hardcover)
ISBN 978-1-4555-1555-4 (paperback)
ISBK 978-1-4555-2242-2 (large print)

For Lynn, as ever, with love—M.P.

Acknowledgments

Many thanks to James Patterson for taking me on the roller coaster, and to Susan Sandon and Paul Sidey for making sure I had my belt buckled!—M.P.

Introduction

WHEN THE RICH and famous are in trouble, their first call isn't 911. They call my team at Private. In the handful of years since my father left me the agency—a first and last attempt at reconciliation from his prison cell—Private's reputation has taken off. And with demand from elite clientele all around the world, we've opened branches globally, from Los Angeles to New York, Paris to Tokyo. But it's the London office that always seems to have its share of some of the highest profile cases the firm investigates.

It was the Private London office that took down the madman who threatened London's Olympic Games. But before that, before the tragedies that took place during that case, Private London had an especially challenging case on their hands. For me, this case was deeply personal, and it involved a young woman by the name of Hannah Shapiro.

I met Hannah before I was even running Private, three days after her thirteenth birthday. I helped to rescue her from a kidnapping that had quickly turned tragic. Afterward, the girl had a rough time of it. Then, she was twenty and headed to London for three years of school, and I had to do everything in my power to make sure she was safe. With a million dollars on her head, I needed to put her under the protection of someone we could trust. The only man for the job was the head of the London Private International office, Dan Carter.

This was back in 2010, but it's only now, a few years later, that I feel enough distance to be able to talk about it. It's strange, though. In so many ways it still feels like just yesterday. The day that I burst through that door to find a thirteen-year-old girl whose life would never be the same.

Jack Morgan

Part One

Part One

Chapter 1

9 April 2003—Los Angeles, USA
The day everything changed.

Morning

HANNAH SHAPIRO WAS having a wonderful day.

Presents and mimosas at breakfast. Just the one glass—but a thirteenth birthday needed marking, didn't it? She would become bat mitzvah—a Daughter of the Commandments—this coming Shabbat. But Saturday was three days away!

"Come on, darling, take a sip..." Jessica,

her mother, said, her southern accent sweet and musical. "You'll love it. It tastes just like an angel's tears in a glass."

And so she had. Even though she didn't like the taste of alcohol, Hannah loved her mom more than anything in the world and wouldn't think of disappointing her. She sipped, then half spluttered, half laughed. "I've got bubbles in my nose."

"That's what you pay the good money for, sweetheart!"

Hannah laughed with her.

It was a perfect morning. The only thing missing was her father. "It's a shame Daddy couldn't make it back last night," she said.

"It's government business. He'd have been here if he could, darling."

"I know."

"And he promised he'll try to make the three o'clock flight. Even if he has to fight the chief of staff to do it!" her mother said, hugging Hannah and ruffling her hair.

Hannah giggled again. She couldn't imagine her father fighting with anyone.

"Come on, honey. Make a birthday wish on your first champagne."

Hannah thought about it. Her best friends from school, Sally Hunt and Tiffany Wells, had already turned fourteen. Sally had been given a polo pony and Tiffany a diamond watch from Cartier. Both their parents had been divorced more than once.

Hannah looked at the family portrait hanging over the fireplace. Her father and mother so much in love, Hannah in the middle.

She gazed up at her mother, couldn't believe how heartbreakingly beautiful she was. Couldn't believe that her father could bear to spend so much time away from her.

So Hannah took another sip of her mimosa, looked again at the family portrait and made her wish: *Catch that plane, Daddy!*

Afternoon

Crossing Rodeo Drive in Beverly Hills, Hannah took her mother's hand.

They were both laden with packages, bags

from all the best stores hanging off their shoulders.

"We have done very well with the shopping," said Hannah, grinning broadly.

"Daddy said to make it up to you for missing breakfast."

"He's doing a very good job."

"So far. But the day is young."

"Yes."

"And it's good we have the time to ourselves. Daddy doesn't do shopping."

Hannah chuckled. "I know."

Jessica Shapiro winked at her. "But your mother, darling... is a professional!"

Moments later, she fetched out the keys to the Mercedes convertible they were approaching in the underground car park.

She looked up, startled as two men suddenly appeared. They wore black hoods.

Hannah's scream was cut short as a rough hand covered her mouth.

"Tell the little bitch to shut it now! Or I'll blow her brains halfway across California."

Jessica nodded. Numb with fear. Unable to

speak. Staring terrified at Hannah, she pleaded with her daughter with her eyes to be still.

Three Days Later

Hannah wanted to scream again. Scream till her throat bled as she watched what was happening to her mother.

But she couldn't. Duct tape had been wrapped around her head, sealing her mouth shut painfully. Her nostrils bulged wide, as much with fear as the need to suck oxygen into her burning lungs.

She squeezed her eyes shut, images of memory flashing, snapshots of the horror that had led to this moment.

The black-suited hooded men grabbing them. The crook of an elbow jammed tight against her mouth. Throwing her into the back of a windowless van.

Forcing her down on the cold metal floor. Tying her hands with tape. Then her mouth, her feet.

The vehicle moving, bouncing her hard

against the unforgiving side. Tires squealing. Her own muted screams. A dark sack dropped over her head.

Darkness. The sound of her mother sobbing nearby. A mewing, hurt sound.

Her bladder voiding. The awful shame of it.

A world of hurt later.

Her mother lay naked on a bed. Her hands above her head tied cruelly to the headboard.

One of the men was on top of her mother now. Grunting as he raped her. Feeding on her pain, her humiliation, her helplessness. It didn't take long. He stood up and gestured to the other hood leaning against the far wall.

"You want a go now?"

"Not on mommy I don't," said the second man flatly. "I like my meat fresher."

Hannah whimpered, horrified as she realized what he meant.

He raised the gun that he held loosely in his right hand, tightening a silencer on the end of its barrel. Then he pointed it at Hannah's mother.

"Your husband did this to you, not me. He wouldn't pay the ransom."

Hannah shook her head violently, begging

with her eyes, screaming out to her father as she had been doing since the horror had begun. Why hadn't he paid them the money? Why hadn't he saved them? Where was he?

The gunman's eyes were so cold. "He had his chance," he said simply.

Then he pulled the trigger. He shot Jessica Shapiro twice. The shots made a sound like a nail gun.

"Can't say we didn't give daddy a chance," said the hood.

Hannah slumped back in the chair, reeling. Her system shutting down in shock. The grip of fear holding her heart so tight that she couldn't breathe.

The man holstered his gun and undid his trouser belt. "Untie the girl," he said.

At that moment, a lifetime too late, the door to the loft was smashed off its hinges.

As the gunman turned, a high-velocity bullet punched through his forehead, knocking him off his heels. His head exploded.

The sound of the shot still rang deafeningly in the air as his dead body slid down the wall.

The other kidnapper took a step toward his partner before three shots from the semi-automatic weapon cut him down. He crashed to his knees, tumbled sideways, dead before he hit the floor.

A fine mist of red seemed to hang in the air for a moment and then a tall man stepped through it, lowering the gun that he was holding in a two-handed grip.

He looked down at the girl with desperately sad, apologetic eyes.

"You're safe now, Hannah," said Jack Morgan.

Chapter 2

Seven years later. Somewhere over the Atlantic.

MY NAME IS Dan Carter. I run the London office of Private International.

At that moment I was sitting in first class on my way to New York to meet with my boss. I'm ex-military—ex-Royal Military Police, to be specific. Late thirties. Shade over six foot, dirty blond hair, blue eyes; 185 pounds in weight. I can run the mile in under five minutes and bench-press 240. I could build up to more but I like the way my suits fit me just fine. In my line of work it's not all about brute strength. I don't scare easily.

But I don't like flying.

"Sorry, what did you say?"

"I said would you like another drink, sir?" asked the air hostess. She had a smile that could have lit the pitch at Wembley Stadium but I wasn't even registering it. Like I said, I'm not a good flyer. The man I was on my way to meet was. But then, he was an ex-military pilot. Served his time in Afghanistan. Jack Morgan who owned Private worldwide. Hell—Jack Morgan *was* Private!

The air hostess moved away and I took another small sip of beer. I didn't want to overdo it. Not good form, turning up drunk for an important meeting. I didn't know if my boss was well known for giving people a second chance—somehow I doubted it—but I didn't plan to find out.

One of the reasons he'd hired me was because I had rescued an American soldier over in Iraq. Saved his life. I don't talk about it, but he had known the real story behind it. Suffice to say I wasn't following standing orders—could probably have been court-martialed and dishonorably discharged.

Might have been better that way. Eventually

I was invalided out and had to ride a wheelchair for a while. Jack Morgan had checked my references pretty thoroughly. Going so far as to talk with the injured young GI I had carried through a kill zone to medical help.

The fact that I had killed two other American soldiers who had shot him and were raping a suspected bomb maker's wife didn't faze him. He knew why, even if the people who gave me a medal for the rescue didn't. And I sincerely hope they never did. But Jack Morgan approved, he knew the circumstances and he wanted to have a man capable of making his own decisions heading up his London operation. Getting the job done—whatever it took—and living with the consequences.

I guess I had proved that I could do that. To him, at least.

For me, though, things are never as black and white as I would have liked. Moral certitude is something that gets blown away pretty damn quickly when you take the King's shilling and march overseas to another man's war.

Or fly.

Like I was doing.

Chapter 3

ON THE STEADY tarmac of the JFK runway, I resisted the urge to drop to my knees and kiss the ground.

People were watching, after all, and small children were running ahead of me laughing and giggling as if they hadn't been through seven hours of ordeal. Too young to realize the dangers, I rationalized, and headed for the airport entrance.

An hour later and I was waiting in the Blue Bar in the Algonquin, sipping on a chilled Peroni. I'd been treating the woman serving behind the bar to some of my wit but it was like bouncing pebbles off concrete. But suddenly she smiled.

Not at me. She was looking at the entrance

and the man who was walking up to join me at the bar.

Jack Morgan.

He's used to it. Let me tell you, Jack is a man to have as a friend not an enemy—but you don't want him by your side if you're in a bar looking to meet a nice lady for a dance.

"Dan," he said, smiling, and stuck his hand out.

"Jack," I said back and shook his hand. He was about an inch taller than me but built bigger. Could have played pro ball, one of his colleagues once told me and I didn't doubt it. His uncle owned the Raiders for a start which probably would have helped.

He smiled at the woman behind the bar. "I'll take my usual, please, Samantha," he said to her.

"Coming right up, Mister Morgan."

She flashed her dentistry again. That's something the Americans are definitely world class in. Teeth.

"I appreciate you coming out here, Dan."

I turned back to Jack and shrugged. "You're the boss."

"You're the boss of London. I guess you're wondering why I needed you for a simple baby-sitting job."

"I am a little curious," I admitted. "Couldn't someone from the New York office have brought her over? We could have met her at the airport."

"The truth is," he replied, "there's nothing simple about this case."

Chapter 4

"WHAT DO YOU know about Hannah Shapiro?"

"Nothing at all. Your assistant said you'd fill me in, just told me to meet you here."

"Good. This is clearly on a need-to-know basis. Safer that way."

Jack took the drink from the bar lady and laid his briefcase on the counter. Popping open the locks. "Apart from her first name, she has a completely new identity—surname, passport. Everything."

"Witness-protection program?"

"Something like that."

"Only not government-sanctioned?"

"In fact it is."

"She's how old?"

"Hannah is twenty."

"And I'm taking her back to England?"

"You are."

"For how long?"

"Three years, Dan."

I looked at him quizzically and took a sip of beer. Then nodded. "Long enough to get a degree, I guess?"

Jack Morgan nodded, pleased. "You catch on fast."

"Where's she going to be studying?"

"Chancellors."

I nodded right back at him. One of the oldest, one of the best. I looked down at the documents. Money was clearly not a problem. Private didn't come cheap—even if it was for just a hand-holding job on a flight over the Pond.

"This isn't just a hand-holding exercise, Dan."

I fought the urge to react. "It's not?"

"She's extremely valuable cargo. I need an eye on her the whole time she's over there in England. Looked after discreetly."

"Hard to be discreet if she goes round

like Madonna with a crew of bodyguards the whole time."

"Indeed. Less of a bodyguard, more of a companion. Let us know if she starts falling in with the wrong kind of crowd. Discreetly. Eyes and ears."

"So discreet even Hannah herself doesn't know about it?"

"Right again."

"When's her course start?"

"September."

I took a sip of my lager. "I might need some strings pulling."

"Way ahead of you." Jack nodded at the briefcase. "I've spoken to the dean of admissions."

"What's she going to be reading?"

"Psychiatry."

I nodded thoughtfully again. "That could work."

"She's had some issues in the past that I can't talk about. Maybe this will help her deal with that."

"And we make sure she has the space to do so."

"Her father is a major client of ours, Dan. Seven figures major. So she's important to us."

"What does he do?"

Jack looked at me with a small quirk of a smile. "He pays the bills."

"Like you said. *Need-to-know basis.*"

"You got it, bubba." He clicked his glass against mine and drained it. "Okay. Let's go meet the million-dollar baby."

Chapter 5

I HAD EXPECTED the precious cargo I was going to be babysitting to be just that.

West Coast precious. Serious money, serious *Valley* attitude. I had her pictured pretty clearly in my mind's eye—young, tanned and beautiful.

She was young, I got that much right at least. Looked even younger than she actually was.

Hannah's hair was mousy brown, tied back. She wore tortoiseshell glasses, a simple skirt and blouse with a cardigan, flat shoes. I don't know the name of the geeky girl from Scooby Doo, but she was like a thinner version of her without the confidence. Maybe a taller Ugly Betty. No makeup discernible to my eye, and my eye was pretty good in that respect. Nervous.

Hannah Shapiro looked like she wouldn't say boo to a waddling duck, let alone a goose.

"Hi, I'm Dan," I said. "Dan Carter." I held out my hand.

She shook it with her own small, delicate hand but didn't say a word or make eye contact.

Maybe it was down to the confident air of masculine authority I exude. Maybe—but she looked as though a strong wind could knock her over. If she was going to be studying psychiatry I was surmising she had ambitions for the research side of the business. I couldn't see her as a practitioner, with the couch and the reassuring voice and the leading questions. You had to be comfortable around people to do that kind of work.

Perhaps she was right to be nervous—she was standing next to Del Rio, after all.

Del Rio, one of Jack Morgan's right-hand men from the West Coast office. He'd done four years' hard time at the state's pleasure, and looked perfectly capable of doing so again. But he was on our side of the law nowadays, if not exactly working within it.

But that was the whole point of Private, after all. We weren't constrained by the same rules and regulations that restricted our uniformed counterparts. That was how we earned our money. And if half the rumors I had heard about Del Rio were true, he was more than willing to take the law into his own bare hands—take it with lethal consequences.

I held my hand out and shook his. If the girl's grip was feather light, this guy had a grip like an anaconda. Del Rio nodded. He didn't say anything either but I don't think it was from a lack of self-confidence. I don't think you could dent his self-confidence with anything short of an oak pickaxe handle.

"Dan will take care of you now, but if you ever need to speak to me you've got my number, right?" said Jack Morgan to the girl, who still seemed more interested in her feet than in anything else.

"Yeah, Jack," she said. "Thanks." Then she looked up and smiled. She had a nice smile.

"Anytime, night or day." Jack slapped me on the back. "Take good care of her, Dan. I'm counting on you."

"You got it," I said, falling into the native lingo. I turned to the young woman. "We good to go?"

See.

"Sure," she replied. I didn't get a smile but figured it was just a matter of time. A six-hour flight is plenty of time to get to know people. I'd break her in under four, I reckoned. The old Dan Carter charm. They should put it in a bottle.

Chapter 6

A COUPLE OF hours later I sighed an inward breath of relief and undid my seat belt.

It took a couple of tugs. I turned to look at the young woman next to me who was effortlessly undoing hers, her attention never wavering from the e-book she was reading.

I had let Hannah Shapiro have the window seat and she had pulled the blind down, which had suited me just fine. A little bit of turbulence had been predicted and the fasten-seat-belt sign had lit up. I had got mine on a lot quicker than it took to get it off. Luckily the threatened turbulence hadn't arrived!

I craned my head to look at the book that

Hannah was engrossed in. "What are you reading?" I asked her.

She didn't look up. "*The Beautiful and the Damned*," she said.

"*Tender is the Night* is my favorite novel," I said.

She looked up then, surprised. "Really?"

"Really. And I know what you're thinking."

"And what's that?"

"That a big man has no time really to do anything but just sit and be big."

There was a slight crack in the corner of her mouth. It might even have been a smile.

"F. Scott Fitzgerald?"

"The same."

"*Tender is the Night*—my mother's favorite book."

"Are you going to miss her?"

"I already do. She died, Mister Carter."

"I'm sorry to hear that."

"It was a long time ago. I was a child."

"What happened?"

"I grew up."

I decided not to press the point—Hannah clearly didn't want to talk about it. Looking at her it seemed to me that whatever had happened it hadn't been so long ago. She might have been twenty but she still looked like a child to me.

"Losing a parent is never easy," I said gently. "No matter how old you are."

"Are your parents alive, Mister Carter?"

"My father died a few years back. My mother is still with us, thank God."

She looked at me unblinking for a moment, as if searching for something in my eyes.

"You should thank God indeed. You must cherish her, Mister Carter," she said finally. "There is nothing in life more precious than your mother."

"I do," I said, feeling a little guilty. I hadn't spoken to my mother in over a week.

Hannah nodded as if my answer satisfied her.

"It was cancer," she said quietly. "There was nothing they could do."

"I'm sorry," I said again.

She shook her head. "It wasn't anybody's fault, was it?"

I didn't reply.

"My father is a scientist, did you know? Extremely rich. Extremely clever. He couldn't do anything, either."

I nodded. She was right. Death just came at you sometimes. Sideways, from behind, head-on like a high speed train. And whichever way it came at you there was nothing you could do about it. I knew that better than most.

"My father gave Mom a first-edition copy of *Tender is the Night* on their twentieth wedding anniversary. She treasured it like it was the most valuable thing in the world to her."

"Maybe it was..." I paused for a moment. "After you, I should imagine."

And got a smile this time. A sad one, though.

"When she went it was like the light had gone out of the world, Mister Carter. All the warmth."

"Call me Dan, please."

Hannah didn't seem to be listening, lost in her own memories. "I feel sometimes that I'm still walking in the shadows, waiting for dawn," she said.

I thought of my mother and my dear departed dad and I knew how she felt. "The dawn does come," I said. "Eventually it always does come."

"Hope is the feathered thing."

"Emily Dickinson."

"You are a man full of surprises, Mister Carter."

I let the *mister* ride and held my hand out. "It's Dan, remember?" I said.

"I certainly do," she replied, shaking my hand and meeting my eyes this time and holding the grin. I smiled back at her myself. I was ahead of schedule.

"I shouldn't have told you my dad was a scientist," she said.

"That's okay. I know how to keep a secret. Kind of goes with the job."

"I guess so. I didn't know they had private detectives in England. I thought it was all bobbies and police boxes."

"And some of us."

"Are you ex-police?"

"Royal Military Police. Redcaps, we call them."

"You served overseas, then?"

"I did."

"Like Jack Morgan?"

"Jack was in Afghanistan. I was in Iraq."

"So what made you leave the military?"

I looked at Hannah for a moment or two before replying.

"It's too long a story for this flight," I said. She seemed to accept that and returned to her novel.

I closed my eyes and leaned back, the memory of that day flashing into my mind as clearly as though it had been yesterday.

The pain every bit as fresh. Remembering.

I didn't know it at the time but it turned out that Hannah and I had a lot more in common than I thought.

Chapter 7

9 April 2003. Baghdad City, Iraq.

THERE WERE FOUR of us in the jeep that afternoon.

Three men, one woman. One mission accomplished. Operation Telic. Signed, sealed, delivered. The end of the war.

At least, it felt like that. We were on our way to check into some reported post-conflict celebrations that were maybe getting a little rowdy. We couldn't blame the boys—and had no intention of any strong-arm stuff. Enough people had been hurt as it was. Enough bodies sent home to be buried way before their time.

You couldn't blame the lads for having a drink or two. Letting off a little steam. If you couldn't celebrate today—then when could you?

The sun was shining as it had been every day since I'd started this tour of duty. But even that seemed different somehow. A brighter, cleaner, excoriating light. I knew that was nonsense but it felt that way.

The excitement in the air was certainly palpable. I hadn't felt anything like it since I'd been a very small child and my whole street had turned out for a party to celebrate the Queen's silver jubilee. That had been a hot, glorious day too.

The Jesuit poet Gerard Manley Hopkins once wrote some lines: "*The world is charged with the wonder of God. It will flame out, like shining from shook foil.*"

Well, God's grandeur wasn't evident around us then, truth to tell. We were in a particularly devastated area on the western outskirts of the city. Blown-up buildings left, right and center, their roofs and top floors shattered and cracked like a scattering of ruined teeth. The scars of incendiary bombs and smoke and ash and wreckage strewn all around.

The city had been literally smashed apart. But what was in the air that day was hope. Hope—maybe that was what God's grandeur really was all along. Because without hope what do you have? The three other people in the jeep with me all had fixed grins on their faces.

In the front passenger seat was Captain Richard Smith. He was in his thirties, a husband, a father, my superior officer and a man I would have followed into the very fires of hell. And sometimes in the last few weeks it had felt as though that was just where we'd been.

Beside him at the wheel was Lance Corporal Lee Martin, in his twenties. An irrepressible practical joker, a man who never had a bad word to say about anyone and would give you the last pound in his pocket.

Sitting by me in the back was my fellow sergeant, Anne Jones. Cropped blonde hair, could drink pretty much any man in the unit under the table and beat most of them at arm wrestling—but had a secret passion for the romantic novels of Catherine Cookson. I'd caught her reading a copy of *The Cinder Path* one day and she had threatened to cut off my manhood with a rusty knife if I told anyone about it.

Each one of us had a smile on our faces as we bumped along the uneven track through the bomb-blasted area. And it wasn't just to do with the sun beating down and the banter and jokes as though we were on our way to a barbecue. It was do with the sense of achievement. A sense of closure.

Had I been consulted I would have said that I was against us ever coming to Iraq in the first place, but it wasn't my place to say so and I was certainly never asked for an opinion. I was in the service. I did what I was told. That was what being in the army meant.

What felt so good that day was knowing that it was all over. Finally. There would be a clean-up operation for sure, but the armies had done their part. The weapons of mass destruction would be found now. No one had any real doubt about that—not on our side, at least.

The combined forces of mainly American and British troops had brought down a despotic regime. Justice was going to be seen to be done, finally, for the long-suffering people of this blighted land.

I looked across to my right where Sergeant Jones was flicking through some photos she had taken on a small digital camera. She paused at one photo and zoomed in a little. The huge twelve-meter-high statue of Saddam Hussein, erected in 2002 as a celebration of his sixty-fifth birthday, being pulled down by U.S. troops in Baghdad's Firdus Square.

She had photographed it as it was being broadcast live on the TV of a small coffee bar, the set on the wall dwarfing the counter it was mounted behind. She had caught the statue mid-descent and the image was surprisingly clear.

An iconic picture. Countless hundreds like it no doubt flying round the world news, the World Wide Web. It was one of those moments in time, I thought, when everything changes. The Berlin Wall coming down. Armstrong walking on the moon. Kennedy being shot.

The fact that it had happened right across from the Palestine Hotel where the world's reporters had been stationed didn't even occur to us at the time, or the fact that there didn't seem to be huge numbers there celebrating the fact.

U.S. tanks circled the area, and rightly so: sniper fire had already stopped Marine Lieutenant Tim McLaughlin from raising an American flag the first time he had tried to do it. The war might have been over but not all the combatants knew that yet. Corporal Jones closed the camera and smiled again, shielding her eyes as she looked up at the sun.

9 April 2003, the day everything changed.

"It's going to be another scorcher," Anne said, surprising no one, as the jeep bounced in the road and the landmine buried beneath it detonated and exploded in a white-hot burst of pain and light and death.

Chapter 8

I FELT AS if I had been put in a sack and kicked around the locker room by the full linebacker defensive of the Miami Rangers.

I could feel the harsh sand clogging my nostrils, the flayed skin of my cheeks hot. My head throbbed like the worst hangover imaginable.

My eyes were screwed shut and I couldn't bring myself to open them. I didn't dare. I was terrified of what I might see. I could hear a low moaning sound like that of a whimpering animal and it took me a moment or two to realize that it was me who was making the noise.

I blew out a deep, ragged breath and finally opened my eyes.

The sunlight skewered them. Searing needles of pain stabbing into them. I closed them again till the pain receded.

I waited a few moments, breathing deeply, and then, shielding my eyes with my hand, I opened them again.

I was lying on my side by a burned-out old Volvo estate that I remembered passing before the road bomb had exploded underneath us. I put my arm across my forehead to shield my eyes further from the blinding light. My whole body protested against the slightest movement. Nothing felt broken, though, as I rolled onto my hip and looked across the street.

Some fifteen feet away the hulk of our jeep was pouring thick black smoke into the blue sky like a distress signal being sent way too late.

Certainly far too late for the young driver. His right hand stretched toward me as though begging for help. His eyes lifeless as a fly crawled across his face.

Further out in the road lay Sergeant Jones. Only moments ago she had been celebrating the downfall of Saddam Hussein. Now she was as motionless as the toppled dictator's statue. Her neck twisted at an impossible angle. Dead on the streets, killed by the same regime she herself had played a part in overthrowing. Dead before the new era she had wanted for the troubled country had even begun.

I dragged the back of my sleeve across my eyes and squinted into the sun again as I scanned back and forth around the jeep. There was no sign of my CO.

I levered myself clumsily up on one knee, wincing as the pain spiked through me again. My body was going to be black and blue with bruises, I guessed. But at least I was alive. Miraculously—I was still alive.

I took a breath and stood up. I regretted it immediately. Gasping in agony as my ankle gave way. I fell sideways—part instinct, part simply collapsing—at the same time as the shot rang out. A single sharp crack.

A fraction of a second later the bullet

slapped into my left arm, hitting it just below the shoulder. Spinning me round and dropping me back to the ground like a tenpin nicked on a split.

I winced and clamped a hand to the wound. I shouldn't have been surprised. Standard procedure to keep a man behind to pick off the loose pieces the bomb hadn't dealt with, and to take pleasure in their explosive handiwork.

"Keep down, Carter!" shouted my CO from somewhere behind the ruined jeep. "The shooter's in the building behind that Volvo," he added somewhat unnecessarily. I held my hand to my wounded arm—I already had that particular intel. I snapped open the holster on my belt and drew out my service revolver.

"Just stay where you are," Richard Smith called out again. "He's got you in his sights."

"Sir!" I shouted back and craned my head up to see over the top of the vehicle.

Another bullet thudded heavily into the metal of the car and I dropped down to the ground again. Captain Smith fired a shot back at the sniper—he was in a covered position in a burned-out shell of a house.

Always listen to your commanding officer— don't think about it, just do what he says. Pretty much summed up what they'd drummed into us at boot camp before I'd specialized with the RMP. Stay where you are, he'd said. Certainly seemed like good advice just then.

Until Sergeant Anne Jones moved her head.

Chapter 9

I ROLLED ONTO my side again and hoisted myself up.

Stretching out my good arm, I pushed the revolver over the top of the wrecked Volvo and fired a shot in the general direction of the insurgent sniper.

For God's sake, didn't these people know the war was over?

An immediate hail of bullets rocked the Volvo. I was glad that whoever it was that had me locked in his sights wasn't carrying a rocket-propelled-grenade launcher.

"What in the name of holy Christ are you up to, Carter?" my CO bellowed.

"Anne, sir," I replied. "I saw her move."

"Shit!"

There was no response for a moment or two. "We can't leave her here, sir."

"Yes, thank you, sergeant. He's at ten o'clock to you, first-story window, right-hand side. On three I am going to come out shooting. When I get to Sergeant Jones, cover me. One, two, three..."

A quick succession of shots rang out as he burst from around the side of the shattered jeep, pistol held in both hands as he crabbed across toward the fallen sergeant. His shots peppering the wall and windows of the sniper's building.

I groaned as I stood up, rested my arms on the roof of the Volvo and steadied my aim. Captain Smith reached Sergeant Jones, dropped his pistol and bent down to pick her up.

There was a movement in the window that I was aiming at and I squeezed the trigger. The shot was returned—I squeezed again three or four times and caught sight of some more movement. Had I hit him?

"Clear," Captain Smith shouted behind me.

I was about to lower my gun when the sunlight glinted on the barrel of a weapon that had just appeared in the window again. It jerked upward and I guessed the shooter was reloading.

Without thinking too much about it, I stumbled round the remains of the Volvo and limped as fast as I could toward the building, ignoring the shouts from my CO behind me.

Counting off in my mind the seconds it would take to reload whatever weapon the sniper had, 1 half-stumbled and fell over the entrance step into the building. I replaced the cartridge clip in my own pistol and held it steady, pointing up the staircase as I rose to one knee and then stood up.

I leaned against the wall, keeping the pistol as steady as I could manage with a wounded arm. A trickle of sweat ran from my forehead and into one eye. I dragged the sleeve of my shirt across my eyes again as quickly as I could.

The house, like most of this area on the outskirts of the city, had been hit by heavy mortar fire. The walls were smoke-damaged, any surviving furniture had long since been looted and the staircase in front of me tilted dangerously.

Moving forward, I kept the gun raised at shoulder level, double-gripped and straight out. I climbed each step slowly, aware of the unsteadiness of my left ankle but not conscious of pain any more.

I leaned against the right-hand wall to make myself less of a target. I held my breath as I inched upward.

I was on the fifth step, about two-thirds of the way up the stairs, when the surface beneath my right ankle gave way. My leg dropped through the shattered wood as my body crashed sideways, my arms flung out to try and keep my balance, my pistol banging against the side of the wall as I slumped against it.

Another trickle of sweat ran into my eye and I looked up to see the muzzle of a rifle aimed square at my face.

Chapter 10

THE AIR WAS loud with gunfire.

A bullet slammed into my thigh, knocking me backward, my right leg wrenched out of the damaged staircase as I tumbled down the stairs to land on the concrete floor. Captain Smith stood in the doorway, his automatic rifle blazing away.

Moments later the body of the Iraqi insurgent crashed down the stairs to land beside me, his head slapping against the hard floor. He didn't cry out. He was dead.

I looked up at the doorway. My CO was silhouetted in a nimbus of light. "Thanks for the assist," I called out to him through clenched teeth.

"*De nada*," he said and then dropped to his knees, his weapon clattering to the floor.

"Captain," I said, dragging myself up and limping over to him.

"Anne didn't make it," he said, his voice a wet rasp. "I guess I didn't, either."

He fell forward and I held him to stop him collapsing to the ground. "Looks like it's just you, Dan," he said.

"Don't say that. We'll get help. You're going to be okay."

He shook his head weakly. "There's been too many lies in this damn war already. Truth is, we shouldn't be here in the first place and I don't think today is going to change anything."

"Just hang in there," I said. "I'll get help."

He shook his head again. "Do me one favor." His voice was a low croak now.

"Anything," I said softly.

"Look out for Chloe for me," Captain Smith said. Then he breathed out and died in my arms.

"You got it, boss," I said, tears pricking in my eyes. "You got it."

Chapter 11

I WAS STARTLED out of my reverie by the buzzing of the seat-belt sign flashing overhead once more.

We were about half an hour away from Heathrow by my reckoning. I checked my belt again, something you learn in the military: take care of your equipment and with luck your equipment will take care of you. The clasp was working fine.

I glanced across at Hannah. She didn't seem too bothered that turbulence ahead had been announced, and was listening quietly to some music on her iPod. Some thrash rap, no doubt—or whatever the cool kids were listening to nowadays. I guess you could call me old-fashioned but I like my music with a melody to it. Maybe I *was* getting old.

I aged five years in the next five seconds, though, when the 787 hit an air pocket. It might be called a Dreamliner but air pockets are my worst nightmare. The state-of-the-art plane dropped like a stone. I felt a small hand holding my own and looked across to see my young charge watching me, concerned.

"It's all right," I said. "Statistically you have a lot more chance being killed crossing the road than you do flying."

Whoever comes up with these sayings should be taken away and shot, if you ask me.

"I know that," she said. "But you looked like you were just about to have a heart attack."

Hannah was trying to put a brave face on things, I could tell that. I forced the corners of my own mouth to form a smile. "Indigestion," I said. "I should have turned down that lobster sandwich. I never do well with crustacean-based food at altitude."

"I'm Jewish," she said.

I obviously looked puzzled.

"Jews don't eat shellfish," she explained.

"I knew that, and very wise." I nodded. "Can play merry hell with the gastric juices." I winced as the plane was buffeted again.

"If it lives in the sea it needs fins and scales to be kosher. But I don't care—I love lobster."

"Not Orthodox, then?"

She looked at me again. "I'm not sure what I am any more. I didn't make bat mitzvah, even."

A sadness seemed to fill her eyes again. I looked down and saw that she was still holding my hand.

Then, as suddenly as it had appeared, the turbulence cleared. She smiled up at me, but the sadness in her eyes didn't go away.

"So, you're going to take care of me in England?" Hannah said, letting go of my hand.

I couldn't be sure but I thought I detected an amused quirk in the set of her mouth as she asked the question.

"Yes," I said. "I'm going to take care of you."

Part Two

Part Two

Chapter 12

Present day: London, England

LONDON IS THE greatest city in the world and don't let anyone tell you different.

It is in May, at least. When the sun is shining.

I was standing by the panoramic window of my office, looking out over New Oxford Street.

Private has grown into a worldwide private detective agency. We have offices in Los Angeles, New York, Rome, Dublin—and right here in London, of course. We are expanding all the time. We are the biggest and we are the best. Our clients range from rock legends and movie stars to government departments. From a wife suspicious of her philandering husband to the Metropolitan Police itself.

One of our biggest clients was the woman I was watching from my office window as she walked across the street.

Alison Chambers, chief "Rainmaker" from the law firm occupying the four stories below us—Chambers, Chambers and Mason—hips swaying as if she knew she was being watched. Of course she was being watched! Alison Chambers drew glances like a foxglove draws bees.

She pushed the button on her key to open the car locks and then held her right hand facing back above her head and extended her middle finger. I grinned. She was having dinner with me later. It was her idea of a joke. I liked that about her. Always the tease.

I looked over at the framed original film poster of Bogart and Bacall in *The Big Sleep* hanging on the wall by the window. As ever, Bogey seemed to be judging me. I couldn't see Bacall ever flipping him the bird. The print was a gift from an ex-wife who, I guess, thought she was pretty funny. I'm a private detective, after all. But that's where the similarity ends. The difference between Dan Carter and the man in the hat is that I just have my wits to live on. I'm an Englishman—we're not licensed to carry a gun!

I had just finished a video conference with Jack Morgan. He was a material witness in a big case just coming to trial in Los Angeles. A Supreme Court judge charged with the murder of her lesbian lover. And so he would be off the radar for a while. The case was drawing more attention than the O.J. Simpson trial, and, even if he could have done, Jack would never have walked away from the free publicity.

He couldn't walk away, though. The judge was a friend of his, and the men in black suits had slapped a subpoena on Jack. Putting him in a hotel with a couple of FBI agents babysitting him. Monday morning he'd be in court or he'd be in jail for contempt of it.

But Private London had nothing that needed his attention. We'd had a good month, settled a couple of long-running corporate cases and had plenty more business lined up on the books. Nothing that needed drastic action. For once—once in a blue moon—Dan Carter had a work-free weekend lined up. And I intended to make the most of it.

That guy leaning out from the prow of the *Titanic* probably felt just the same kind of optimism I was feeling. I'd never seen the film but I'm guessing it didn't work out too well for him, either.

The phone on my desk rang. I picked it up.

"Dan, it's Wendy Lee. I've got a problem."

Chapter 13

A HALF-MILE ACROSS London from the offices of Private, heading south and east. A barman in his late twenties called Ryan pushed a tray of shot glasses filled with tequila toward a red-faced pair of students.

They carried them to a nearby table and handed them round to a group of equally flushed young men. They were all wearing the university rugby colors and were chasing pints with slammers. One of them dropped his glass into his pint of lager and shouted: "*Depth charge!*"

Contempt was too mild a word for what the

barman thought of them. He was a postgraduate student who had worked two jobs while getting his first degree and was still left with a mountain of debt. This lot of braying jackasses wouldn't know a day's work, or debt, if it bit them on their privileged arses. He looked across at a pretty dark-haired woman who was standing further along the bar. Sometimes he hated his job. Sometimes he liked it.

Chloe Wilson didn't even notice the barman looking at her. She was feeling hot.

And not in a sexy manner, but in a sweaty, giddy kind of way. The three of them had come out all heels, squeals and ready to *partay!* At least, that had been the plan. Her two friends, Laura Skelton and Hannah Durrant, had been knocking back the vodka and Red Bulls since six o'clock like they were going out of fashion. And why not? They were all twenty-something-year-old students in the heart of the fine city of London on a Friday evening in spring—what the hell else were they supposed to be doing? But Chloe had held back on the booze. She had to. Someone had to keep a clear head. London could be a dangerous place, after all. Even on campus.

Chancellors University London, also known as CUL or Chancellors, was spread throughout the capital—as were most London-based colleges. But CUL dated way back to the sixteenth century. It had been founded by Henry VIII's Chancellor—Cardinal Wolsey. It had a central block or two of ancient residential buildings and lecture halls in a warren of inner connecting squares and passages. In the sixteenth century it had been a theological school set to rival Magdalen College at Oxford University.

Nowadays it had a more secular curriculum. After the Reformation the Chapel of the Blessed Virgin had been one of the first to go under the sledgehammer. All trappings of Catholic worship stripped out. Now it was simply the Chapel Bar. It was at the northern end of Chancery Square beneath the main rectory and was a stone-flagged cellar that on this evening was packed wall to wall with animated young adults.

Like the three beautiful young women near

the busy bar—making hay while the May sun shone bright.

Ryan stepped over to ask if they needed any more drinks. The dark-haired woman he had been watching earlier shook her head. But her friends drained their glasses and held them out for a refill. Not so much as a "please" or a "thank you."

Some of them were coming to the end of their time at college, Ryan knew. Some of them were coming toward the end of their first year. All of them with a bright future ahead. Their confidence was evident in their loud voices, their designer wear and perfect teeth. The privilege that they had inherited would be passed on through generations to come, as it always had been.

Some of them, though, had no future.

They just didn't know it yet.

Chapter 14

ADRIAN TUTTLE, A tall, gangly, floppy-haired man in his late twenties, pushed the passenger door of my car shut with a bit more force than he probably intended.

It slammed closed. The sound of it echoed all along the street.

"All right, Adrian," I said. "Take it easy. You sign on for Private, you're on call twenty-four seven. Love life always takes second billing. It's in your contract."

"What love life?"

I looked at my watch. Adrian had had to cancel a date when the call from the Met had come in, but I had no intention of missing mine.

Adrian was Private's forensic photographer. He had his own company car waiting for him but had failed his driving test six times. His luck with the ladies was equally as spectacular. Wendy Lee, his line boss, a five-foot bundle of Chinese energy and an ex-Forensic Science Service pathologist, had called in from Holborn. Her car had broken down so I'd agreed to drive Adrian to the crime scene and meet there. I didn't like his chances taking a taxi through London traffic on a Friday night. Official business meant I could put the detachable blue light on the roof of my BMW 4x4, blast the siren and cut through the commuters like a hot knife through butter.

I could have got one of my operatives to take him, but I like to go out with my agents in the field regularly. Let them know we are a team at Private. Besides, if I'd wanted to be a desk-jockey manager shuffling paper I would have joined a bank. But that night I'd told Wendy I'd swap her taxi for my car and leave them to it. Forensic examinations were definitely not on my agenda for the evening.

Ahead of us the familiar blue lights of

parked police cars flashed, and yellow tape blocked the public from the crime scene that lay beyond it.

"She could have been the one," continued Adrian morosely as he unzipped a large carry-case.

"You'll get another chance," I said, slapping him on the back as he stepped into his scene-of-crime overalls. "There's someone for everybody, you know. Even you."

Most people assumed that the white-suited forensic photographers and videographers seen on the TV news photographing and recording crime scenes were members of the police force. And sometimes they were—but sometimes they weren't. The Metropolitan Police, and the other forces throughout the country, also used independent companies. Like us.

The forensic division of Private London had a contract with the Metropolitan Police, purely in the photographic area. Forensic pathologists themselves were still under the direction of the Forensic Science Service, which was an agency of the Home Office working with the police.

Adrian's boss Wendy Lee had been a popular and highly respected pathologist at the FSS before I recruited her to head up Private's forensic unit. Some cases required independent forensic analysis before they came to court—and the resources that Private offered Dr. Lee tempted her away almost as much as the far higher salary I dangled under her nose. We gave her access to the kind of superior technology that the Met could only dream about.

The detective in charge at the scene, DI Ken Harman, nodded to me as Adrian and I walked up. We'd worked together before.

"Dan."

"Ken."

We shook hands briefly. And he held up the tape for us to cross under.

POLICE—DO NOT CROSS THE LINE

Somebody *had* crossed the line, though, I thought ironically as I straightened up again on the other side of it. As ever, it was the smell that hit me first.

Someone had crossed the line big time.

Chapter 15

SCENE-OF-CRIME OFFICERS STOOD to one side, ready to start processing the site once it had been thoroughly photographed.

Bright lights had been mounted on tall stands, illuminating the area as if it were a film set. Adrian fired up the light on his handheld HD video camera and started shooting.

I looked down at the body, wrapped in translucent plastic. The features just about discernible as a woman's. Maybe.

"Who found her?" I asked.

The detective grunted in what could have been ironic amusement, could have been something stuck in his throat. "Little toerag by the name of Jason Kendrick. Fourteen-year-old

one-man sodding crime wave. Raped and
stabbed a teenage prostitute just two streets or
so across. Scuttled here just like a rat when he
heard the blues-and-twos. Then ran back out
again as soon as he saw this," Harman said,
pointing at the mutilated corpse.

"Can't say as I blame him," I said.

The detective grunted again. "He does. He
ran straight into a police car." Harman smiled
grimly.

"And the girl?"

"She'll live. She fell on her own knife as she
tried to fight him off but missed all her major
organs. She was lucky."

"I guess, but that's the kind of luck I can
do without."

"I hear you."

"And the boy rapist?"

"Again, he'll live. Scrapes and bruises. Hit
the side of the car and was winded, apparently.
Couldn't breathe and thought he was going to
die." Harman twisted his mouth into something between a scowl and a smile. "Can't say
the world would have been the poorer if he
had done."

I didn't comment. Seems to me there's all kinds of bad luck in the world. The kind that gets you working the streets selling your body while you're still little more than a child. The kind that gets you into trouble with the law when you are five years old and have been taught no different. The kind that gets you running into speeding police cars nine years later after upgrading to the sort of crime that means you'll live out the rest of your childhood—and then some—in an institutional correction facility.

The kind of luck that gets you laid out on the cold floor of an old workshop. Being the center of attention in a way that no one would have wished upon themselves in their worst nightmares.

I watched as Adrian put down the video camera, unzipped his case, took out his stills camera, screwed a lens onto its body, and stepped over to begin photographing the corpse.

He was using an MD180 which, according to Jack Morgan, was the best damn camera ever manufactured for the processing of crime scenes. He had insisted that Private London's forensic unit should use the same and I reckon that Adrian would have kissed him for it. He certainly handled the camera as reverentially as he would a lover.

Wendy Lee stepped under the tape, suited-up but gloveless. I tossed her my car keys.

"I'll leave you to it," I said.

"Boss."

I looked down again at the dead body. Like I said, it had been wrapped in heavy plastic. But rats had eaten away the central section, exposing the torso, pelvic area and upper rib-cage. Bones protruded and much of the soft inner flesh and organs had been eaten away. There was no pooling of blood around the area.

A uniformed constable suddenly held a hand to his mouth and dashed out of the room.

I followed him out.

Not the start to the weekend that I had planned.

Chapter 16

"WHO'S BEEN ASSIGNED to processing the body?" asked Dr. Lee.

She was looking at the sallow-faced DI who was pointedly not looking at the horror show that lay at his feet.

Ken Harman gestured as a tall woman entered. Wendy nodded at her pleased. Doctor Harriet "Harry" Walsh had been her assistant at the time she had left the FSS when she'd been seduced by Private. And Wendy had never regretted her change of employer. Sure, she may not actually process the bodies at scenes of crime any more, but that was just data collection, after all. And it wasn't the collection that was important—it was what you did with it afterward that mattered. And Wendy Lee could now crank that data faster than the FSS by an order of magnitude.

"What have you got for me, Ken?" asked the pathologist as she snapped on the obligatory latex gloves and walked over. She dipped her head forward and tied back a glorious tumble of red-gold curls, causing them to sparkle momentarily in the bright artificial light before hiding them under a protective cap. She stood up again and at five foot eleven in her flat-soled shoes she made Wendy Lee feel dwarfed, not for the first time that evening.

"Looks like a Jane Doe," said the detective. "Hard to tell for a layman like me. Whoever it is has been feeding a family of *Rattus norvegicus* for quite some time, by the looks of it."

"You don't look too well," said Harriet Walsh.

"Just finished a large doner kebab when the call came in," he explained. "Wish I hadn't had the extra chili sauce now."

Doctor Walsh gave Harman a brief sympathetic smile and nodded to Wendy Lee.

"What do you think?"

"Just got here, Harry. But female...looks to be in her early twenties."

Doctor Walsh looked down at what was revealed of the body and sighed. "And out of hunting season, too."

She gestured to a couple of her SOCO assistants who were standing by, waiting for the nod. Then she kneeled down to peel back the plastic sheeting that partially covered the dead body. Using a scalpel to slice the plastic and peel it back as delicately as possible.

Any evidence could be vital—the merest speck of fabric or mud or blood. Nothing could be taken for granted. The whole scene would be processed, photographed, recorded, analyzed. And it all took time.

Some half an hour later the plastic sheet that had once wrapped the body now lay either side of it. The gruesome package opened up like some macabre gift.

Adrian Tuttle moved in closer, the flash mounted on his camera making the bright light intermittently even more glaring as he shot photo after photo. The white skin of the dead woman almost bleached in the flashes.

It was now quite evidently a woman, likely in her early twenties as Doctor Walsh had concurred. Impossible to tell her exact age without proper forensic analysis. But the long dark hair, the exposed pelvic bone, the remains of her breasts that hadn't been mutilated or cut or simply eaten away, all pointed to the sex of the victim.

A young woman. Taken. Murdered. And left for rodents to feed on in the squalor of a backstreet lock-up.

Chapter 17

"WHAT?" CHLOE WILSON practically shouted the word but she might as well have whispered for all the difference it made.

Loud music still played continuously in the underground student union bar and the noise of it reverberated off the thick walls like a swelling, bouncing wave of sound, making it hard for Chloe to think, let alone hear what her friend was trying to say to her. She had to shout again even more loudly against the music and the raucous conversation that surrounded her. "I can't hear you! What did you say?" she said, feeling the strain in her throat.

Her friend Hannah leaned in closer, attracting the attention of two young first-year students. Flushed with acne and alcohol, they tried surreptitiously to peek down her low-cut blouse at her ample bosom. Hannah flicked them a finger and put her arm around Chloe's shoulder. "I said it's my shout, Chloe," she said, her accent pure West Coast of America—the rich part of it. "Like another vodka?"

Chloe took a sip of her half-finished drink and shook her head. She was a little dizzy again. Feeling the heat flash through her face, she put a hand on the cool marble surface of the bar to steady her balance. "I need something to eat," she said. "I'm feeling a little light-headed. Let's get a pizza first and then hit some bars in Soho."

"Good thinking, girlfriend," said Hannah. "Bunch of goddamned horny schoolboys in here, is all."

Chloe nodded again, not quite as vigorously this time.

"I need to pee first, though, honey."

Chloe watched as Hannah looped her arm through the arm of her other friend, Laura. She dragged her away from a shaggy-haired gangling youth wearing a tweed jacket with elbow patches, who was attempting to chat her up, and headed off to the ladies'. Chloe took another small sip of her drink and flapped her hand in front of her face. Christ but it was hot in here, she thought for the hundredth time in the last half-hour. Maybe it wasn't food she needed, just some fresh air.

"You all right, love?"

A male voice, friendly enough—but Chloe would have snapped back, telling the guy to get lost. Not in the mood for being chatted up herself. Then she saw that it was just the barman who was speaking to her. A reasonably good-looking guy, she supposed, in his mid-twenties or thereabouts. A post-graduate student reading history of art, if she remembered correctly. He was quite smitten with Laura if Chloe was any judge, watching her with puppy-dog eyes whenever they came into the union. And who could blame him? Laura was gorgeous. Bright, clever, gorgeous. Dangerous things in a woman, as Chloe's godfather would say—thinking himself quite the comedian.

She shook her head at the barman, trying

to remember his name. "I'm fine, thanks. Just need some air."

"Sorry, we don't sell that."

Chloe laughed and regretted it immediately. The room seemed to spin a little more again and she took a deep breath and steadied herself. Back on the wagon tomorrow, she thought. She couldn't afford to get drunk. "No, I'm good, Ryan," she said, finally remembering his name.

"Have a glass of water," the barman said, handing her a glass he had just poured out.

"Cheers." Chloe said, taking a grateful sip of the water.

"Chloe, isn't it?"

"That's right."

"Reading psychiatry and law?"

"You been researching me?"

The barman flushed a little. "No, your friend Laura told me."

"Come on, Chloe, stop chatting up the help," Hannah called out to her as she led Laura through the heaving masses toward the door. Chloe caught Ryan watching the two of them leave, Hannah putting on the extra bit of wiggle, giving it the Shakira shimmy—knowing that Ryan would be watching. Chloe felt a twinge of sympathy for the barman. He wasn't even watching Hannah, his gaze was fixed on Laura. Fixed on her with the wet-eyed, puppy-like devotion of the truly lost cause. Chloe smiled ruefully. Laura was going to break a lot of hearts at CUL over the next two years before she finally tossed her mortar board in the air. Hell, Hannah would too. The pair of them drew attention from the men in the bar as they passed like a powerful magnet draws iron filings. Some of them getting an angry look or an elbow in the ribs for their trouble from unhappy girlfriends.

"Catch you later," Chloe said to the still-distracted barman. Finishing the glass of water, she turned to leave but her right leg seemed to give out under her and she crashed toward the floor.

Chapter 18

"DAN CARTER," I said to the willowy blonde standing imperiously behind the counter at the reception of Scott's restaurant.

Might seem strange to some to come straight from a murder scene in King's Cross to a swanky restaurant in Mayfair. But the sad truth was that you got used to it. You had to. Otherwise you didn't function. It wasn't that you didn't care. It was that you couldn't make it personal. You couldn't afford to.

Scott's had always been popular, but the currently highest-paid actress in the world— you know, the brunette with the killer smile— had recently declared it her favorite restaurant in London. And now Scott's had taken over from The Ivy as *the* place to be seen dining.

I flashed the receptionist a charming grin. She didn't exactly sneer as she looked down at her bookings list but the fraction of a millimeter that her left eyebrow moved conveyed just the same emotion.

I looked down at the deck shoes I was wearing. Maybe she thought I should have been wearing socks?

"Don Cotter?" said the receptionist.

"That's Carter," I said. "Dan Carter."

She beckoned us forward, led us into the restaurant proper and up to our table.

"See, Alison?" I said. "As good as my word. Private appreciates the business you throw our way."

"You and your associates do a good job, Dan. It's that simple. Keep doing it and we'll keep hiring you."

Alison Chambers was the niece—and the apple of his eye—of Charles William Chambers of Chambers, Chambers and Mason. Private London operates in a number of diverse areas. Personal security and detective work for people rich enough to afford us and who don't want police involvement for whatever reasons. And on the other side of the coin we worked with the Metropolitan Police on contract with our forensic division. But we also did a great deal of financial and corporate investigation. Industrial sabotage, intellectual theft, fraud. Computer forensics.

So it suited us well to keep in with the firm that occupied the offices below and it suited me to keep in with Alison Chambers. Her uncle might have had his name on the front of the building but Alison was the powerhouse in the firm.

I watched her studying the menu, multi-colored reading glasses perched delicately on the end of her shapely nose like an exotic butterfly ready to take flight. Her large, brown eyes as she considered the entrées as intent as if she had been scrutinising a million-pound contract.

"I've heard the prawn cocktail is good here," I said.

She didn't laugh. "How about you make

yourself useful and order some wine? Something with bubbles in it," she said instead.

I held a finger discreetly in the air and beckoned a waiter across. He smiled professionally as he approached and then for real as he saw Alison.

She has this effect on men. Even gay men. *Especially* gay men, come to think of it. And this in a restaurant where three tables across Liz Hurley was sitting with some actress whose name I couldn't place. But she was tipped to be Doctor Who's next traveling companion and was wearing a skirt even shorter than that worn by the current one.

I notice details like that. It's my job. I'm a detective.

"Could we see the wine list?" I asked the smiling waiter. "And what beers do you have?"

Alison Chambers tutted pointedly. "I don't need the wine list," she said. "Do you still have any of the Henriot Enchanteleurs 1990?"

The waiter positively beamed. "Indeed we do, madame."

"Then I'll take a glass of that."

"I'm afraid we only sell it by the bottle."

"We'd best have the bottle, then," she said.

"And a bottle of Corona for me," I said. "If you've still got it?"

A short while later the waiter returned with a chilled bottle of three-figured fizz for the lady and a bottle of ice-cold beer for me. I poured it into a glass, at least.

"How's the honeytrap case coming along?" she asked me.

"Let's not talk shop, Alison. This should be about pleasure, not business."

She pointedly held up the ring finger of her left hand.

Did I mention that she was married? Alison and I have been best friends since university and flirt with her I might, but I'd never do anything to jeopardise that friendship.

I pulled out a digital voice-recorder that Suzy, one of our operatives, had given me earlier and pushed the play button. Suzy was speaking, her voice husky. The honey in the trap smoked with hickory chips. Whatever she was selling men were going to buy it.

Alison listened to Suzy working the guy. She was good.

A couple of minutes later and she had heard all she needed to.

"The video footage has already been e-mailed to you."

"Good. Let's celebrate," she said. "I'm going to start with something to go with the excellent fizz. My friends tell me the beluga is very good here with blinis and sour cream."

"What about a drop scone and a dollop of jam?"

Her smile broadened. "What say we go with the fifty grams?"

My own smile held, just about. Six hundred smackeroos in and she hadn't even got to the main course yet. But dinner was on Private so what the heck, we could afford it. I flashed her a couple of kilowatts of smile. I could afford that as well.

The weekend was definitely getting better.

Chapter 19

CHLOE PUT A hand out to the bar and steadied herself, brushing away the arm of one of the rugby players who had come across to help her up a minute or two earlier.

"I'm okay now," she said, irritated. "Was just a bit dizzy, is all."

The rugby player held his hands up in the air and moved aside.

Chloe fought her way through the crowds to try and catch up with her friends. They were at the other end of the room now. Arm in arm and singing "Swing Low, Sweet Chariot" at full volume, as if the ale-fueled rugger buggers in her way needed any more encouragement! A group of them had linked arms too, and were joining in the song at full volume, blocking her way through to the door. It took her a while to fight past. She had to slap away one highly amused prop forward who took the opportunity to push up against her in a manner that was just a shade short of criminal assault in her book. Another day she would have done more than just slap the idiot, but she wanted to get out and get some air.

She finally made it to the entrance and closed the door firmly behind her. The noise thankfully muted as she walked up the steps leading to the quad above. The cool night air clearing her head a little. Her friends' raucous singing, some distance ahead of her now, was echoing loudly around the quad. No doubt setting the ghost of the Cardinal spinning in his grave.

"Hang on. Wait for me," Chloe called out, but her voice was hoarse now from all the shouting she'd done in the bar and her friends showed no sign of having heard her. She shook her head a little to clear the vodka cobwebs from her brain and quickened her pace as she climbed the stone steps. She was glad at least that she didn't have high heels on. At five foot ten she didn't need them. In the main men didn't like her towering over them—she had found that out at fifteen years old when she was the same height as she was now.

Out on the quad she could see her two friends turning right into one of the passages that linked the warren of buildings. Chloe stumbled a little as she started to run to catch up with them and had to take a moment to steady herself. But she soon came up to the turning and moved quickly round the corner. It was darker as the lights from the quad fell behind her. The lane dog-legged after a few yards and cut off the lights from the college quad entirely. One of the Victorian street lamps that dotted the lanes in seemingly random fashion was out at the elbow of the bend. Chloe looked up at it unhappily. The university had a duty to keep the area lit. The tall buildings on either side of the narrow street made it darker than it would otherwise have been. A muffled scream ahead snapped Chloe out of her thoughts, sobering her in an instant.

She charged round the next corner, breathing quickly to pump some oxygen into her blood.

Ahead of her was a group of five hooded and dark-clothed men, three of whom had grabbed her friends. Two had hold of Laura and one had a chokehold on Hannah. The remaining two were leaning against a black van.

"Let them go, you *bastards*," Chloe tried to scream, but her voice came out in a hoarse, painful croak again. Adrenaline kicked in. She ran toward them. One of the men turned to face her. A disdainful sneer on his lips, although she couldn't see his eyes that were shaded by the hood he was wearing. She kicked him hard in the groin and the sneer vanished as he crumpled, groaning, to to the ground.

She felt an arm pulling her back and she spun round, knocking the arm away, spearing a hard fist into her assailant's sternum and then uppercutting him as he doubled forward. But she was sluggish, far more sluggish than she should have been. The uppercut was off target, and the man moved aside so that her punch only grazed the side of his head. He snapped a blow straight back at her. But Chloe had anticipated it—she stepped inside his swing, grabbing his arm and using the momentum of the missed punch to pull him forward toward her. She lowered her head as she did so and smashed her forehead into the bridge of his nose. There was a satisfying crunch of cartilage. The man squealed like a stuck pig and dropped to his knees, hands cradling his wrecked nose that was now spilling blood.

Chloe breathed deeply and turned toward the van. Two of the remaining three men moved toward her—more cautiously than their colleagues had. One of them holding Laura tight to his body with a muscular arm wrapped around her. She saw the flash of steel as that man pulled a long-bladed knife from his jacket, watched Hannah stumble, heard a scream. Laura fell down and was yanked rudely up.

"What do you want?" Chloe shouted at the men, holding her hands forward ready to strike.

"Just leave now and you won't get hurt," came a quiet hiss from the hooded figure who now held a terrified Hannah against the side of the black van.

Chloe shook her head. "Just let them go!" she said, putting one foot forward, hands held like blades as she moved slowly toward the two men facing her. Her head was clearing now. Something the man holding Hannah had said triggering some kind of memory. She tried to catch hold of the thought but couldn't, the synapses in her brain still not firing at a hundred percent—despite the adrenaline that was coursing through her blood now.

She moved forward slightly again, her foot not leaving the ground as she slid it along the uneven surface of the street, doubly glad now that she hadn't worn heels. The hooded man who didn't have hold of either Laura or Hannah took a step forward himself. Chloe tilted sideways quicker than he could register and snapped out her right foot, slamming it into his knee.

"It's okay, Laura," she said to her terrified friend. "Everything is going to be all right."

Laura shook her head, her eyes widening with panic, with shock.

"Trust me, babe," Chloe said, misunderstanding her friend's reaction. "They are not getting away with this!"

She saw the man holding Laura take a step backward as she inched her foot forward once more. She felt the movement of air behind her. But before she could react a baseball bat swung against the back of her head, crunching into the fragile bone. She collapsed forward and hit the cold cobbled ground.

Chapter 20

DOCTOR HARRIET WALSH knelt down and examined the gaping wounds.

"Cause of death?" asked DI Ken Harman.

Doctor Walsh looked back over her shoulder and shrugged. "Can't tell at this stage. No bruising to the neck, no evidence of gunshot damage. The soft tissue and organs have been eaten away in the main."

"Murder, though?"

She shrugged again. "Maybe. She died, that much is evident, and was then wrapped in this plastic sheeting—left here until she could be disposed of somewhere else, I guess. But then again, it's my job to give you facts, not to speculate."

The detective shook his head, disagreeing. "Speculating is good. At this stage..." He cleared his throat. "We're not in a court of law presenting cold facts and hard evidence. We're pissing in the wind, hoping its direction doesn't turn against us. So speculate away, give us a thread to start pulling on and we just might unravel the whole damn thing before someone gets hurt again."

Wendy Lee looked over at him. "Do we know who owns the lock-up?"

"Not yet," said DI Harman. "But we're on it." He turned to the pathologist. "Is it possible she was suffocated by the sheeting?"

Dr. Walsh ran her hands gently over the dead woman's cheeks and shook her head. "No indication of it."

"If it wasn't murder...why wrap the body up and hide it away like this?"

Wendy looked down at the woman's face for a moment or two without responding. Then she said, "She looks Middle Eastern to me. Egyptian, perhaps. Jewish?"

"Maybe Eastern European?" said Doctor Walsh.

Wendy shrugged. "Maybe. Could be an illegal immigrant. Could be she died from natural causes but whoever brought her in couldn't afford to deal with her death through the official channels."

"Human trafficking?"

"It's a possibility. We all know that organized criminals out of Eastern Europe and Africa, but not exclusively from those parts of the world, have been bringing in large numbers of women. Holding them to ransom with threats against their children or family back home."

Harman nodded thoughtfully.

"It's a trade worth billions of pounds. And this is an area pretty well know for the seedier side of the prostitution business."

Harman looked over at the dead body. "You think she was a prostitute?"

Dr. Walsh looked back at him and shook her head. "Just *speculating*. We haven't even begun to do a post-mortem on the poor woman. One thing I learned really early on in this game, detective, is—if you leap too early to conclusions…"

"You can end up landing on your arse!" Wendy Lee finished for her.

Harriet Walsh turned back to the dead woman and looked at her left hand which was curled into a semi-fist as if she was holding something. The pathologist opened the hand gently.

"Rigor mortis has set in and then softened so I can tell you she has been dead for a number of days..." she said and then trailed off. She looked up at Adrian Tuttle and said, "Get a shot of this."

As Tuttle leaned in, his flashgun firing off mini-explosions of light, Wendy Lee leaned forward to look as well.

"What is it?" asked Harman.

"The *digitus anularis*. The *phalange quartus*, if you like, on the hand sinister."

Harman grunted again. "I don't like. What's it mean in plain Anglo-Saxon?"

"The ring finger to you and me, detective," explained Wendy Lee.

Dr. Walsh held the dead woman's wrist and showed the others the left hand. "The phalange or fourth finger on the left hand, counting the thumb as the first finger. It's been cut off at the second knuckle."

The detective squatted down, groaning a little as his knees creaked. "I'm getting too old for this job," he said. "You sure it has been *cut* off and not gnawed?" he asked. "Our hungry rats?"

"I'll get it under a microscope but these are clean lines around the knuckle and there has been no rodent activity anywhere near it."

"Why have bony gristle when you can have the prime meat?" said Harman.

"Not delicately put, inspector. But you make a valid point."

Harman stood up, groaning again as he did and holding his hands to his suffering knees.

"How old *are* you in fact, detective?" Wendy Lee asked him.

"Forty-two next month," he replied.

"Maybe you want to think about doing some exercise," she said pointedly.

"It's all right for you, Dr. Lee—you're a lot closer to the ground."

Harriet Walsh stood and nodded to her

team. "Let's get her down to the workshop. See what we can see."

"So what are we looking at, detective?" asked Tuttle, the first time he had spoken since they had entered the crime scene. "Prostitution, trafficking, ritualistic killing. Or an accidental death covered up and the wedding ring removed as possible evidence of her identity?"

"Could be any of the above." The detective inspector shrugged. "Truth is . . . as of this moment I don't have a clue."

Tuttle nodded sagely.

The difference between him and Harman was, he *did* have one. He had a very big clue.

"Well, let me tell you something else, then," he said.

Chapter 21

DI KIRSTY WEBB pulled the zipper on her coat up firmly.

She was leaning against the wall of a building, built sometime in the sixteenth century, and watching her people process the crime scene.

Such as it was. A poorly lit cobbled backstreet off one of the quads of Chancellors University. At least, it would have been poorly lit if the police hadn't mounted bright halogen lights to photograph and work the scene.

Three female students from the university had been viciously assaulted. One of them kidnapped. One of them slashed with a knife.

One of them beaten with a baseball bat and even now fighting for her life in the hospital.

Could be a murder case before the night was out.

DI Webb took a sip of her coffee and scowled. The crystal-ball gazers at the Meteorological Office were promising a sunny day for Saturday and she was supposed to have the weekend off. She'd hoped to get in the garden and sort things out.

Fat chance of that now. This case would put paid to all that. Chancellors University was all about old money. And that meant pressure from above. It always did.

So the garden would go untamed for a while longer. Which would have suited her ex-husband, Webb thought bitterly. Her mood worsening as she took another sip of coffee and wondered why she was even thinking about the bastard.

But she knew exactly why. Goddamn him! Tomorrow was their wedding anniversary. Ten years ago instead of punching him on the nose like he so richly deserved, she had simply slapped him and said yes.

She crumpled the styrofoam coffee cup in her hand and watched as the ambulance drove away. Its sirens shrieking into the night air and the noise bouncing of the cloistered walls of the warren of buildings that made up that part of the university.

The lead scene-of-crime officer ducked under the police-line tape and approached. He was followed by DS Andy Crane, Kirsty's partner.

"You got anything good for me?"

The SOC officer smiled. He was a handsome man, tall, lean, in his late twenties. "Detective Inspector Webb," he said, grinning wider. "I thought you'd never ask."

"You're funny, Richard. Funny like chlamydia."

"They say God loves a trier."

"They say God loves everyone. Me, I hate most people, so stop flapping your lips like a fishwife and tell me what we've got."

DS Crane shrugged. "The paramedic sedated the first one—the knife victim—so we didn't get much from her. A black van. Hooded men. She wasn't sure how many. More than three."

"They say anything?"

"No. The one they beat up with a baseball bat tried to stop it, apparently. Some kind of karate nut or some such."

DI Webb gestured to the taped-off area of the road. "Any sign of what we might call clues?"

"There are some faint tire marks, and some blood droplets which we are pretty sure are going to turn out to have come from the injured girl's arm."

"Who phoned it in?"

The detective sergeant pointed across to the pavement where a woman in her thirties was drinking a mug of tea, a female uniformed officer speaking to her. "Jane Harrington, lectures here at the university."

"What did she see?"

"Nothing. She was on her way home after a late tutorial. The van had gone before she got here. Found one student unconscious and the other hysterical and screaming, with blood pouring down her arm."

"Cut badly?"

"Her wrist was sliced, is all, as the other girl

tried to fight them off. Not too deeply. Nothing arterial."

DI Webb made some notes in a small black book that she pulled out of her coat. "Names?"

"Chloe Wilson is the girl hit with the baseball bat, the woman knifed is Laura Skelton and the woman they took is Hannah Durrant."

"All students here?"

The detective sergeant nodded again. "Coming to the end of their first year. Chloe Wilson reading law and psychiatry, the other two just psychiatry."

DI Webb nodded to her assistant. "Okay, stay with it, sergeant. I'll check back later."

"Where you going, boss?"

"The hospital. See if Sleeping Beauty or her sedated friend are ready to be interviewed."

Kirsty Webb nodded to the uniformed officer—another sergeant—who was standing by one of the police cars. "Come on then, Buttons—you get to take me to the ball."

Chapter 22

LAURA SKELTON WAS sitting up in the bed, her face as pale as the case on the pillow propping her up.

Her right arm was bandaged and tears had streaked her mascara, giving her a bedraggled, gothlike appearance.

DI Webb flashed her warrant card at the doctor and nurse who were standing by Laura's bed. "I'm Detective Inspector Kirsty Webb. Is it okay to speak to Laura?"

The doctor looked across at the young woman who nodded weakly.

"Thanks," said Kirsty. "I know you must be pretty shaken up by what happened."

"Have you found Hannah? Is she okay?"

"I'm sorry. But we're doing all we can. Which is why I need you to try and remember everything that happened."

"I told the others all I know."

"I understand that. But I want you to go through it again—some detail might be essential."

"It all happened so fast."

"I know. Start with you leaving the university grounds. You'd been drinking in the union bar?" Kirsty prompted.

"Yes. Since six o'clock. But Chloe wanted to get something to eat. She was feeling a little dizzy."

Kirsty checked her notebook. "That would be Chloe Wilson?"

Laura looked over at the doctor, tears starting in her eyes. "Is she going to be okay?"

The doctor made a calming gesture with his hand. "She's being closely monitored, Laura."

"He hit her with a baseball bat. The sound it made..." Laura wiped her eyes again, fresh tears running down her face.

"Take your time."

Laura gulped some air into her lungs. "The street lamp was out and when we turned the corner there was a bunch of hooded men who jumped on us."

"How many?"

"I don't know," Laura said, clearly distraught. "It all happened so fast. One of them had a knife." Her hand went unconsciously to her bandaged arm.

"What happened?"

"Chloe came round the corner. She ran straight at them—kicking, punching. I've never seen anything like it. I didn't know she could do that."

"Do what?"

"Kung fu. Whatever it was. Martial arts. She was amazing—and then one of them hit her with the baseball bat."

"And they took Hannah away in the van?"

"Chloe must have spooked them. The one who had hold of me pushed me away, cutting my arm. Then they threw Hannah in the van and drove off." Her face paled even more as the reality of it all hit home again. "It could have been me."

"What was the van like?"

Laura shrugged apologetically. "Just a black van. No windows. It looked quite new. A Ford, I guess."

"You didn't get its number?"

Laura shook her head. "No. I don't think there was a number plate." She squeezed her eyes shut. "I can't remember."

An alarm went off from the next room. Shrill. Insistent. Laura looked across for a moment and then screamed.

Chapter 23

DI KIRSTY WEBB ran out of the room.

She was moved to the side and had to look through the window of the intensive-care room as the crash team went in.

The bed was disconnected from most of the monitoring equipment, turning it into a mobile gurney, and was wheeled out of the room.

Kirsty Webb looked at the unconscious woman who was in the bed. Half of her long dark hair had been shaved away and there was a thick padded bandage on the back of her skull.

Kirsty drew a sharp breath as the team hurried the woman toward the theater.

"Shit!" she said, not realizing that she was speaking aloud.

"What is it?" the sergeant asked.

"That girl..."

"Boss?"

"She's not Chloe Wilson," she said simply and pulled out her mobile phone.

Chapter 24

I LOOKED AT the caller display on my mobile phone.

Whatever my ex-wife wanted to tell me it wasn't going to be good news. I ignored the hostile glares from the other diners, then clicked the button.

"Dan Carter," I said pretending not to know who was calling.

I listened to what Kirsty was saying for a moment and her words took a moment or two to register. I mumbled something or other thanking her for letting me know, and clicked the phone closed.

"We have to leave," I said. I stood up, pulled out my wallet and chucked a bunch of fifty-pound notes on the table. Our main course hadn't yet arrived but I had suddenly lost all appetite. I felt sick to my stomach. "Did you drive here?" I asked Alison.

"No. Strangely enough, I don't usually order a bottle of champagne if I'm driving," she said dryly. "What's going on?"

I shook my head and slipped my jacket on. "I need to get a taxi," I said simply.

Alison hurried after me and slid her arm through mine.

"What's wrong, Dan?" she pressed, the concern clear in her voice.

"Everything," I replied.

Chapter 25

I CURSED AS the taxi pulled to a stop at yet another traffic light.

I leaned back, closing my eyes. Willing my heart to beat slower. Thinking of the young girl I had fetched across the Atlantic to London.

The worst possible thing had happened. She'd been kidnapped on our watch. Taken by violent men. Had her cover been compromised? Was it a random attack?

I remembered her small hand holding mine. I had said I was going to take care of her.

I felt sick as I played over in my mind what Kirsty had told me had happened to the other girl. Another girl I had also promised to protect. A promise made long ago in a foreign land when her father, who had given his life to save mine, had begged me to look after her.

Twenty minutes later I stood outside the intensive-care room looking through the slatted blinds at the frail, young woman who lay in the hospital bed. Surrounded by wires and drips and monitors.

Chloe Smith. Who had just as much heart and guts as her father.

Jack Morgan had wanted somebody undercover at the university to keep an eye on Hannah. A companion, he'd said, not a bodyguard. And I had thought Chloe was the perfect choice.

She'd had a gap year traveling round the world and was going to sign up to join the police. She was as bright as a button and fearless in the way that only youth can give you.

Her mother and I had discussed it. University would be an ideal opportunity for her. She would come out with a law and psychiatry degree and should she still wish to join the police she would be fast-tracked as a graduate and get where she wanted to be far quicker. Private would pay all her fees and a salary as well. Jack Morgan had sanctioned that and Hannah's father had gladly written the checks. There would be a job for Chloe in the company if she changed her mind about joining the force. It was win win all round. Or should have been.

Chloe had enrolled at Chancellors under a cover name, much as Hannah had. She had befriended the American girl as planned. It wasn't hard to arrange.

The same course, the same accommodation. Private has connections. The strings were pulled and it was supposed to be straightforward. Chloe was meant just to keep an eye on Hannah, report back if there was any trouble. Chloe was clearly her father's girl, though. She had gone in, guns blazing, to the rescue and to hell with the consequences. I had done something similar all those years before and her father had come to my rescue. If it hadn't been for him I wouldn't be alive today.

But because of me his daughter was now comatose in an intensive-care hospital bed.

Jack Morgan had told me to keep a special eye on the million-dollar baby. He'd told me it was personal to him. Well, it was just as personal to me now.

Chapter 26

IT TOOK ME a moment or two to realize that someone had slid their hand into my own and was squeezing it.

Sympathetically. As a friend would. I turned round, a little dazed, shaking my head as if to clear my brain from the dark thoughts that were dancing around inside it.

"Who is she?" asked Alison Chambers.

"She's my god-daughter," I said.

"I didn't know you had a god-daughter."

"I don't. Not really. 'Godfather' was kind of a nickname she had for me. I was an unofficial godparent—a guardian angel, she would call me. Teasing me." I shook my head again. "Some guardian angel."

"So who is she?"

"Her name's Chloe, Alison. Chloe Smith."

"Why did you never tell me?"

"You remember my best man at the wedding?"

"The wedding I wasn't invited to!" she said pointedly

I nodded, thinking back. It was a year before the Second Gulf War. May the twenty-first 2002. Richard Smith had just made captain and I was getting married. A double celebration.

I remembered looking over my shoulder at the people who had filled every seat in the room. Some more had had to stand at the back. Admittedly it wasn't a large room. On one side, dotted among the civilians, a number of men and women in the full-dress rig of the RMP and on the other side of the divide, and likewise among the civilians there, the blue serge uniforms of the capital city's finest.

There was a bit of a low murmur and I turned back to face the serious-looking minister who was giving me an unimpressed look.

"And do you, Daniel Edward Carter, take

Kirsty Fiona Webb to be your lawful wedded wife?" he said.

I looked across at the woman standing next to me. Her jet-black hair cut in a bob that would have put Louise Brooks to shame. Her brilliant green eyes sparkling, her Cupid's-bow lips painted a dark red, the 1920s gown she was wearing a miracle of lace and white satin hugging her toned body like a second skin. Cliché, I know, but she had never looked more beautiful to me. If I was Eric Clapton I could have written a song about it. But I wasn't. I was Sergeant Dan Carter of the Royal Military Police and I was about to marry the girl of my dreams—Police Constable Kirsty Webb of the Metropolitan Police.

"I do," I said and beamed at her.

It wasn't, on reflection, the best of times for my mobile phone to ring. The shrill retro sound of an old telephone bouncing off the walls.

"Sorry, I thought I'd turned it off," I mumbled as I fumbled the phone out of my pocket. But Kirsty was too quick for me and grabbed the phone out of my hand like a heron spearing a trout. She looked at the phone, turned it off, threw it to the side and slapped me hard across the face.

Behind me I could hear my best man fighting hard to suppress a laugh. But Kirsty fixed him with a basilisk stare and any thought of laughter disappeared like a candle flame snuffed out in a high wind. She turned back to her uncle, the minister.

"Get on with it, then," she said.

The minister, Reverend Crake, cleared his throat and then smiled at her. "And do you. Kirsty Fiona Webb, take Daniel Edward Carter as your lawful wedded husband?"

She waited long enough to twist the hook and then nodded. "I do," she said.

It hadn't been the best omen for our marriage.

I remembered Richard Smith's amused, laughing eyes that day. And then I looked down at his daughter's eyes nine years later. Closed now. Machinery keeping her alive.

I'd find the sons of bitches who'd done this to my beautiful god-daughter and make them pay, I swore to myself.

Or I'd die trying.

Chapter 27

I FOLDED MY other hand over Alison's and gave it a squeeze. "Kirsty didn't want you there, you know that."

"Of course I knew that. I'd told her plenty of times that there was no reason to be jealous."

I grimaced slightly. "Yeah. That probably didn't help."

"I know."

"My best man at the wedding was Captain Smith. Her father." I nodded at Chloe. "The man who saved my life."

"The war," she said.

"Yes."

I had never spoken to Alison about the

war. Never spoken to *anyone* about it. They tried to get me to have counseling. But Dan Carter is strictly old school.

As I said, I'd come home invalided out. Eventually I was out of the wheelchair. But I swapped my baton for a bottle and tried to chase the demons away with that. I wasn't the first and I sure as hell wouldn't be the last.

All I managed to do, however, was chase away my wife, my family, my friends.

Like I say, it's a familiar story, not one I'm proud of. Not one I beat myself up over, either.

Look closely at who most of the homeless in London are, or at those who are languishing in prisons when they should be in hospitals. Military men and women who had given more than they were asked in service to their country and got short shrift for change.

I was one of the lucky ones. I didn't end up freezing to death on a West End backstreet while the civilians walked by with their gazes averted. Eventually I came to terms with things. I realized I was carrying the guilt like a lame man who'd been cured hanging onto a walking stick that he no longer needed. But it wasn't my guilt to carry and so I tossed it down and started living again. I went back into work. I turned my life around.

But not in time to save my marriage.

On cue, like the devil you speak of, my ex-wife turned the corner of the corridor at that moment and walked toward us.

My hand flew guiltily away from Alison's. Stupid, I know, but it was a knee-jerk reaction and I could see that Kirsty had noticed it. Some emotion was playing in her eyes—was it a frown or was it a smile? I couldn't tell. Maybe that was the problem. I never could tell with Kirsty. Never sure whether she was going to slap me or kiss me. Or both.

But I had a notion of what the look in her eye was that Friday evening. It looked a lot like sympathy.

"Alison," she said simply.

"Kirsty."

Kirsty looked at me, hesitating for a moment, and I felt a chill dancing over my heart. Someone walking on my grave.

"I've got some bad news, Dan," she said.

Chapter 28

IT WAS DARK outside now.

I leaned against the cool brick wall of the hospital and took a couple of breaths. Alison was inside, trying to find a coffee machine, and Kirsty had left to pursue her own investigations.

I was still taking in what she had told me but couldn't make the connection. After what I had seen earlier that evening I *refused* to make a connection.

Someone had taken Hannah Shapiro, we knew that much. We didn't know if she was the primary target. Whether she was just in the wrong place at the wrong time. I needed to know what the motive was and I needed to know soon, because one thing I did know for certain—the longer it went on without her being found the worse it would be for her. Statistics wouldn't lie in this case.

I pulled out my phone and hit speed-dial. After a few rings I heard the smooth, unmistakably West Coast accent I had been expecting.

"Jack Morgan."

"Jack," I said. "We've got a major problem."

"What is it, Dan?"

"Hannah—she's been abducted. Just outside the university campus. A group of hooded men. Unmarked van."

There was a long silence on the other end of the line. Then: "When did it happen?"

His voice was as tight, as serious, as I'd ever heard it.

"An hour or so ago."

"Have you heard anything?"

"No ransom demand as yet."

"Maybe they're not after money."

I didn't respond. I knew all too well that young women were abducted for all kinds of reasons. By no means all of them financial. I closed my eyes, trying to shut out the memory of what I had seen in the lock-up at King's Cross. Failed.

"I want you to drop everything else, Dan! Everything. That girl is your only priority, you hear me?"

"You don't have to tell me, Jack. The people who took her also put my god-daughter in intensive care."

"I'll be getting on a plane as soon as the FBI let me loose. Meanwhile Private worldwide is at your entire disposal. You need anything—anything at all—you let us know."

"I appreciate it."

"Just get the girl home safe, Dan. Money isn't an issue."

"You think it's a kidnapping?"

There was another pause on the end of the line and I could hear the frustration in Jack's voice. "There are things you need to know about Hannah Shapiro," he said. "It all goes back to April 9, 2003."

Some minutes later I hung up. I looked

down and opened the hand clenched tight around my car key. The metal had cut into my flesh. I held the wound to my mouth and tasted the iron in it.

Like I said. Someone was going to pay.

Part Three

Chapter 29

I LIVE IN a small apartment in Soho, on the third floor of an old building on Dean Street.

I have a lounge, a bedroom, a small kitchen that I rarely use and a bathroom. I had the front window double-glazed shortly after I moved in and the place is snug. I have a small television and a digital internet radio.

Dean Street is one of my favorite places in the world. Home to The Crown and Two Chairmen, the Groucho Club and the best bar in the western hemisphere—The French House—even if it does sell beer only by the half-pint and you have to steer well clear at lunchtime when it's packed with media types and tourists.

But at half-six in the morning the pubs are closed tighter than a drum. The little Italian café around the corner was open early, though. I bought an espresso to go, which I sipped as I walked across town to the office.

I was short of the recommended eight hours of shut-eye—by about seven hours, I reckoned—and the sharp, bitter jolt of the caffeine was kicking in fine. Normally, before going into work, I'd have gone to the gym I used just off Piccadilly Circus near the Café Royal. But Chloe was still unconscious in intensive care, Hannah Shapiro was still missing and we still didn't have a clue why she had been taken.

Jack Morgan had been straight in touch with Hannah's father, Harlan Shapiro, who was getting on this evening's flight to London.

Her abductors had made no contact. We didn't know if Hannah's cover had been blown or if a ransom demand was imminent. Given what Kirsty had told me last evening I very much hoped that was the case. If she hadn't been taken for money...I shook the thought away, dropped my empty espresso cup in a litter bin outside a newsagent's and picked up my pace. The clock was ticking and we didn't have a minute to waste.

Ten minutes later I sprinted up the stairs to my office. I never take the elevator if I can help it. I don't like elevators.

Lucy, my PA, flashed her cut-glass smile as me as I punched in the security code and stepped through to the open-plan reception office. She was blonde, beautiful and had a top-drawer accent to go with the smile.

"Morning, Lucy. Everyone in yet?"

She shook her head. "Dr. Lee is on her way in but Sponge won't be coming in today. The rest are in the conference room."

"What do you mean, he won't be coming in?" If my tone was a tad sharp I didn't apologize for it

"It's his mother."

Vladimir Kopchek, or "Sponge" as he was known because of his ability to soak up every bit of information and retain it, was our computer and technical support expert. He defected to the west before glasnost. He's in his fifties now and has a mind sharper than an ex-wife's tongue. His mother back in Russia had fallen ill and he was awaiting the results of tests. "What is it?" I asked.

"They don't give her very long. Maybe three months. He's booked himself on the first flight over."

I nodded, resigned. I couldn't blame the guy, but he was going to be hard to replace.

Wendy Lee came through the door, carrying a paper sack. "I got you coffee," she said.

We walked into the conference room. About twenty foot by eighteen. A long walnut table running to the wall opposite the door. Flush with the end of the table and rising up the wall some ten foot by eight was a state-of-the-art LED television screen. Fractions of an inch thick.

When it was switched to video-conference mode it connected to Private's other offices around the world. So that the table seemed to carry on beyond the screen into an identical office. Except in that office it would be Jack Morgan's team sitting around the table in his octagonal war room, or the crew of our outfits in Rome—or Paris or New York.

Today, though, it was just my team who were there for the briefing.

Chapter 30

AROUND THE TABLE were Adrian Tuttle, Wendy Lee, Suzy Malone, Brad Dexter and Sam Riddel.

Sam is my number two at the agency. He was wearing a coal-black three-piece suit and a dark blue tie. He's a six foot four ex-copper and ex-boxer, and he's black. He'd never killed a man in the ring, but I wasn't so sure about out of it. He grew up on one of the worst estates in South London. Two of his brothers were killed before he was ten years old. Killed in the drug-turf wars that were still a feature of everyday life in that part of London. The fact that Sam had survived it, had never turned to the dark side as it were, meant he could pretty much survive anything in my book.

Suzy was in her early thirties. Ex-Metropolitan Police. Five foot six, auburn hair, fifth-degree black-sash Wing Chun kung fu, Third Dan kick-boxing, a marksman, a loyal friend, a deadly enemy, openly bisexual and one of my favorite people in the whole world. The Met Police's loss was decidedly our gain. Likewise Brad Dexter. Early fifties, built like an American-style fridge, he had taken early retirement from the close-protection unit of the Met. He now headed up our personal-security division.

"Okay, guys," I said as I picked up a small white remote-control unit from the desk. "Everything else is off the agenda. What I am going to tell you about now needs our total focus. Jack Morgan would be flying over himself to head this up, but he can't. He's subpoenaed to appear in federal court and can't leave the country."

"What's going on, Dan?" asked Wendy Lee.

I pointed the remote control at the TV and clicked the on button. I would say it was state-of-the-art Apple and Sony TV technology—

but it wasn't, Apple wouldn't be bringing their version out for a year or so.

As it was, I wasn't using the sophisticated conference facility—I was just using it for a slide show.

First up was a recent picture of Hannah Shapiro. I couldn't believe it was the same nervous girl I had brought over from America less than eighteen months ago. Chloe had told me that Hannah had come out of herself a lot, becoming more confident and outgoing. But the transformation was incredible, even so.

Hannah looked bold, comfortable and gorgeous. Her hair now full and wavy, a tumble of deep brunette curls. Her eyes bright, a killer smile. Her figure was more shapely, filled out—she had become a woman. A very sexy one at that.

I felt guilty thinking it. Remembering the small nervous hand holding mine on that bumpy flight. She was like a completely different person.

"Hannah Shapiro," I said. "Registered at Chancellors University under the name 'Hannah Durrant.'"

"Why the name change?" asked Lucy.

"Her father is Harlan Shapiro. A very wealthy West Coast industrialist. Electronic systems. Communications."

"And...?" Wendy Lee asked.

I took a sip of my coffee, remembering what Jack had told me the night before. Hannah's mother hadn't died of cancer like she had told me on the flight. She had died in circumstances almost too horrific to take in.

"A good few years ago," I replied, "on Hannah's thirteenth birthday, she and her mother were kidnapped. A ransom was demanded. A ransom that her father didn't pay."

"What happened?" Lucy again. Sam wasn't saying anything—I'd briefed him last night. He knew who Chloe was, too—and what she meant to me.

"The people who took them, Vincent Cabrello and John Santini, were a couple of low-life hoodlums who had fallen foul of some connected people in New York State. They hightailed it over to the West Coast to lie low, enjoy some sunshine and make what they figured would be some easy pickings."

"And they picked on Hannah Shapiro and her mother?" Suzy asked.

I nodded. "The kidnapping wasn't planned. Hannah and her mother weren't specifically targeted."

"Opportunistic?"

"Seems that way. They were just in the wrong place at the wrong time. Cabrello and Santini, pumped up on speed and bourbon, waited in their van in an underground car park. They just planned to take the first likely candidate they saw. They figured that anybody shopping in this particular mall would have serious money, and they were right..."

I pointed at the picture of Hannah. "They hit the jackpot with Hannah and Jessica Shapiro. Only trouble was, they were bringing another lightning storm down on their heads at the same time. And this one they wouldn't be able to run away from."

"Jack Morgan," Sam grunted.

Chapter 31

I NODDED.

"Jessica Shapiro told her captors exactly who she and Hannah were, what they were worth and said she was a hundred percent certain that her husband would pay the ransom."

"But he didn't," Wendy Lee said.

"No. John Santini contacted Harlan Shapiro and gave him a couple of days to come up with the money. No police or all bets were off and then he would be collecting his wife and daughter in plastic bags. Given their history as enforcers for East Coast organized crime it was no idle threat. Not that Harlan Shapiro knew that, of course. He is a man used to getting his own way."

I took a sip of my coffee. "Harlan Shapiro decided to make a stand. Like his government he was going to stand firm in the face of terrorism, as he saw it. He needed a private detective agency known for getting the job done. One that would not hesitate if lethal force was required. One that wouldn't be hamstrung with legal bureaucracy and Miranda rights, etc., etc. One that would get his wife and daughter back safe. He never believed that if he paid the money the kidnappers would make good on their promise. Most likely he was right."

"Wouldn't be the first time," Sam agreed.

"Yeah, so he went to a private-investigation outfit he had used a few times before. Run by a guy called Prentiss who assigned Jack Morgan to the case.

"Right off the bat Jack advised Harlan Shapiro to pay the ransom. From what he had heard of the operation he deduced they were dealing with a couple of chancers whose ambitions far outstretched their likely experience. Pay the ransom and he could practically guarantee they would trace the kidnappers down, recover the money and deliver them to justice."

"But Shapiro didn't listen to him?" asked Suzy.

I shook my head. "No. He didn't."

"Jack obviously managed to get them back, though?" asked Lucy puzzled.

"Not entirely. He saved Hannah. But not before she was forced to watch her mother being raped by Vincent Cabrello and murdered by John Santini."

"That's awful."

"You've got to remember that Jack didn't have the resources of Private behind him at the time, Lucy. When he got there he was too late for Jessica but at least he saved Hannah."

"What happened to the kidnappers?"

I smiled bleakly. "Let's just say they didn't make it to trial."

"You reckon the two cases are connected?" asked Brad Dexter.

Chapter 32

I SHOOK MY HEAD.

"I can't see how. Cabrello and Santini were operating independently. Their ties to the East Coast were cut. This was their cock-up, pure and simple. So whoever has her now has nothing to do with that first abduction. That's the one thing we can be a hundred percent sure of."

"Still no ransom demands?" asked Sam.

"Not so far."

Adrian held up his hand.

"You don't have to put your hand up, Adrian." I gestured at him to spit out his thoughts.

"Maybe it isn't a kidnapping as such."

"Go on?" I prompted.

I knew where he was going with this and I didn't like it one bit.

"Maybe it's not a kidnap for ransom as such, like the last time was. The murder scene I was called out to last night. A young woman...she *maybe* had organs harvested from her."

"Maybe?"

"We're waiting on the post-mortem," added Wendy Lee.

"The tip of her wedding finger was missing," added Adrian Tuttle.

"And this relates to Hannah Shapiro how?" asked Sam.

"Because it's not the first time, Sam," I said. Facing the fact that it might already be far too late for Hannah.

Wendy Lee nodded and put it out there. "It looks like there's a serial killer," she said. "In the city. Targeting healthy young women."

"Women like Hannah," said Adrian Tuttle, looking at the picture of the beautiful young American woman that filled the video screen.

Chapter 33

PROFESSOR ANNABELLE WESTON was older than Hannah but every bit as striking.

I'd have placed her in her mid-thirties if I'd had to guess. Five seven or eight, give or take the heels on a pair of court shoes. Long strawberry-blonde hair, lively, almost turquoise eyes. A light splash of freckles across her shoulders but her face was alabaster-clear with high cheekbones. Her teeth wouldn't have looked out of place in a San Diego beauty pageant—and she certainly wasn't dressed like any professor from my day!

She was wearing skintight jeans, cowboy boots and a pastel-blue cashmere sweater that did nothing to distract from her womanly figure.

Her hair was tied back in a loose kind of scarf, and she had a pair of glasses perched on the end of her nose, just the way Alison wore them. These were tortoiseshell, giving her an academic look, which I guess she was entitled to. The eyes behind the lenses of those glasses were deadly serious.

"You're not working with the police on this, then?" she asked.

Her voice was as English as her strawberries-and-cream complexion. Home counties. Money. Pound to a penny she had polo ponies featuring somewhere in her childhood.

I shook my head. "No," I said leaning forward and handing her my card. "We often work with the police in an official capacity, but in this instance we are pursuing a separate investigation."

"I don't understand. We have had the proper authorities talking to everyone here already. What is your interest, specifically?"

She glanced at my business card, then looked at me challengingly. There was steel behind the beauty. I wouldn't like my chances if I was one of her students trying to bluff my way to an extension on an overdue assignment.

"We're representing Hannah's family," said Sam Riddel who was sitting beside me.

"And we have a personal interest too," I added.

"And what would that be?"

"You were Hannah's tutor, is that right?" I asked.

"Yes, I was." She caught herself. "That is to say, I *am* her tutor."

"And likewise Chloe Wilson's?"

"Yes. Both of them."

"Chloe Wilson is my god-daughter, Professor Weston."

"Oh…"

She reacted, taking it in, and the hardness in her eyes softened to genuine concern. "How is she? Has she regained consciousness?"

"She's stable but still critical. They are keeping an eye on her round the clock."

"If there's anything I can do…?"

"That's why we're here, professor. Whoever did this isn't going to get away with it. I can promise you that, and I can promise we will find Hannah and bring her home unharmed."

I don't know why I said that last part. Or rather I did—I wanted to impress the woman, I guess.

"Poor Hannah. I can't bear to think what she is going through."

"She will be safe for the moment, professor. I know that much." I almost believed it myself.

"Call me Annabelle, please."

I resisted the urge to say it was a pretty name. But it was. "They will be keeping her safe, Annabelle," I said instead. "She's precious goods to them. Until we hear their demands I am pretty certain they won't harm a hair on her head."

"There has been no contact with the family, then? No ransom demand?"

I shook my head.

I didn't tell her the other possibility that Adrian Tuttle had raised in the morning's briefing. That she had been taken for body parts and for all we knew was already dead.

"I'm sure we'll hear something soon," I

said. "And the entire resources of Private worldwide are at my disposal to get her safely home."

"Shouldn't the police be left to handle it?"

"The police will be doing everything they can. But sometimes we can do more."

"How so?"

"Each year in London alone there about one hundred and seventy homicides," I said. "That's more than one every three days. And that's just homicide. If you take into account every other crime, from theft and assault to rape, that occurs in this city, never mind the ongoing threat of terrorist attacks that have to be investigated—if you think about that, then you can see that we can bring to bear on this case something the Metropolitan Police could never hope to."

"Which is?" the professor asked.

"*Absolute* focus." I said

And it was true.

Professor Weston looked down at my business card for a moment and then nodded, lifted her head and looked me straight in the eye.

"Just tell me what you need."

Chapter 34

SUZY CRADLED THE phone to her ear and typed on the computer keyboard in front of her.

"Copy that, Dan," she said as the crest of Chancellors University appeared in the center of the screen above the word SECURITY printed in block capitals.

She clicked on the crest and the image fragmented into a thousand pixels floating off the screen, leaving a plain password box in its place.

"Okay, I got it," she said. "I'll get back to you." She clicked her phone shut as Lucy came in.

"What have we got?"

"Dan's been to see Hannah and Chloe's tutor. She's the faculty liaison officer with security at the college."

"Which means?"

"She has access to the security files online. Including CCTV footage."

Suzy quickly typed in the password. Flicking through several screens and pulling up a list of digitally stored data. She clicked against yesterday's date and then against the cameras marked for the union bar and then the quad outside. She right-clicked and saved them as AVI files.

She stood up and grinned. "Come on."

"Where to?"

"You haven't seen this yet. It's fun."

Lucy followed her, puzzled, as she walked away from her desk and led her back to the conference room.

Inside, Suzy opened the top drawer of a storage unit and took out two pairs of what appeared to be lightly tinted sunglasses. She threw Lucy a pair, slipped hers on and picked up the thin wandlike remote control that operated the television that dominated the far end of the room. She stepped to the side and flicked a switch. Shutters dropped over the exterior and interior of the windows and the lights dimmed to almost darkness.

"Lights, camera, action," said Suzy, pressing the control, and the Union Bar of Chancellors College filled the screen. Suzy freeze-framed the image and pulled out her notebook.

She pointed the control at the monitor again, clicked the button and light danced into the room, transforming the two-dimensional image in a full holographic-style 3D effect as the tape played and a burst of motion surrounded the on-screen figures.

"Last night's footage," explained Suzy. "The computer takes the feed from each camera and triangulates it, making the image three-dimensional."

Lucy held out her hand and flinched as a large and extremely drunk young man seemed to walk straight at her.

"The police will have this footage as well but they have nowhere near this kind of image-enhancement and three-dimensional-projection technology."

Lucy nodded, impressed. It really felt as if she could reach out and pick up a glass off one of the tables.

"Sound as well. Chancellors recently had their whole security network upgraded."

Lucy pushed another button and the deafening noise of the bar filled the room. She adjusted the volume to a reasonable level and used the control to navigate around the room, coming to the entrance door where she fast-forwarded until Chloe and her two friends came in and walked up to the bar.

Two brunettes and a blonde. Young, vibrant, beautiful.

Dressed up for a night of partying, by the looks of them. There was no shortage of young men hitting on them and they particularly drew the attention of a large crowd who were wearing CUL rugby shirts. They seemed perfectly capable of deflecting the unwanted attention. Suzy guessed they were probably used to it.

Lucy and Suzy let the tape run and the events unfold around them. The girls were downing vodka and Red Bulls like they were going out of fashion. At least, Hannah and Laura were. Dan's god-daughter Chloe seemed to be holding back.

After about an hour Suzy paused the tape—she had watched it up to the girls leaving the bar—and then rewound. She zoomed in a little on Hannah and Chloe who were talking. Having to shout to make themselves heard. Suzy killed the volume from the other cameras, turned up the one focused on the girls and let the sequence run again.

Chapter 35

"Good thinking, girlfriend. Bunch of goddamned horny schoolboys in here, is all. I need to pee first, though, honey."

Hannah looped her arm through that of Laura who was being chatted up by a lanky youth and headed to the loos.

Chloe put a hand on the bar, seeming to steady herself.

"She look all right to you, Lucy?" asked Suzy as she paused the footage again.

"No. Not for the amount she's had. She's not been drinking as much as the other girls."

"No. She's keeping herself sober. Or trying to."

"Always on the case."

Suzy nodded. "She's a pro. You figure her drink was spiked?"

"Looks that way."

Suzy nodded and ran the tape again, watching as the barman chatted to Chloe who then nearly collapsed as she walked away. She stood up unsteadily and brushed away the hand of one of the rugby players who had come across to help her.

Chloe was five foot ten in her bare feet and the man seemed surprised at her strength. He backed off, holding his hand up, and Chloe stumbled through a crowd of his friends who were singing loudly. She lurched through them, through the door and up the ancient stone steps out into the night.

"Someone spiked her drink," said Suzy. "I guarantee it."

"Maybe it was caught on camera?"

"Let's find out," said Suzy as she rewound the footage and fast-forwarded it again. Slowing it down as drinks were poured and handed over.

Some half an hour or so after the girls had entered the bar she paused it again. Then ran it backward and forwards a few more times. The crowd of rugby players and another bunch of male students were at the bar and the barman was obscured from view for a while. When the crowd cleared, Chloe had a new drink in front of her.

"One of those men at the bar?" asked Lucy.

"Could be." Suzy tried to adjust the angle of view but there wasn't a camera behind the bar pointing down, only one pointing out-wards, so there was no way they could see what had happened to Chloe's drink. She pulled out her phone and hit a speed-dial but-ton. She listened to Dan's recorded voice as the call went direct to voicemail.

"Dan, it's Suzy," she said after the beep. "Get someone onto Chloe's blood works at the hospital. It looks like she was slipped a Mickey of some sort."

She closed her phone and turned back to the screen.

"Why would someone have just targeted Hannah?" asked Lucy.

"I don't know. Unless they knew who she was."

Suzy pressed the remote again and they sat and watched as the external security cameras picked up the action. Switching data files as Chloe came up the steps leading into the quad, walking across it and out into the side street.

She flipped the control again and called up the earlier footage as Chloe left the bar. She watched her leave, weaving through the group of drunken rugby players. One of them was watching her very closely.

Suzy let the tape run for a few moments more and then whistled quietly.

"Well, well, well," she said.

She clicked another button and the printer standing in the corner of the room beeped and hummed into life.

Chapter 36

THE UNION JACK Café near Shaftesbury Avenue was one of the last of a dying breed in the capital. A proper greasy spoon.

I had ordered the full monty—eggs, bacon, sausages, hash browns, mushrooms, black pudding—but when it arrived I pushed it aside. The memory of Chloe lying in bed with a tube in her mouth kind of spoiled my appetite.

Sam Riddel was carving his yolk-free scrambled eggs on wheat toast with surgical precision. He laid his fork carefully aside and took a sip of his chilled organic tomato juice. His breakfast went against all the principles of the café, but we had been coming here long enough for the owner to compromise for Sam. Besides, most people didn't argue with my colleague. Apart from his boyfriend and me, that was.

Suzy came in, carrying an A4 manila envelope.

"What have you got?" I asked.

"Not sure yet, but you'll want to see this." She opened the envelope and put a photo in front of me. "This is the guy serving Chloe and the others last night in the union bar. I've heard back from the hospital..."

"And?"

"And Chloe's blood work was showing traces of an intermediate-acting three-hydroxy benzodiazepine."

"Which means?"

"Temazepam," said Sam and took another delicate sip of his tomato juice.

"Someone slipped her a Mickey. Lucy and I went through all the footage, there were a couple of possibilities," Suzy said, tapping the photo. "This guy had ample opportunity and he's out of sight of the CCTV easily for long enough to spike her vodka. He leaves the bar shortly after Chloe. He doesn't show up in the quad but there are other exits not covered by any camera."

"And the other possibility?"

"A group of men at the bar. Rugby team— one of them shows a very keen interest in her."

Suzy flipped a couple of photos down. The young men from the security footage. Early twenties, big, boisterous by the look of it, wearing the university rugby colors. And a further one. A close-up shot of one of the men. A degree more serious than the others, his eyes unsmiling as he looked at Chloe leaving. An intense, predatory look.

"Good job. We got names on these people yet?"

"The barman's called Ryan Williams. He's being interviewed down at Paddington Green even as we speak."

"He's been arrested?"

"No. Helping with enquiries."

"Why take him down there, then?"

"Don't know, boss. But you probably know someone who does." Suzy smiled pointedly. She was right. I did.

I tapped the pictures of the rugby players. "And the merry gentlemen here?"

"We're on it, Dan."

"Good."

"But there's more," she added.

"Go on," prompted Sam.

Suzy picked up the envelope again. "I went back to the footage from the quad, wound back a couple of hours. The university had a visitor you both might recognize, and I'm guessing he wasn't there because he had a tutorial on Spenser's *Faerie Queen*."

She slipped the final photo out and flipped it down on the table.

She was probably right about the tutorial. The man in the dark suit and matching sunglasses was about Sam Riddel's height but a good few stone heavier, and certainly no vegetarian. His name was Brendan "Snake" Ferres and he was one of the most unpleasant men to walk the planet.

"Not good," I said simply.

"Not good at all," agreed Suzy.

"As far from good as it can get," added Sam.

Brendan Ferres was the right-and left-hand

man of Ronnie Allen. And Ronnie Allen was a very serious customer. He was the go-to man north of the river for drugs, prostitution, guns, murder. You name it—if it was illegal his fingers were going to be in the pie somewhere. But not kidnapping, so far as I knew.

I picked up the photos, sliding them back into the manila envelope.

"You see Allen mixed up in this?" I asked Sam.

He shrugged and finished his drink. "Not his usual thing. But then again, we don't really know what this thing is. We don't know who has got Hannah Shapiro and as yet we don't know why."

He had a point.

Or he did. Until my phone rang, jangling on the Formica-topped table. I looked at the caller ID.

Jack Morgan.

Chapter 37

DI KIRSTY WEBB desperately fancied a cigarette.

She hadn't smoked in over ten years, but she reckoned she could kill for one now as she watched the forensic pathologist preparing to examine the corpse.

It was supposed to be Kirsty's weekend off. Fat chance of that now with a girl gone missing, abducted right off the street, and another woman found eviscerated and dumped. Murdered, most likely.

Three weeks earlier Kirsty had been the lead DI called to the Putney rowing club on the Surrey side of the Thames.

Six-thirty in the morning on the first of May, Dr. Jonathan Brown, a twenty-seven-year-old academic specializing in medieval hagiography, had been preparing to go on the water. He was a hotly tipped single-sculls hopeful for the 2012 Olympics and pretty much every minute of his spare time was spent training for the event.

As he was putting his scull onto the water that morning, however, Dr. Brown saw something that caused him to step back, make the sign of the cross and mutter a prayer to Saint Andrew the Apostle, the patron saint of fishermen. What he was looking at was the mottled arm of a dead woman.

The woman was lying at the end of the ramp running down to the river, looking as though she was trying to pull herself out of the water. Dr. Brown looked at the arm, horrified for a moment, unsure what to do. Then, as the tidal waters gently rocked into shore, the body was lifted and turned by the swell.

The medieval scholar saw that her body had been cut open. A gaping wound across her torso. He staggered back, gagging—and for the first time in over five years he didn't do any training that morning.

Kirsty Webb had been trying to track the identity of the woman ever since.

Chapter 38

THE WOMAN WAS estimated to be in her mid- to late twenties, was naked and had no identifying marks or tattoos on her body.

Her fingerprints didn't show up on any database. Neither did her DNA but it had taken three weeks for DI Webb to get that information: the report had landed on her desk only that morning. The dead woman's teeth were intact but were useless for identification purposes—unless they found a candidate to match them against.

The only significant clue apart from the fact that she had had her heart surgically removed was the fact that the third finger on her left hand had been severed at the second knuckle. If she had been married there was no evidence of it now.

The press had run wild with the story. All manner of theories were put forward. The most lurid of which was that the woman had been slaughtered in some kind of blood sacrifice or voodoo ritual.

It wouldn't be the first time. Kirsty remembered the West African boy that the Metropolitan Police had called Adam. His torso had been found in the Thames. Chemicals in his stomach had been identified as a so-called "magic potion" containing traces of pure gold, a clear indication that his murder had most likely been a ritual killing.

And now, three weeks since the first mutilated woman's body had been discovered on the banks of the Thames, a second had been found a few miles away in King's Cross.

Organs removed, wedding-ring finger amputated. Kirsty Webb had no doubt they were dealing with a serial killer.

Or killers. If the same people had taken the young student Hannah Shapiro last night—

then the police were definitely dealing with a group of them.

Remembering Hannah made Kirsty think of Dan Carter and his god-daughter, still lying unconscious in an intensive-care room. And thinking of him made her remember that today was their wedding anniversary—and then she really, really did want that cigarette.

Damn the bloody man! Everywhere she turned in London he popped up like the proverbial bad penny. But fingers crossed that all that would change soon. Kirsty was on the shortlist for a new initiative being set up to coordinate worldwide information on serial murder. It was a prestigious job, carrying with it a promotion, a commensurate salary hike and, most important of all, it was based in Manchester! About two hundred miles north from Dan bloody Carter as the crow flew.

If she could crack the mystery wide open she had a far better chance of getting the post. The only thing was, of course, that the serial-killer element had taken her off this case as lead. She was just a cog in the machine now.

So Kirsty needed to make things happen—which was why she was here on her day off watching the post-mortem on the unknown woman found in a vermin-riddled lock-up in the King's Cross area.

She had tracked down the owner of the garage. A certain Edward Morrison, a retired motor mechanic from Paddington. They had arrived at the address with enough blue lights to decorate Oxford Street. However, a startled Mr. Shah and his young bride, the new occupants of the ground-floor flat, had informed them that Edward Morrison no longer lived there.

He had died of a heart attack some six months earlier. There were no living relatives and no one had been officially aware of the lock-up until the Met had traced its ownership. It was another dead end in a series of dead ends.

Doctor Harriet Walsh looked over at the detective. "Still no idea who she is?"

"None at all. We're going through the missing-persons register, obviously, but she could be from anywhere in the country. It's going to take time."

The doctor nodded thoughtfully. "Or from another country."

"Exactly. There anything you can tell me ahead of the post?"

"Are you lead on this?"

"No. Just conscientious."

The doctor smiled. "Fair enough."

"We know about the finger being cut off. Are there other similarities?"

The doctor walked across to a cabinet and picked up some photographs.

"There was extensive damage done to the soft tissue, as you know."

"The rats."

"Yes. I took some photos and then had them enlarged. If you look here on the third rib you can see a definite scratch."

Kirsty took the photo and looked at it. "And this tells us what?"

"It tells us that this didn't come from a rat's teeth but from a man-made item."

"What kind of item?"

Doctor Walsh walked over to her instrument tray. "One of these," she said—and picked up a scalpel.

Chapter 39

KIRSTY SHUDDERED AS the doctor replaced the instrument.

"How long ago?" she asked.

"I'll know more when we have done the proper post-mortem."

"And the scratch?"

"Most likely from an operation."

Kirsty Webb nodded. It confirmed her worst fears. "And how long ago would that have taken place?"

"Probably a number of days. Maybe up to a week. But no longer."

"Somebody killed her and then removed her organs."

The doctor put the scalpel back on the tray and put a mask over her mouth. Then she turned back to the DI. "Let's hope he killed her first!" she said before picking up the hand-held, powered circular saw.

Chapter 40

JACK MORGAN HAD received a textmail from whoever had taken Hannah Shapiro.

It had been sent from an untraceable phone and it was flagging up as an overseas call. It said simply that an e-mail would be sent to the London offices shortly and a phone call would follow this afternoon.

Ten minutes after the call from Jack and we were sitting back in the conference room.

An hour later and the screen at the end of the table beeped again. We'd already had five false alarms. The screen was set to computer mode, the bottom quarter of it a large monitor now. I used the handheld gizmo to move the mouse over incoming mail and clicked on the new message.

The sender's address was a series of capital letters and numbers: KJP9OU56KL@hot mail.com. The subject line read DAMAGED GOODS.

With a sense of dread I moved the cursor and clicked to open the mail. It revealed a hyperlink: http://www.youtube.com/watch?v=118ecF3VzMM

I puffed out a sigh and clicked on the link. It led to a YouTube video. Darkness for a number of seconds. A faint, whimpering, mewing sound in the background.

Not good.

A bright light came on. Throwing a spotlight on Hannah Shapiro sitting against a plain wall, a window beside her with its slatted blinds closed. The darkness surrounding the pool of light on Hannah indicating that the time was late night.

Hannah was dressed only in her underwear: black silk matching bra and boxer-style briefs. Some rope was hanging from her left wrist. A ball gag lying on the floor.

Her hair was tangled, her face was distraught, deathly pale. Makeup running around her tear-stained reddened eyes like one of those Japanese Noh dancers caught in a rain shower. She had a piece of paper in her hand. She looked up at the camera, heartbreaking desperation in her eyes.

"Please do what they say," Hannah said. "They will hurt me. They have made that very clear. Hurt me in terrible ways. Do not contact the police. Do not attempt to find me. They will be in touch with instructions in due course. Do not contact the police."

The light went off. It was dark for a few seconds and then came the sound of Hannah crying before it was suddenly muffled.

I played the clip back again: there was an option to play it at HD, which I clicked on, but the quality wasn't greatly improved.

I turned to Adrian Tuttle, our only remaining computer expert now that Sponge had gone back to Russia. "Adrian, get out there and see if you can track the traffic line on this. And burn the footage from YouTube. I want to put it in our system. See what we can do with it."

"Boss."

He hurried his gangling frame out of the conference room, back to his workstation. A real-life Ichabod Crane. I would have smiled at the thought but seeing Hannah Shapiro humiliated, trussed up and scared for her life had left me too furious for levity.

I used the remote to click back to our e-mail in-box. Nothing there.

I'd promised I'd take care of Hannah. Doing a fine job of it so far, I thought sourly. I slammed my hand down on the conference table in frustration and looked around at my colleagues. "Any ideas?"

"I'd say the ball is in play now. That's something," said Sam.

I nodded. Hannah was unhurt thus far. That was important—our job was to make it stay that way. And Sam was right: the ball was in play. We had something to focus on now. They had made contact: that was far better than the alternative.

We watched the tape through a couple more times, blowing it up to full-screen. Learned nothing more.

"So, we sit and wait?" Suzy asked.

"No," I said. "We need to get down to the college, look into those rugby players. This barman. We need to keep moving, guys."

"I'll get on it," she replied.

I nodded. "Take Lucy with you, Suzy. Get down to the bar. You might find out something that the police haven't picked up on."

"You got it."

"But be careful, okay?"

"Boss."

She stood up and left and I turned to Sam. "Why don't you and I go and have a word with Brendan Ferres and his puppet master?"

"That wise? Before we know what the deal is?"

"Probably not. But we're going to do it anyway. Let's kick the apple tree a little, see what drops," I said.

Then all hell broke loose.

Chapter 41

THE DOOR FLEW open and a flustered Lucy hurried in.

"Sorry, sir, there was nothing I could do," she said.

Following in behind her was my ex-wife, DI Kirsty Webb of the Metropolitan Police, and several of her colleagues in smartly pressed blue uniforms.

"Dan Carter," she began ominously. "I am arresting you on suspicion of interfering with the course of justice."

"You are shitting me," I replied.

She gave me a pointed look of the kind that I remembered only too well. "You do not have to say anything, but it may harm your defense if you do not mention when questioned something which you later rely on in court. Anything you do say may be given in evidence."

Kirsty waited for me to come back with a smart remark. I didn't give her the satisfaction.

She nodded to one of the burly uniformed officers. "Cuff him, George."

I held my hands out and smiled sweetly at her as the cop slapped the cuffs on my wrists.

"What did I do? I forget it was our anniversary?"

I couldn't help myself.

"Take him down the nick," she said tersely to George. "Make sure he doesn't fall down too many stairs."

Chapter 42

HALF AN HOUR later I was in a holding cell.

It was painted a sickly pale lime green. An inset concrete bed with a thin pallet on it. No windows. I had checked the door—it was locked.

Kirsty hadn't said a single word to me on the journey over. It would have been hard to—she'd been traveling in a separate car. I had been bundled unceremoniously into the backseat of a modified Range Rover with caged partitions. It felt like I'd been picked up by the police dog-handling unit. Maybe I had been.

I'd taken my jacket and shirt off. Kept my

white cotton T-shirt on to spare the blushes of any visitors, and was doing press-ups. I had done about a hundred and twenty when I heard the viewing hatch slide open and a voice announce, "You got a visitor, Carter."

I got a faint hint of perfume, something floral and musky, and considered moving onto finger-and-thumb press-ups, but thought better of the idea.

Was I any fitter now than I'd been before an Iraqi roadside bomb and a couple of well-aimed insurgent bullets had seen me hospitalised for two months all those years ago? The truth was that I probably was.

I didn't take my immortality for granted any more, that was for damn sure. And I kept my body in as fit a condition as I could manage. Doing press-ups in the cell gave me something to do other than think of Hannah and Chloe. Didn't work, but when you get dealt a crap hand you've got to play it the best you can.

The door opened and I stood up.

It was Alison Chambers. Black suit, white silk blouse. Her makeup perfectly applied and the perfume as heady as that from a field of poppies.

"What the fuck have you done now, Dan?" she said, kind of spoiling the moment.

I shrugged as the thickset uniform shut the door on us. "I'm sorry. I can't offer you tea," I said as I sat down on the pallet and patted the space beside me for her to join me.

She folded her arms and gave me the kind of look my beloved ex had given me earlier. You know the kind—the sort a judge might give you before slamming down the gavel and sending you off to the colonies for fifteen years' hard labor.

"Just tell me what's going on," she said.

"Alison," I said. "I honestly don't know."

And I honestly didn't.

Chapter 43

I TOOK A sip of tea.

It was awful. Too much sugar, too much milk. I made a tutting sound and got a reproachful look from Alison Chambers.

She was now sitting next to me on the bed. A businesslike notebook open on her lap, on the pages of which she was writing businesslike notes, I assumed. The nib of her Mont Blanc fountain pen appeared to scratch into the paper a tad deeper than was probably necessary.

"The tea not to your satisfaction?" she asked coolly.

"It's not PG Tips, I can tell you that much," I said.

"And this isn't the Ritz either, if you hadn't noticed. It's the Paddington Green nick."

"Yeah, I did notice that. The last time Kirsty took my trouser belt off on our wedding anniversary she didn't take the shoelaces as well!"

I looked down at my brogues. Without the laces the tongues of both shoes flopped out like those of overheated dogs.

"You don't seem to be taking this seriously, Dan. So I am not sure I can help you."

"Oh, I'm taking this deadly seriously, I can assure you."

"You bring a woman into this country under a false passport. You enter your so-called god-daughter into the same college as her, also under a false name, but at least that's not a crime so far as I know."

"Nor me," I agreed.

"But you had Chloe working for you, didn't you?" Alison pressed angrily.

I didn't respond.

"And now the girl you smuggled in illegally," she continued, "has been kidnapped and you refuse to tell the police a damn thing."

"I'm taking the Fifth."

She sighed, exasperated. "This is Paddington Green, Carter! Not Prairie Fart, Idaho. You don't have the option to take the Fifth. There is no Fifth!"

"You know, your eyes really do go green when you're angry."

"For God's sake! Are you even listening to me?"

"Like they said when I was arrested, Alison, I don't have to say anything."

"Well, you bloody do to me! And stop with the flip bloody act, Dan. I know you're beating yourself up about what happened to those girls. I know you're angry and want to get out there and do something about it."

Alison knew me pretty well. "I do."

"And I am trying to help you do that. So why don't you throw me a bone here?"

I sighed and shook my head. "If you don't know then you can't be compromised."

"Then what am I supposed to do?"

"Nothing. I'll take care of it."

"How?"

"I don't know."

The door opened and Kirsty walked in. She looked at us both for a moment without speaking.

"Isn't this cozy?" she said finally. "The Thin Man and his lawyer. All we need now is a little dog and it would be a perfect picture."

Kirsty was a big fan of old black-and-white films.

"Are you going to charge my client?" asked Alison, a degree of frost creeping into her voice.

Kirsty smiled but there wasn't a lot of warmth in it, either. "Client?" she said, rolling the word around on her tongue as if trying it on for size and not finding it to her liking.

"If you have something to say, how about we expedite matters and simply say it, Kirsty?" said Alison.

Kirsty looked at me, ignoring her. "Just so you know. It was never my idea to arrest you in the first place."

"Fair enough."

"The second murder and now this abduction. My hands were tied. The big guns were wheeled in and my boss DSI Andrew Harrington ordered you brought in. There's promotion written all over this case."

"I see."

"No way around it. You brought her here under a false passport, Dan. There's stuff going on that you know and we don't. And that's not right."

I nodded. Hard to argue with her. "Sorry." I said simply.

"So...is there anything you want to tell us?"

I shook my head. The message had been very clear. If the police became involved then Hannah would be hurt. Hurt in ways that did not bear thinking about. There was no option.

"Then you leave me no choice..." said DI Webb.

"Than to do what?" asked Alison Chambers.

"Than to let you go," said Kirsty. Surprising the pair of us.

Chapter 44

IT WAS JUST shy of one o'clock.

The union bar was starting to fill up. It was a Saturday. Lucy and Suzy had positioned themselves at the far left of the bar, perched on stools that gave them a good view of the room.

They had been chatting to Carol, a third-year history student who was working the shift with the older full-time manager called Sian.

Sian had told Lucy that Ryan would be coming on shift from one o'clock. It wasn't the first time she had been asked that particular question over the couple of months that Ryan had been working for her and she very much doubted that it would be the last. Ryan, it seemed, was very popular with the female students.

Carol handed a soda-and-lime to Suzy.

"Thanks. Terrible thing about what happened to those girls last night."

"It's disgusting," agreed the barmaid. "A couple of *No Means No* leaflets and that's all the protection they reckon we need."

"Too true," agreed Lucy.

"I certainly won't be working any more night shifts."

"Were you working last night, then?" asked Suzy pretending ignorance.

"No. And I'm bloody glad, too. It could have been any one of us."

"Yeah," agreed Lucy. Although she had her doubts.

She sipped on her own soda-and-lime and wondered how much more of the stuff she could drink. She looked across to the doorway and nudged Suzy with her foot as Ryan the barman came in.

He waved at a group of three women who were sitting at a table with papers and books spread out before them. They waved back enthusiastically.

"Popular lad," said Lucy quietly.

"I wouldn't waste your time," said Carol, amused. "That boy's in lurve."

"Oh yeah?" replied Suzy. "Who with? Himself?"

Carol laughed. "No, Ryan's all right. But it seems it's unrequited love, so who knows?"

"Who's the lucky lady, then?"

Carol nodded to a young woman who had come in while they were chatting. She was sitting alone at a table partly hidden from view by one of the carved stone pillars holding the roof in place.

She was strikingly attractive, with long blonde hair, baby-blue eyes set in a creamy complexion, Cupid's-bow lips painted pillar-box red. She wore jeans and a short-sleeved rugby shirt. The only thing marring the perfect image was the bandage she wore on her lower right arm, although she made even that look like a fashion statement. But there was also a sadness in her big come-to-bed eyes.

Laura Skelton.

Chapter 45

NO WONDER THE barman had the hots for Laura, thought Suzy.

She liked the look of her herself. And when she did go for women she normally went for brunettes. Dan Carter and she had that much in common.

Ryan stood with his back to them, talking to Laura Skelton for a few moments, then headed to the side of the bar, lifting a flap to swap places with Carol who sketched a wave to Lucy as she left. "Good luck," she said as she passed.

Lucy nodded back, pretending to be a little flustered and letting the barman catch it. All good cover, she thought. Besides, if the barman was innocent, and single...

Suzy flicked her a half-smile, snapping her out of her reverie. "Be interesting to hear what he said to her."

Lucy nodded to the security camera. "Be on tape. Can't see him incriminating himself if he is involved, though."

Ryan Williams came across at that moment and gave them a smile of his own, but an almost apologetic one. "I don't believe I have seen you ladies here before," he said.

"No," said Suzy, giving it the full tilt with her chin. "We're virgins."

"To the bar, she means," added Lucy.

"Can I see your NUS cards then, please?" he said.

"What kind of girls do you think we are?" said Suzy in mock outrage. "I've never had an STD in my life."

The barman didn't smile. He'd heard it plenty of times before. "I said NUS. No ID and I will have to ask you to leave, I'm afraid. Particularly after what happened last night."

"It's not safe, you mean?" asked Lucy, giving a good impression of a nervous woman.

"No, you're perfectly safe. We've just had a lot of journalists trying to blag their way on campus today. It's been all over the news."

Suzy laughed. "Do we look like journalists?" She held up her hand before Ryan could reply. "It's okay, sheriff, you can keep your weapon holstered for now."

She pulled out an NUS card and held it up as Lucy rummaged in her bag for hers. It had taken them less than five minutes to get them mocked-up back at the office earlier. "See?" she said. "We're both pickers of apples from the tree of wisdom."

Ryan looked at the cards briefly and nodded. "Sorry. I have to ask."

Suzy nodded too, all serious now. "Absolutely. And I'm glad you did. God knows, we all have to look out for each other. Especially now," she added as Laura Skelton approached the bar.

"Can I just get a coffee, please, Ryan? Cappuccino," she said.

"It's on the house." The barman beamed at her and hurried off to the other end of the bar where an espresso machine was set back on the counter."

"I'm sorry," Suzy said to Laura.

"For what?"

"You probably heard us talking. Saying we all had to look out for each other. I didn't mean to be insensitive."

"It's okay," said Laura. "I just wish I could have looked out for them better." She ran a hand reflexively along her bandaged arm.

"Do the police know any more?" asked Lucy.

Laura shook her head. "I still can't believe what happened. Why take Hannah, why leave us behind? God, they could have killed Chloe." Her eyes welled. "What are they going to do to Hannah?"

Suzy stroked her arm. "Hey, it's going to be all right. I am sure she is going to be fine."

"Did you know her?"

Suzy shook her head.

"So how do you know that she's going to be fine?" Laura snapped.

"If she's been kidnapped it wouldn't make sense to harm her."

192 • James Patterson

"But she's not rich. Her father has *some* money, but he's just a car dealer back in San Diego. He's not a multimillionaire or anything."

Ryan came back with the coffee and Laura nodded at him, not really registering his presence.

"We were just about to have lunch," said Lucy. "Why don't you join us? I'm Lucy by the way."

"Thanks."

"And I'm Suzy Malone," said Suzy, smiling as she held out her hand. Laura took it and held on for a while, and when Suzy looked in her eyes there was a definite charge.

Suzy let Laura's hand go. She was working. Never mix business with pleasure. Wasn't that the golden rule?

Chapter 46

ALISON CHAMBERS STRODE forcefully across the car park toward her parked car.

There was very little swish to her hips this time, although her hair tossed a little angrily from side to side. I couldn't help watching her and grinned a little guiltily as Kirsty came out through the entrance doors and up to me.

"Enjoying the view?" she said curtly.

I was standing in the car park of Paddington Green police station, having had my belt and shoelaces returned to me and been released some ten minutes earlier.

"Isn't it time you let it go?" I asked.

"More to the point, isn't it time *you* did?" she snapped back.

I sighed. I had no burning desire to have another ride on that particular carousel. "Thanks," I said simply, instead of pushing it.

"Thanks for what?"

"For not wanting to arrest me."

"I'd watch your back if I were you. DSI Harrington is spitting feathers in there."

"Sorry to ruin his day."

"I mean it, Dan. He's got a serious hard-on for you."

"All I care about is finding that little girl."

Even though I had seen the recent pictures of Hannah and the footage of her dressed up like some kind of sick Bettie Page caricature, I still thought of her as the young girl who had discussed F. Scott Fitzgerald with me on that flight not so very long ago.

"I know you do."

I looked across at my ex-wife. For a moment there I thought I had detected a little tenderness in her voice.

Of course I had. Kirsty didn't hate the world. She just hated me. She wanted Hannah Shapiro found every bit as much as I did. Policing wasn't just a job to her. It was her vocation. Her life. I felt the familiar stab of guilt I always felt when she showed her softer side.

"I'm sorry," I said. "If I could go back in time."

"It's not your fault, Dan. You didn't kidnap the girl, did you?"

"I wasn't talking about that..."

She held up a hand to stop me saying any more.

"Yeah, yeah. I know what you were talking about but I don't want to hear it. Not any more. Too much water. Too many bridges."

I nodded, reminded of a line from an old situation-comedy theme tune. *"What became of the people we used to be?"* I looked at Kirsty, remembered the hurt I had caused her, knew I could still cause her when she looked at me with those green eyes that a man could lose himself in, and felt as low as she usually made me feel.

A honk sounded from across the car park as a black BMW 4x4 pulled in and approached. Sam Riddel, my ride back. I realized I was a little disappointed that he had arrived so quickly. And that thought scared me more than anything that had already happened that weekend.

"What I want to know is…" said Kirsty, snapping me out of my reverie.

"Go on?" I prompted.

"How in the name of the crucified and risen savior did you get the Home Office to spring you?"

Chapter 47

PENELOPE HARRIS COULD never have been described as a cheerful woman

And that Saturday was no exception. She worked as a dental nurse in a small clinic in Old Amersham and was due to have the Saturday off. But due to staff shortages—caused by a stomach bug that had been doing the rounds though had mercifully passed her by—she had swapped her rota and agreed to come in.

Most lunchtimes she would have had a packed lunch in the staff room. A cheese-and-pickle sandwich with a packet of potato chips and a black-cherry yogurt. She never varied her routine. Routine was important to

Penelope. Without routine you had chaos, as far as she was concerned, and Penelope Harris abhorred chaos as much as nature abhorred a vacuum. And one of the things Penelope did every Saturday afternoon was her weekly shop at the big Tesco.

So that Saturday lunchtime found her there—pushing her trolley round in a foul mood.

The place was busier than ever and Penelope had to maneuver her way around hordes of extremely overweight shoppers. But Tesco stocked a ready meal called Finest Spaghetti Bolognaise, perfect for one. It was her Saturday-night treat when she settled down to watch *Casualty*, her favorite soap, and she would be very put out if she missed out on it. Luckily they had some in stock. She had backup in the freezer, but it wasn't the same thing as fresh. Not the same thing at all.

Still, she was a bit flustered, a bit hot and not in the best of tempers when she returned to the surgery.

She had left her mobile to charge and there were three missed text messages on it waiting for her return, and one voice-recorded message.

As Penelope listened to the message the fragments of any remaining hope of a better day vanished quickly. The phone fell from her hand to clatter on the hard floor of the dental surgery's staffroom.

Her colleague Debra Brooking turned in surprise as she poured hot water from the kettle into a Pot Noodle.

"Everything all right, Penelope?" she asked. "Not bad news, is it?"

Penelope nodded, her face ashen. "It's my brother. He's just been run over by a train."

Chapter 48

HALF AN HOUR later Penelope Harris was standing in front of the reception desk at the Stoke Mandeville hospital, her face flushed with anger.

"What do you mean, I can't see him? He's my brother!"

"I know that," said the increasingly flustered receptionist on the general admissions desk. "You are aware of the circumstances of the accident?"

"His car was on the railway line. A train hit him."

"Yes, I'm sorry."

"I know he was badly mutilated. But I should still be able to see the body."

"It's not so straightforward, I'm afraid."

"Why the hell not?"

The receptionist reddened and shrugged apologetically as a man in his fifties, wearing a white coat and with the obligatory stethoscope round his neck, appeared. "It's okay, Maureen," he said. "I'll take this."

Penelope turned to him. "Are you in charge here?"

"I'm Mister Ferguson, one of the surgical registrars," he said.

"Good. I want to see my brother."

Ferguson nodded. "Please come with me." He gestured with his hand and led Penelope into a small room with a couple of sofas and a cold-water dispenser.

"I don't understand. Why can't I just go and see him?"

"He's in surgery, Miss Harris."

Penelope stepped back. "What are you talking about? They told me he's dead."

"I'm sorry. I didn't mean to confuse you. He had a donor card. His heart was viable. He's going to save a young woman's life."

Penelope shook her head, not believing what she was hearing.

"I understand that your brother was a teacher. The young lady receiving his heart is a gifted young pianist. She's recently been given a musical scholarship to Corpus Christi College at Cambridge University."

"No," said Penelope.

"I'm sorry?"

"My brother would never have carried a donor card. We have discussed this."

The surgical registrar gestured apologetically. "I can assure you that he had a card in his wallet..." He hesitated. "And he left a note."

"What note?"

"I'm sorry, Miss Harris, but your brother committed suicide."

"No...there's been some mistake. It's not my brother. You've got the wrong person."

"The man had your brother's wallet and was driving his car."

Penelope shook her head again. "Maybe they were stolen."

The registrar didn't respond and Penelope

tilted her chin defiantly. "Well, if it is him, then I don't want the transplant to go ahead. He wouldn't have wanted it—I know that for a fact."

"It's too late, Miss Harris."

"I refuse. Let us be very clear about this: I am not giving you permission."

"The girl's heart has already been removed. They are in the process of replacing it with your brother's now."

"Well, I want it stopped!"

Chapter 49

SAM TURNED THE steering wheel and glanced across at me.

"Friends in high places, Dan?"

"Seems that way. Jack Morgan has, at least."

"The Foreign Office?"

"Homeland Security stateside contacted their opposite numbers here. They arranged the passport for Hannah Shapiro in the first place. All above board."

"The ex not too pleased, I take it?"

"Actually, Kirsty was fine with it. Her boss wasn't quite so."

"Shame."

"Shame indeed."

My phone rang and I looked at the caller ID. It said withheld. "This better not be a bloody marketing company," I said and clicked the green telephone on. "Dan Carter."

A mechanical voice spoke. "Be at your office in two hours. We'll give you instructions then. If you have just been speaking to the police you've signed her death warrant."

The line went dead.

Sam looked across. "That them?"

I nodded.

"What's the plan?"

"They're calling back in a couple of hours with details."

"What did he sound like?"

I shrugged. "They used a voice distorter."

"How did they get your number?"

"I would imagine Hannah gave it to them. She knows who we are, after all."

"They say anything else?"

"They said if I'd been speaking to the police about it all bets were off."

"They knew you'd been arrested?"

"Yup."

"Sophisticated operation, then?"

"Maybe."

"Which is a good thing, I guess."

"I guess so too," I agreed. Thinking that Hannah Shapiro already knew only too well how messy things could get with amateurs.

A short while later Sam pulled the car to a stop in the car park of one of the CUL sports grounds. It was based off the city center and had a brick-built single-story clubhouse and two rugby pitches. One of them was being used by the CUL squad who were running training exercises.

We walked over to the sidelines and watched for a while. Suzy had learned that they would be playing later that afternoon, in the annual grudge match between them and UCL. Just like the annual boat race between Oxford and Cambridge. If you added the victories up, then Chancellors would be slightly ahead, but UCL had beaten them in the last two encounters and they were keen to redress the balance, as I explained to Sam.

"They're so keen to redress the balance," replied Sam, "you'd think they wouldn't be out partying the night before."

I looked at him and grinned. "College boys. They have a quicker recovery time. You're getting old, is all."

"Old nothing. I could give those silver-spoon-eating bookworms a two-minute start and still beat them over a mile."

He probably could have, too.

"You ever play rugby?"

"Rugby? Are you out of your Caucasian mind?" Sam said, laying it on thick. "I went to the college of hard knocks, my friend. We don't got no rugby in that particular school."

I smiled. I knew for a fact that he had gone to a Catholic grammar school, could have gone to a university of his choice. He'd chosen Hendon Police College instead. Something about growing up on an estate with limited life expectancy, I reckon. Where he'd watched two of his brothers getting themselves killed. Like I said earlier, he could have gone either way. Lucky for us he chose as he did.

The practice session finished and the young men started walking toward the clubhouse. I jogged across to join them.

"Hold up a minute."

They stopped and looked at me curiously. One of them, a tall guy—taller than me at least, but not as tall as Sam—stepped forward. He was about twenty-three had corkscrew-curly hair cut short, and a jagged scar on his forehead. Made him look like Harry Potter's barbarian cousin. The guy who had been paying a lot of attention to the girls as they left the bar last night. Ashleigh Roughton, according to the details that Lucy had forwarded to my BlackBerry.

"Don't tell me," he said, giving me an unimpressed look. "You're scouting for the Saracens and want to sign us up."

"No. I want to talk to you about the three girls from your university who were attacked last night."

"You the filth?"

I smiled. Hard not to. He was trying to sound tough and down with it. But his accent was preppier than an Abercrombie and Fitch crew-neck sweater—in pastel.

"In a manner of speaking, Ashleigh. In the private sector."

"You know who I am?"

"We know who all of you are. We're not here without sanction."

"You're not the police, then we got nothing to say to you! We've already told the proper authorities all that we know. Which is nothing."

He turned his shoulder and nodded to his teammates. I stepped up quickly, put my hand on his shoulder and turned him back.

"Hang on, I'm not done here."

"Get your hands off me," he said, brushing my hand away.

"Like I said, I've got a couple of questions," I replied, stepping forward, getting into his face.

"Hard to ask questions with a mouthful of broken teeth."

I laughed. "That supposed to be a threat?"

He took a step back. A cocky smile playing on his lips. "What? You don't think I could take you."

"You might be able to take a couple of the Wendys from the backs on your rugby squad there. But I hit people for a living, son."

Which wasn't true, but hey—truth is

always the first casualty in a conflict, isn't it? That was what I'd heard. The "son" bit had the desired effect. Maybe I should have said "I push buttons for a living." His shoulder hunched forward and he might as well have written on a postcard what he was about to do and mailed it to me yesterday.

Chapter 50

I TILTED MY head back so that Roughton's roundhouse punch sailed past my chin, and as he struggled to keep his balance I stepped forward quickly and jabbed my first two fingers hard into his solar plexus.

He doubled up, making a sound like a broken washing machine, and fell on his side to the floor, his face turning purple.

His teammates stepped forward and I held my hand up. "He's just winded. He's going to be fine."

"More than you're going to be, mate." One of them had found his voice. Another preppie trying to sound tough.

Sam took off his jacket. "Any of you care to hold this for me?"

The guy who had spoken up was Tim Graham, according to my notes—five foot eleven and half the weight of Sam, by the looks of him. Graham stared across at my partner, his expression suddenly not so confident.

I held my hands up, placatingly. "Hold on, now. You lot could rush us and—who knows—eventually you might take us down. But not before some of you get hurt. I mean *seriously* hurt."

I looked down as Ashleigh Roughton got to his feet, breathing deeply, moisture in his eyes.

"You're only winded," I said to him. "I sucker-punched you."

He nodded. I hadn't done any such thing, of course, but I figured it might help defuse the situation if I gave him some of his face back. I wasn't going to be doing much good finding Chloe's attackers if I was in an intensive-care bed myself.

Another guy stepped forward, five nine but enormous. I figured him for a hooker. Rugbywise that was. He had the kind of face that even a mother would find hard to love.

"You the Riddler?" he asked, ignoring me and looking straight at Sam.

"I never liked that nickname much," he replied.

The ugly man's face broke into a grin. "My dad took me to see you fight once. Years ago. You were awesome. Met Police against the RAF. You won."

"I remember. Who was your dad?"

"Chief Superintendent Patrick Connolley. He's retired now."

"He was a good man."

The guy nodded, still grinning. "Awesome," he said again.

I sensed a shift in mood. I held my hands out. "What say we just ask you all a few questions? Then you can channel your aggression into kicking ten shades of crap out of UCL this afternoon."

Half an hour later we had spoken to each member of the team and were heading out of the sports ground, back to Sam's car.

"Well, we didn't learn much from that," he said.

I jumped in the car and pulled my seat belt across. But Sam was wrong, I figured we *had* learned something. Something important.

The guy I'd floored, Ashleigh Roughton, had something to hide or my name wasn't Dan Carter. I was very far from smiling but things were starting to get shifting now. The opposition had the next move but I could feel the tide turning. So far they'd been calling all the shots. I intended to change that.

Chapter 51

MISTER ALISTAIR LLOYD gestured to his assistant, a thirty-year-old Canadian woman.

"Close her up, Michaela," he said.

As he walked out of the theater he was surprised to see a couple of police officers, his colleague John Ferguson, and an animated young woman with an unhappy expression on her face waiting to see him.

"There's a bit of a problem, Alistair," said Ferguson.

"Oh?"

"My brother would never have signed a donor card. There's been a mistake," said Penelope Harris.

"I'm sorry? I don't follow."

"I want the operation stopped."

The surgeon shrugged. There wasn't much apology in the gesture. "It's too late, I'm afraid. The transplant has been done. It was clearly what your brother wanted."

"I don't believe it. I want to see him."

"Of course. You have to understand that he was in a serious accident. He suffered major injuries."

"I know that. I need to know it's him."

One of the police officers stepped forward. "We need a formal identification."

"Of course you do. Come with me, then."

A short while later Alistair Lloyd nodded at the mortuary assistant who slid open the drawer and revealed the body. The dead man had suffered considerable trauma but his face, although lacerated, was recognizable. Penelope gasped holding a hand to her mouth. Then she nodded, unable to speak.

The surgeon gestured to the assistant to close the drawer again. As he did, Penelope's brother's left hand flopped loose from the covering sheet.

"What happened to his hand?" Penelope asked, puzzled.

John Ferguson looked down, shocked. The third finger of the dead man's hand had been severed at the second knuckle.

"It wasn't like that when he came in," he said.

Chapter 52

SAM WAS PARKING the car as I jogged up the stairs to our office.

There was some activity in the offices of Chambers, Chambers and Mason. But not a great deal of it. Lawyers, it seemed, were not always on the case. Not on Saturday afternoons, at any rate.

Lucy was back at her reception desk, typing on her computer.

"Where's Suzy?" I asked her.

"She's still down at the university."

"You get anything more?"

"We made contact with Laura Skelton. She's pretty shell-shocked by what happened."

"She would be. She add anything new?"

Lucy shook her head. "Suzy's still with her. They seemed to be getting on pretty well. She thought it might be useful to strike up a friendship."

"Keep me posted. And tell her to dig into a meatball by the name of Ashleigh Roughton while she's down there. Captain of the rugby team. Make him a priority."

"On it!" She snatched up the phone.

Maybe we'd make a field agent out of her yet. I walked across the office to the water cooler, pulled a cup out of the dispenser and poured myself some.

Sipping on the water, I strolled over to Adrian Tuttle's workstation. He had three computers on it, a big Apple cinema display screen and two laptops. The footage of Hannah bound and reading the message that her captors had given her was freeze-framed. Adrian looked up from the laptop he was working on as I approached.

"You got any good news for me, Adrian?" I asked.

He shook his head apologetically. "The e-mail address is a hotmail account, as you know. Use it and lose it kind of thing."

"And the YouTube account?"

"Linked to that address. I'm trying to get the computer signature but I'm not having any luck."

"YouTube won't release it?"

"Not short of a warrant. And the original film has been taken down."

"You can't trace the ISP remotely?"

Adrian shook his head. "Sponge might have been able to but..." He shrugged. "Outside of my pay grade."

I nodded. Nothing I didn't expect. "Keep on it."

The phone rang. Lucy answered it and waved me across.

"It's them," she said.

"Put it through to my office, Lucy, I'll take it there."

I gestured to Sam to follow me and headed into my office. As Sam closed the door behind me I hit my speakerphone button.

"It's Dan Carter. Talk to me."

"*There's a trade on the table if you're interested.*"

"Of course we're interested."

"Good. Ten o'clock tomorrow morning. Parliament Square. There is a statue of Sir Robert Peel on the southwest corner of it."

"I know it."

"Good again. Be there then. Be alone. And have one million pounds' worth of cut diamonds with you."

I looked at my watch. "That might be tricky to arrange in time."

"Your problem, not mine. And make sure they are perfect. No flaws. After all... neither of us want to be left with damaged goods when this trade is completed, do we?"

"No," I said. Picturing Hannah Shapiro dressed in her underwear, terrified. I gripped the phone tighter.

"Then we have an understanding?"

"I'll be there," I agreed.

"Any..." there was a slight hesitation *"...woodentops, as you call them, show up... and it's on your head, Mister Carter. Don't let her down. She's counting on you."*

"I want to hear her voice."

The line went dead.

I clicked on my computer screen and pulled up the incoming-call register. Nothing. I slammed the phone down. "Son of a bitch!"

"At least we know something from that."

"What?"

"It's not an American outfit that's taken her."

"How so?"

"He said *woodentops*. Quite pointedly. Not likely an American would use the expression."

"Not impossible. They have English cop shows over there too, and he said *as you call them*. Meaning the British, as though he were foreign."

"It's more a term used in the force than out. And it's hardly a current one, is it?"

"True."

"Could have been deliberate."

"I'm pretty sure everything he said was deliberate."

"What are we going to do?"

"Get the diamonds. Make the trade."

"No cops."

"Absolutely no cops. We can handle this," I said with a degree of confidence that I certainly didn't feel.

Chapter 53

PROFESSOR ANNABELLE WESTON
looked at her watch and pushed aside a second-
year student's essay that she had been marking.

Jungian archetypes in contemporary
graphic novels. She sighed dismissively and
picked up the telephone, tapping in some
numbers. After a while, the phone she was
calling clicked into a recorded message—she
waited for it to finish.

"Laura, this is Professor Weston, just to
remind you that you were due for a tutorial.
I can understand if you're not coming in but
I just wanted to make sure you're all right.
Please give me a call."

She hung up and twirled a perfectly manicured finger around a lock of her strawberry-blonde hair. She looked at the first paragraph of the essay again and put it to one side once more, unable to concentrate.

She snatched the phone up again, consulted a business card that was sitting on her desk and dialed another number. After a second or two it was answered.

"Dan Carter."

She smiled a little hesitantly. "Dan, it's Professor Weston. Annabelle."

"Hi," he said and she could hear the warmth in his voice, picture the smile at the other end of the line. He had a nice smile. He was bright, too, she could tell that much.

"I just wondered if there had been any developments your end? I have spoken to the police, of course, and all they can tell me is that they are *pursuing all lines of inquiry.* Which I take to mean that they have no idea."

"They'll be doing all they can."

"I guess they are. I just feel so helpless. I feel like I should be doing something."

"I know it's hard. But remember what the poet said. 'They also serve who only stand and wait.'"

"Shakespeare?"

"John Milton. He was referring to his blindness. And even if it does feel like we are stumbling around in the dark, professor, we're not. There is light ahead and we will guide Hannah home by it."

"You sound like something has happened."

"Just experience. Things happen for a reason. And when we understand why—then we can take steps to deal with them."

"And you are close to an understanding?"

"I believe we are working toward that, yes."

"And you'll let me know when you can?"

"We will."

"Thanks, then."

Annabelle Weston hung up, running her thumb and the first finger of her right hand around the wedding-ring finger of her left. There was still a faint white band from where her wedding ring had been removed some years earlier.

A slight smile tugged wistfully at the corners of her lips. I wonder what Dan Carter would be like in bed? she thought to herself.

Her smile faded as she picked the phone up for a third time and hit the speed-dial button.

"Kht Mn Qlby..." she said as the call was answered. "It's me."

Chapter 54

GARY WEBSTER HAD the word *Mechanic* written in the job section of his out-of-date passport.

He also had a medium-sized bodywork and repair shop in Marylebone not far from the thrust and bustle of the High Street that would stand testimony to the truth of it. Certainly as far as the taxman was concerned that was how he made his money. Crash repairs, bodywork, paint jobs, brake and wheel replacements.

In reality, though, he had a number of other profitable sidelines from which he derived his main income. None of them legal.

He was sitting in his local, The Prince Regent—what he called a proper Victorian boozer—on Marylebone High Street, drinking a pint of Abbot Ale when I walked in and went up to him. I sat on the stool next to his.

"Dan," he said, gesturing to the barmaid, and holding out his hand for me to shake. I waved his hand away.

Gary Webster had a grip like a Russian arm-wrestler overloaded on steroids. He was a good three inches shorter than me and a good few inches off the chest too. I'm a forty-four long and he was about a thirty-eight, I reckoned. But his forearms were like legs of pork and I hadn't shaken hands with him since he'd left the fifth form and gone to work with his dad. Not because I hadn't seen him, but because I didn't want my hand mangled.

I slapped him on the shoulder instead and took the bottle of Corona the barmaid had brought across for me. It wasn't the first time I had been in that particular bar.

"How's business?" he asked.

I waggled my hand in a banking-airplane movement. "I've had better days," I said.

"Why you contacted your old pal, I guess?"

I nodded in agreement. "Why I got in touch." I took a long pull on the Corona.

"So . . . this is calling for something outside the legitimate range of your normal operations?" He took a pull of his pint.

"Again, your guess would be correct," I concurred.

"What do you need?"

"Same as last time."

He smiled sardonically. "Nothing for Tonto?"

He was referring to Sam. They didn't get on. "Sam doesn't touch them—you know that."

"Yeah, I know that. Wuss."

"Say that to his face."

Gary grinned. "I would if I could reach that high."

I drained the Corona and he did likewise with two deep swallows of his ale.

"I don't know how you can drink that stuff. It looks like pond water."

He stood up and slapped my shoulder. "It's the canonical ale, Dan. Puts lead in your pencil—and might in your miter."

We took Gary's car. Nothing too flash on the outside: an oldish Mercedes saloon. A

three-liter S320 about fourteen years old—
you could probably pick one up for under a
grand.

You wouldn't get one like this, though.
Gary had tweaked it a little. Putting the kind
of muscle under the hood that can get you
from zero to sixty in the time it takes a patrol
cop to switch on his siren, and out of sight
before he's made it into third gear. It wasn't
registered to him and he never made the mistake of boy-racing it through town. Time
would come when its secret powers would be
needed and when that time came he would
make a nice little earner out of it.

Gary always drew a line between business and pleasure. That was what marked the
difference between the professionals and the
amateurs in his game.

You could feel the sheer power of the engine,
though, even as it purred in low gear through
Marylebone High Street. But it was muscle of
a very different kind that had brought me to
see Gary Webster.

The killing kind.

Chapter 55

TEN MINUTES LATER we were in a lock-up about a quarter of a mile from Gary Webster's garage.

The place wasn't registered in his name. Was registered, in fact, to a bogus person in a bogus company should anyone want to look too closely.

Gary pulled the door shut behind him and flicked on the overhead strip lights. In the center of the room was an almost new Jaguar XK five-liter V8 convertible. About seventy-three grand and upward the last time I looked at one in the windows of the showroom in Berkeley Street, Mayfair.

I'm pretty sure it wasn't there waiting to

have its wheels balanced and a bit of detailing done.

Gary led me past the car to the back of the lock-up. An old-fashioned safe was to one side amidst a pile of used motor parts. He spun the dial and opened the safe, taking out a pump-action shotgun and a semi-automatic pistol that he handed to me. I slipped them into a holdall I had brought along for that purpose.

He reached in again and brought out a couple of boxes of ammunition, which I put in the bag as well. Then I pulled up one of the towels that I had put into the bag earlier to cover everything and zipped the bag closed.

"Is it a good idea keeping stuff like this here, Gary?" I asked.

"The wife doesn't like them at home."

"You're not married."

"Anyway. They're not here any more."

"Just a couple of days."

"You use them, you lose them."

"Goes without saying."

"Yeah, well, a lot of things best said go unsaid."

"You turning philosophical on me?"

Gary gave me a quizzical look, building up to it. Anyone else it would have been no questions asked. But Gary Webster and I had been best friends at school and, even if we hadn't seen a lot of each other over the years since, it was still a bond that would never be broken. We had both had to watch each other's back too many times for that.

"So..." he said finally. "You going to tell me what the gig is?"

I looked him square in the eye. "What's the word on the street with Brendan Ferres?"

Gary reacted. "Snake Ferres?"

"Yup."

He shook his head. "You have got to be fucking kidding me," he said finally.

I shook my own head.

"Well, the word is he's hung like a donkey and has a striking cobra tattooed on it."

"I wasn't talking about the size of his Johnson, Gary."

"Yeah, well, it gives you an idea of his intelligence. His pain threshold too, come to think of it." He grimaced and then grinned. "He had the head of the snake tattooed on his bell end, for Christ's sake!"

I didn't grin back. "Ferres might be mixed up in a bit of business."

"And?"

"A bit of business I'm going to sort."

Gary looked at me to see if I was being serious. I was.

"Have you completely lost the plot? He's Ronnie Allen's right-hand man."

"I know exactly who he is."

"You can't go up against Allen, Dan. Not even you." He shook his head again. "*Especially* not you."

"Brendan Ferres has waltzed into this particular dance. I can't walk away from it, Gary."

"Quite right. You shouldn't walk. You should bloody run!"

"A student was kidnapped last night. Chancellors University."

Gary reacted, shaking his head. "That's not Ronnie Allen's style. Kidnapping. Never heard that."

"Maybe he's branching out."

"Can't see it."

"Brendan Ferres was seen going into the building earlier in the day. The building the students had just left before being assaulted, and one of them taken."

"Maybe it's coincidence."

"I don't believe in that kind of coincidence."

"They happen, Dan. And for the sake of your health I suggest you start believing in them."

"One of the girls was abducted. One of them was cut with a knife. And one of them had a baseball bat taken to the back of her head."

"Jesus. Even so, Dan. Let it go."

I shook my head. "The girl someone took a baseball bat to was Chloe. It was Chloe Smith, Gary."

He took it in for a heartbeat and then his jaw set. "You need backup?"

"No. This is my shout."

"You'll let me know?"

I nodded gratefully but I had no intention of involving him any more than I already had.

"What are you going to do?"

"I'm going to go and ask him. Let him know if the girl is harmed in any way whatsoever . . . that there will be consequences."

"If he's got her, that is. I can't see that. Like I say, it's not his style."

"Yeah," I agreed. "If he's got her."

"Brendan Ferres is a mountain gorilla in a suit. He doesn't do anything unless Ronnie Allen tells him to."

"I know."

"And he's engaged to his daughter."

"I didn't know that."

"Well, he is. And little Becky Allen is the apple of her father's eye."

He was being a little sarcastic. Rebecca Allen was thirty-two years old, five foot ten tall and built like Kirstie Alley at her curvy best. There was nothing little about her— including her sexual appetites if the rumors about her fiancé were not exaggerated. And Gary was quite right—her father treated her like an absolute princess.

"That I did know," I agreed.

"So be careful. Could turn nasty. Face is everything to a man like Ferres."

"Still got to ask the question."

"Yeah."

I hefted the bag. "And I appreciate the assist."

"You got it. You taking Sam with you?"

"Yeah."

"See if you can persuade him to carry, then."

I smiled regretfully. "Never going to happen."

Chapter 56

DI KIRSTY WEBB was wishing she had simply switched off her mobile phone and taken the weekend off.

The drive out of London heading west into the boondocks had been a nightmare, with traffic clogging up Western Avenue and the air-conditioning unit on her car packing up. The first truly hot day of the year and that was when it decided to go on the blink! She had kept the windows open for a while but anyone who has been stuck in traffic in London knows it's not an ideal solution for long.

When she had broken clear of the M25 the roads had cleared, though, and she made better progress. But all in all she couldn't help feeling it was bound to be a bit of a wild-goose chase.

The old market town of Aylesbury is only some forty-five miles north and west of London, but on a good day it could still take an hour and a half to get there. Kirsty would have taken the A41 route but roadworks on the North Circular would have made the journey even more unbearable.

Nice to get out of London, though, she thought, goose chase or not, as she drove into the large car park of Stoke Mandeville hospital and switched off the car radio.

A female DI from the local force was waiting to meet her as she headed into reception. A formidable-looking woman in her late thirties but with steel-gray already dominating her hair.

"Natalie James," she said, holding out her hand.

"Kirsty Webb."

"You'd better come with me."

The DI walked off briskly and Kirsty followed her into the hospital, through reception and down a series of corridors.

The body had been moved to a small side room. A young uniformed officer was standing guard outside. DI James gave him a cursory nod and opened the door, leading Kirsty in.

The corpse was lying on a gurney and had been covered once more with a sheet.

"His car was hit by a high-speed train going at full tilt. Brain death would have been near-instantaneous."

"I can well imagine."

"And his body took a considerable amount of trauma."

"So the injury to his hand could have happened at the same time?"

"We thought so at first," said the gray-haired detective. "But a pathologist took a closer look. The top half of his finger was definitely severed post-mortem. No blood loss, et cetera. There's no doubt about it."

The DI lifted the blanket covering the left side of Colin Harris's body and showed Kirsty the mutilated hand.

Kirsty shook her head, not quite believing it. "Do we know what was used?"

242 • James Patterson

"We think a scalpel."

"Right."

"I understand you have some similar cases?"

"Kind of. Only ours were two women. Early to mid-twenties. Both as of yet unidentified."

"And both had the same finger chopped off."

"The wedding-ring finger. Half of it, anyway. And they both had organs removed."

"What the hell is going on?" The DI was obviously a little rattled. You weren't supposed to have serial killers in Buckinghamshire.

"I don't know, inspector. But we've got a break in the pattern here. That could be significant."

"How could somebody have known, though? Then sneak into our morgue and cut a finger off a dead body in broad daylight!"

"Who was it who authorized the transplant? What's the procedure?"

The DI pulled out a small black book and consulted her notes. "First of all, brain death has to be established by two independent doctors."

"Independent of the hospital?"

"No, of the doctors involved with the donation or the transplantation team."

"So brain death was established by two independent doctors. And then what happened?"

"The body was kept alive by life-support machinery, the heart removed and transplanted into the recipient."

"And the sister maintains that her brother was vehemently against being a donor."

"It's what she says. Although she also says she had become estranged from her brother. They hadn't talked in quite a few years."

"Why was that?"

"She didn't say. I get the feeling that Penelope Harris isn't much of what you might call a people person."

"Can I speak to her?"

"Of course you can. We'll do all we can to help."

"I have to warn you, inspector . . ."

"Go on."

"If this is our serial fruit-loop, or even if it is a copycat, London serious crimes squad are going to be down here en masse. You're going to be kept busy."

"Why didn't they come straight away, then?"

"Because they didn't think there was a connection and my time is a lot less valuable to waste."

"But you do think there is a connection with your two Jane Does?"

"Yes, Inspector James. I do."

Chapter 57

KIRSTY WEBB WAS beginning to dislike Penelope Harris.

The woman seemed to be angry not at her brother's death but at the inconvenience it was causing her.

"I just want to go home," said the woman in question.

"And you will. I just need to go over a few things first," replied Kirsty, trying to keep her own anger in check.

"Oh, for God's sake—I've been over it a hundred times. And it isn't me you should be interrogating."

"It's an interview, not an interrogation..."

"It's those surgeons. They're the ones who

killed my brother, who took his heart like some kind of spare part."

"Your brother was declared brain-dead, Miss Harris. And he carried an organ-donor card."

"It wasn't his."

"They don't just go by the card, Penelope," Kirsty said softly, using the woman's first name to try and get her on her side. It didn't work.

" 'Miss Harris' is fine, thank you very much!"

Kirsty sighed inwardly but kept her expression neutral. "Like I say," she persisted. "They don't just go with the card—they check with the organ-donor registry and your brother's name was on it."

"So that just gives them the right to go ahead and do what they did, does it?"

"Yes, I'm afraid it does."

"Well, it shouldn't."

"Do you have a particular reason to be so against organ donation?"

"We're Jehovah's Witnesses."

Kirsty frowned, puzzled. "I understood that Jehovah's Witnesses aren't against organ donation, just blood transfusions."

"It's a matter of personal conscience and a number of us are against it. And those that are for it still demand that all blood be drained before transplantation."

"I see."

"And was it?"

Kirsty shrugged ever so slightly. "I don't know."

"Well, isn't that what you should be finding out?"

"It doesn't really matter, does it?"

"What on earth do you mean? Of course it matters."

"I'm sorry, I didn't mean to be insensitive. But what I meant is that the woman who received your brother's heart is not a Jehovah's Witness."

Penelope Harris considered it for a moment. "It's the principle," she said finally, putting the detective in mind of a sulky schoolchild.

Kirsty pulled out a piece of paper enclosed in a clear plastic envelope.

"Is that the note he left?" asked Penelope Harris.

"Yes," said Kirsty.

"Can I see it, please?"

Kirsty put it on the table in front of her. It consisted of two simple lines and read: *I am sorry for what I have done. But at least the suffering will stop now. Colin.*

The Harris woman looked at it briefly, then back up at Kirsty, the angry defiance back in her eyes.

"Okay, he may have decided to carry an organ-donor card. I doubt it very much." She shrugged. "But he definitely didn't write that!"

"Why not?"

"Because he never called himself Colin—he absolutely hated the name. It's his real name but he always used his second name: Paul. He only ever used Colin on official documentation because he had to."

Kirsty nodded.

"You don't seem surprised," said the dead man's sister.

"I'm not, Miss Harris," said the dark-haired detective. "I think your brother was murdered."

Chapter 58

WALKING INTO THE Turk's Head Tavern in Tufnell Park with a gun in your pocket is seriously not a good idea.

But I did it anyway.

The conversation didn't exactly stop when Sam and I stepped through the bar's door. But it was pretty damn close.

The Turk's Head was just one of many buildings owned by Ronnie Allen. And every Saturday night the man himself was usually in attendance, playing poker or dealing with business. Not the sort of business the revenue men got a cut of.

Sure enough, that night Allen was at his usual table at the back of the bar. I knew it was his usual table because I had done some business with him before. That is to say Private had. He'd bought a dog-racing track two years ago and had totally refurbished it. He had hired us to overhaul and update all the security. A lot of money changes hands at a dog track, millions of pounds over the year, and there are people in the world stupid enough, seemingly, to try stealing from the man. Brad Dexter had been in charge of the project and we had never had any complaints from Ronnie Allen. He even paid his bill.

Like I said, there were very few people stupid enough to cross him but here Sam and I were, about to beard the lion in his den.

We walked toward his table and a couple of very large men in regulation goon suits stood up and glared at us.

"Bottle of Corona for me, and..." I looked across at Sam.

"Mineral water for me," he said. "Ice, no slice."

"You're going to need a straw to drink it through the face cast, motherfucker!" said the first goon.

"It's okay, Ralph—this man is known to me," said Ronnie Allen.

Ralph, for God's sake. Seems even meatball-headed thugs had designer names now.

Ronnie Allen was sitting with Brendan Ferres. Another dark-suited man with an extremely glamorous blonde was sitting opposite them. I didn't know the other man. He was in his late forties, with sleek silver hair, and was wearing sunglasses. I didn't know his companion either but she looked like she had been poured into her cream-white dress and was nearly spilling out of it.

Ronnie Allen himself was a small man, five seven at a push, with cropped gray hair and amused eyes. Apparently they stayed amused even if one of his associates was taking a baseball bat to someone's knees, or a blowtorch to their bare feet.

I flashed a smile at the blonde woman. "Sorry to interrupt your evening," I said.

"Spit it out, Carter. I'm in a business meeting," said Allen.

"Hannah Shapiro," I said simply.

"Never heard of her."

"She was kidnapped last night."

He shook his head, genuinely puzzled as far as I could tell. "The fuck has that got to do with me?"

I pointed a finger at Brendan Ferres. "Little Boy Blue here was seen at the premises shortly before she was taken."

Allen looked over at Ferres who shrugged. It was like a bison rolling its shoulders. His cold, piggy eyes weren't amused. They were full of hate. I managed to stop my knees from knocking as he glared at me.

"I ain't got a clue what he's on about, Ronnie," he said.

"Chancellors University. Yesterday afternoon. I take it you weren't there getting a thesis marked."

He ignored me and turned to his employer. "How about I just bounce these bozos out and teach them some manners?"

"How about you just answer the question?" Allen replied rhetorically.

"What, I have to answer to some pansy-assed window peeper now, do I?"

"No, Brendan. You answer to me."

He said it quietly but Ferres got the point. He shrugged

"Okay. It's just business. One of the guys there at the college...we have dealings with him. I don't know the first flying fuck about some cooze being kidnapped."

Allen turned to me and flashed me a quick smile. "That answer your questions, gentlemen?" he asked without a hint of irony.

I nodded. I didn't get the sense he was lying.

"That's good, Mister Allen," I replied, showing him the respect he expected. "But if I find out King Kong Junior here had any hand in it, I will come back and put him in the ground," I said, showing a little less respect.

Brendan Ferres would have leaped up but Allen put a quiet hand on his knee and he stayed put. If looks could kill I'd certainly have been dead by then. I returned his look, letting him know I meant every word.

"You let this man come into your place of business and talk this way?"

It was the silver-haired man speaking. He had an American accent—the East Coast, if I was any judge. Italian-American at that. His suit was hand-cut and he wore a watch on his wrist that I reckoned cost more than the Jaguar my mate Gary Webster had squirrelled away in his lock-up. The theme tune of *The Godfather* played in my head and I deduced he probably wasn't here as a food critic for the *Washington Post*.

"Someone took a baseball bat to my goddaughter's head when the girl was taken," I said by way of explanation.

"Family is very important," said Ronnie Allen.

The American guy nodded in agreement.

"I'm telling you, Ronnie. This has got nothing to do with us," said Ferres.

Allen gestured at me, shrugging and holding his hands a little wider apart. "I'm sorry we can't help you."

"You going to give me the name of your contact at Chancellors?" I asked Ferres. He snorted in reply.

"Not prudent business practice—I am sure you can understand why," said Ronnie Allen smoothly. The sort of smoothness a razor blade has.

I could have threatened him with taking what I had to the police, but I couldn't see the point. What I had was bupkis, after all. The square root of sweet Fanny Adams. Nada.

I gave Ferres a final pointed look instead. Letting him know we weren't done. He looked straight back at me—and If I'm perfectly honest I didn't see his knees knocking either. I nodded to Sam and we walked out. I kept my shoulders straight despite the feeling that someone had just painted a bullseye on my back.

As I walked through the bar doors and out into the street beyond I considered making the same one-fingered backward gesture that Alison Chambers had made to me yesterday.

I resisted the urge.

Chapter 59

IT WAS QUIET in the hospital.

But somehow it was still full of sound. Machines in the background. Monitoring equipment beating out a steady rhythm. Life going on. Footfalls in distant corridors. Snoring.

I opened the door to the intensive-care room and walked in. The woman sitting on the chair at the head of the bed looked up at me and smiled. She was pleased to see me, at least. The smile made me feel good for a moment, but only for that instant. The sight of my unconscious god-daughter kind of took the fun out of it for me.

"Mister Carter," the woman said.

"It's Dan, please, Professor Weston," I replied.

"In which case you had better call me Annabelle."

She smiled again but I couldn't smile back. The young woman lying on the bed deserved my entire focus. And Annabelle could prove to be too much of a distraction. Maybe when things got back on an even keel I could try the full Dan Carter charm offensive on her. But for now I had to be all about business. Strictly professional. No time for romance.

I was wrong about that, as it turned out. But not in the way I expected.

I looked down at Chloe. Her eyes still closed. Her breathing even. "Have there been any developments?" I asked Annabelle.

The professor shook her head. "The registrar was just here with Chloe's mother. Chloe is stable but still in a coma."

"Where is Barbara now?"

"She's gone to get us some tea."

Barbara Smith, née Lehman, had driven down overnight from North Scotland, where she had moved a year ago. She'd set out as soon as she had heard what had happened to her daughter. Her new husband Martin Lehman worked in the petrochemical industry and was moved around the country every few years or so. Martin Lehman didn't like me and I wasn't, to tell the truth, too disappointed that he hadn't accompanied his wife.

"I just thought I'd check in on Chloe." Annabelle gestured sadly at some fruit in a bowl on the bedside cabinet. "Bit of a cliché, I know."

"I'm sure she'll be grateful when she wakes up."

The professor nodded and stood up. She was still dressed casually in jeans and a sweater. Still looked a million dollars.

"I'd better leave you to it. I don't think the ward sister will like a crowd in here."

"It was good of you to come."

Annabelle shook her head. "Chloe's one of our students. I'm her tutor."

"Even so."

"She's a very bright girl. Very brave too, from what I hear. She nearly fought them off."

"They weren't playing by the Queensberry Rules."

"No."

She leaned down to smooth Chloe's hair.

"I take it you have no news yourself," she said.

"No," I said. Lying as smoothly as a politician. "But Hannah Shapiro's father will be here tomorrow morning. Maybe the kidnappers will make contact then."

"Annabelle looked at me, a little surprised. "You still think that this is what it was, then? A straightforward kidnapping? Why haven't they been in contact? Made a ransom demand?"

"I don't know."

That's the trouble with lying: once you start you've got to keep doing it—and I didn't like lying to Annabelle. I could see how distraught she was.

"What?" she said.

I guess I had been staring. "Her father has got money," I said. "That's what it usually comes down to. Money."

Money or sex, I thought to myself but didn't articulate the thought.

"I didn't realize she came from a wealthy background."

Saying Harlan Shapiro had money was a bit like saying a forest has a tree or two in it. "Yeah. Her father is pretty well off," I said, not telling her that he had already agreed to pay the ransom and I had the diamonds already stashed in the safe at our offices.

"That's good, then, isn't it? Like we said. I mean... better that the motive is money."

I couldn't keep the image of Hannah Shapiro stripped to her underwear out of my mind and couldn't help agreeing.

"Yes," I said. "It's better than the alternative."

"You'll keep me posted if there are any developments?"

"Of course I will."

Annabelle seemed to hesitate, looking up at me with those almost fey turquoise eyes. There was a definite charge. Then she seemed to catch herself, blushing just a little, but on her alabaster skin it made her look almost unbearably vulnerable.

"Tell Barbara I'll come back tomorrow," she said and hurried out of the room, leaving behind a faint trail of a sweet floral perfume. I looked back at my comatose god-daughter and told myself to snap out of it. Like I said, I didn't have time for distractions.

A few minutes later the door opened again and Chloe's mother walked in. Barbara Lehman was in her early forties and still had the figure of a woman half her age. She was slim, tanned, beautiful. Her hair every bit as dark, curly and lustrous as her daughter's. Her large expressive eyes brimmed as she saw me.

She put the cups of tea she was holding down on a side table and rushed into my arms.

"Oh, Dan," she said unable to hold back the tears.

I pulled her to me, hugging her as tight as I dared, patting my arm on her back as she sobbed against my shoulder.

Chapter 60

SOHO IN THE late evening is always a busy place.

Plenty of the bars remained open and the many restaurants were still alive with chatter and laughter.

I walked along Shaftesbury Avenue, turning left into Dean Street. I had left Barbara some forty minutes ago after giving her as much reassurance as I could. But I was no medical man. Someone was going to pay for it, though, I had told her. Making it a mantra for myself. As if saying it a lot of times would make it so. Coming good on the promise might be a different matter, but I meant every word I said.

Jack Morgan was going to hold me to it, too. This was every bit as personal to him and it was killing him not to be over here working the case with me. But it wouldn't help me, Hannah or Jack himself if he were arrested. A Supreme Court judge gets sent down for a crime she didn't commit because Jack Morgan skips a subpoena and the consequences for Private in the States didn't bear thinking about. So Jack was stuck between a rock and a hard place, so were we.

And time was running out.

I had assumed earlier that there was no connection to the States with Hannah's kidnapping. That it was a local operation. Lightning striking twice and her captors lucking onto a jackpot.

But now I wasn't so sure.

Brendan Ferres going into Chancellors. It was conceivable enough that he did have business there. His lot dealt in drugs. Students used drugs. This wasn't news. But the black-suited man sitting at the table with Ferres and Allen was old school Mafia, I'd put money on it. The first time that Hannah Shapiro had been kidnapped it was by a couple of hoods recently fired from an East Coast outfit. Like I said, I don't like coincidences. If this was all leading back to the States it put a whole new complexion on things. And it was a complexion I didn't much care for.

I strolled past the French House and then the Pitcher and Piano and up to the front door leading into the building where my apartment was.

I looked across at the Crown and Two Chairmen. A group of young men and women stumbled out. Drunk, happy, not a care in the world. I toyed with the idea of going in for a bottle of beer but shrugged the notion away. I had to be up early tomorrow, I had an exchange to make and I needed to have my wits about me. Too much was at stake.

I walked up the three flights of stairs and jiggled the keys into the lock of my front door.

As soon as I walked into the small hallway inside I knew that something was wrong.

Chapter 61

I WAS PRETTY sure I hadn't left my lounge light on.

But there was light coming through the gap at the bottom of the closed door. I picked up an old left-handed five-iron that I kept in a walking-stick holder in the hallway and kicked the door open.

I wasn't expecting laughter.

"You got any idea how ridiculous you look, Dan?"

My ex-wife. Sitting on the sofa, sipping on a generous glass of my Remy Martin Louis XIII Grande Champagne cognac. Retailing at about twelve hundred pounds, depending where you bought it. I didn't much care:

I hadn't bought it, and I didn't drink brandy very often. It was a gift from a grateful client.

I turned around, put the golf club away and crossed to my small kitchen. I opened the fridge, took out a bottle of Corona and popped the cap with a bottle opener I had mounted on the small work surface. With a metallic tingle, the cap tumbled into the litter basket I kept underneath. There were plenty more in there and when the basket was full I'd take it to the recycling center. I'm almost a model citizen. I took a long pull on the cold beer, sighed, then went back into my living room.

"How did you get in here, Kirsty?" I asked.

"I'm police," she replied. "We have ways and means."

"Yeah, you also have a mobile phone—maybe you could have called me."

"Maybe I did. Maybe you had your phone switched off!"

I took out my phone and looked at it. She was right. I had turned it off at the hospital at the request of the ward sister. A two-hundred-and-something-pound African-

Caribbean woman with whom I wasn't about to argue. I switched it back on. Sure enough, there was a message from my ex-wife flashing.

I put the phone back in my pocket. Kirsty took another sip of the brandy.

"Nice drop," she said.

"You can take it with you when you leave."

"You asking me to go?"

"No, I'm just going to stand here looking all masculine until you tell me what you want."

She smiled again. Damn, it was a sexy smile.

And damn again if everything about her wasn't sexy. She had changed out of her businesslike two-piece suit, and was wearing a flouncy white skirt, too short, some kind of peasant blouse laced open at the front and a denim jacket. She was also wearing black Doc Marten boots with blue boot socks and her hair was tied back. The whole outfit should have looked ridiculous.

It didn't.

"I want your help, Dan," she said simply.

It surprised me more than finding her in my apartment in the first place.

"That so?" I replied, master of ready wit that I was, and took another pull on the Corona. Registering that it was nearly empty, I tilted the bottle and finished the job. "I get the feeling I'm going to need another one of these."

I headed back into the kitchen, pulled another bottle from the fridge shelf and held the cold bottle against my forehead for a moment before popping the cap. I went back to the lounge.

"Okay, doll face," I said recovering some of my legendary *savoir faire*. "Spit it out."

Chapter 62

KIRSTY PUT THE brandy snifter down on a small table that she had placed next to my couch.

The sofa itself was positioned under the window that looked down on Dean Street below, and across to Meard Street—which had once been a favored haunt of drug addicts and prostitutes but had gone downmarket now and was favored by media types.

The room was small and contained a three-seater sofa that converted into a double-sprung bed, a thirty-two-inch Sony Bravia HD television which I very rarely watched, and an original Victorian fireplace which, though unused, was stacked with wooden logs. An art deco drinks cabinet which Kirsty had raided. A Moroccan rug on the floor and a bookcase by the television housing most of the books I was supposed to have read when I'd been studying English at Reading University—Dickens, Hardy, Shakespeare, lots of poetry—and which had hardly been glanced at since. When I did read anything nowadays it was most likely in paperback form, and the kind of book that once read you gave away to a friend or dropped off in a charity shop.

So that's my lounge, bijou but comfortable and with everything just as I liked it—apart from the dark-haired woman with dangerously come-to-bed eyes that was sitting on the sofa.

"I've applied for a job in Manchester," she said.

I nodded, although I had absolutely no idea where she was going with this.

"I figured, get out of town," she continued. "You and me won't keep bumping into each other. Take a spade and bury the past where it belongs."

"You always were the romantic one."

"Yeah—it wasn't me taking text messages from your girlfriend when you were supposed to be marrying me."

I took another slug of beer. Kept me from talking, at least, and this was one argument I was never going to win. I swallowed and said, "So you're going to move to Manchester. What do you want me to do, help you pack?" I was being a regular Jack Benny that night.

"It's a new position. They're setting up a serial-killers unit. Worldwide coordination. Profiling. The whole shebang. Bit like the FBI have out at Quantico."

I gestured with the beer bottle for her to continue.

"I'm in with a chance, but there's a lot of competition."

"So why do you need my help, Kirsty?"

"I don't," she said. "I need Private's."

Chapter 63

I GUESS THAT put me back in my box.

"Lay it out for me," I said.

"We're working on a couple of cases. May or may not be linked. Private have already given a forensic assist on one of them. The Jane Doe we found last night in King's Cross."

"Yeah, Adrian Tuttle and Wendy Lee were on it."

"Two women. Both killed. Both had organs removed. Both had half of their wedding-ring fingers removed."

She ran the fingers of her right hand over her own now bare wedding-ring finger. She had bounced the ring that used to adorn it off my face quite a few years ago. Nearly blinded me. I wasn't sure if she was aware what she was doing with her fingers. Either way she stopped doing it.

"We thought there was a pattern. A serial monster preying on women."

"Seems a fair deduction."

"Except we were wrong."

"Go on."

"Earlier today I had a shout. Called out to Stoke Mandeville hospital over in Aylesbury. Division thought it was a waste of time. Turned out it wasn't."

"Another woman?"

"No. This breaks the pattern. It was a man in his late twenties. Colin Harris. A primary-school teacher. His car was parked on the railway line and an InterCity express hit it full tilt."

"Ouch."

"Exactly. The train was traveling at well over one hundred miles an hour. Weighed four hundred metric tons. And even if the driver had slammed on the brakes as soon as he saw the car—it would have taken the train a mile and a half to stop. The Honda Accord had no chance and neither did Colin Harris."

I took another swallow of my beer.

"He was choppered into Stoke Mandeville hospital where a transplant patient was waiting. The incident had left him brain-dead. He was on the organ-donor register so when he had been certified as officially so, his heart was removed, transplanted and the life-support mechanisms were switched off."

"Suicide by Network Rail?"

Kirsty shook her head. "Somebody wanted us to think that. He had taken sleeping medication, left a note. But it turns out he didn't commit suicide. He was put there and left to die."

"So what's the connection with your Jane Doe times two?"

"The third finger of his left hand was cut off at the second knuckle. Post-mortem."

"Which means it was done at the hospital?"

"Yes."

"The same guy?"

"Or group of them. It was a group who took Hannah Shapiro remember, Dan. What if the two cases really are connected?"

I shook my head. Given the exchange that was scheduled for tomorrow morning I thought it extremely unlikely.

"It doesn't feel connected to me. Seems like two different things going on here."

"What if someone is harvesting organs? People rich enough not to want to go on a waiting list?"

"The old urban myth."

Kirsty shrugged. "If people think of things, Dan, it can usually be done. You know that."

I did know that but I didn't want to think about it.

Kirsty finished her brandy and poured herself another healthy slug. By my reckoning, you got fourteen ordinary bar doubles out of a seventy-centiliter bottle of spirits. The one she had just poured was probably double that again. So I guessed that so far she had helped herself to about five hundred bucks' worth of my brandy.

"Hannah has disappeared into the ether.

It's been over twenty-four hours. If it was a kidnapping for ransom we would have heard something by now and we haven't," she said.

I shook my head. She looked up at me sharply.

"Unless *you* have heard something?"

I shook my head again—I was turning into one of those nodding dogs you see in the backs of cars. "No. All I know is her father gets here tomorrow morning. If they have contacted him, I don't know about it."

"Right," she said, not sounding a hundred percent convinced.

"He lost his wife to kidnappers, Kirsty," I said. "She was raped and murdered in front of his daughter. If her abductors have told him not to speak to the authorities, I for one wouldn't blame him if he just paid what they wanted and took her home. Would you?"

She took another hit of brandy. "I guess not."

"So where does Private come in?" I asked. Changing the subject.

"We're running a DNA analysis through the system on the second Jane Doe. The first one came back with nothing, but it took over three weeks to do it. I haven't got three weeks. Whoever is doing this needs to be stopped. And it seems to me he's escalating."

"You want to use our labs?"

"Yeah. And in return I'll get you everything we've got on the Hannah Shapiro case. Off the record."

"I'd appreciate it."

"Chloe means a lot to me too, Dan."

And she did. Chloe's father had been my best man and Kirsty had loved him as much as I did. His death had sent me off the rails and I didn't see at the time that she was grieving too: I'd been too selfish to share my own grief. She hadn't been to Iraq, she hadn't seen what I had. I'd been too wrapped up in my own self-pity to see how much I was hurting her. I was destroying our marriage but I didn't care. Caring meant feeling.

We talked some more. I don't know for how long. Ten minutes? Twenty minutes? Kirsty drank more brandy and I had a couple more Coronas. I lost count.

I remember opening the fridge door and taking the last bottle off the shelf. I turned round to open it and there she was, in the small kitchen with me, and I had nowhere left to run.

Somehow she was in my arms, our lips were on each other's. Our breath hot. Her tongue flicking in my mouth. She fumbled loose my belt and undid my trousers so that they pooled around my ankles. She reached in and took hold of me with her familiar, knowing hand. She bit into my neck as I cupped my hands on her perfectly toned buttocks and pulled her against me. I was already rock-hard.

I hadn't expected to be making love to my ex-wife on our wedding anniversary.

It turned out that was the least of my problems.

Part Four

Chapter 64

I OPENED MY eyes with a start.

The clock on my bedside cabinet read 05:59. I watched it for a few seconds and it clicked over to 06:00. The radio alarm switched on. I tapped the button to turn it off and closed my eyes again.

I did that most mornings. I don't know why I bothered with the alarm. Since my army days I could pretty much tell myself when I wanted to wake up. And I did.

My head didn't feel as bad as it should have done. I had drunk far too many beers. Maybe the workout had compensated.

I smiled a little. Little bit guilty. Little bit

pleased with myself. Little bit confused about what I was feeling, if I'm honest.

Kirsty had gone at about four o'clock. She had been groaning when she awoke. She didn't kiss me goodbye when she left. In fact, she didn't say a word. I remember her picking up her boots and almost tiptoeing out of my bedroom like a naughty adolescent. I smiled briefly again but couldn't afford the luxury of letting my thoughts linger. I opened my eyes again. Time to go to work.

I swung my legs out of bed and yawned, turning it into a shout and shaking my head as I did so. I wasn't feeling as bad as I should have been, but there were a few cobwebs to shake loose.

An hour and fifteen minutes later and I was on the treadmill at the gym. I had already done a full workout—weights and cardiovascular—and was warming down.

Sam Riddel was on the treadmill next to me. He hadn't had as long a workout, but then again he probably hadn't drunk a shed-load of Corona beer. Far as I knew you don't get hangovers from mineral water. We hadn't spoken. He'd just nodded at me and gone through his weights routine.

Sam looked across at me now. There was a slight, questioning wrinkle on his forehead.

"You seem in a particularly good mood this morning," he said.

"I just got a call from the hospital. Chloe has come out of the coma. She's still critical. Still in intensive care, but she spoke to her mother and is sleeping naturally now."

"That's great news, Dan."

"Word," I said. I can be down with my homies when I want.

He looked at me again, even more suspiciously. "You get your ashes hauled last night?" he asked.

"A gentleman never tells."

"Saying you did—who would the lucky lady have been?"

"Ah . . ." I said.

"Ah?"

"It's a long story. And we haven't got time," I said, all business now. The treadmill slowed to a walking pace and I picked up my towel and headed for the showers.

Half past eight and back in the office, I watched as Alison Chambers parked her car on the double yellow line below, tossed her keys to one of her flunkeys to park it and headed toward the building.

If she could see me watching her she didn't show it. I wondered what she would make of what had happened with Kirsty last night. I didn't figure I would be telling her. I also wondered what she was doing at work on a Sunday, but I guess some lawyers are like some private detectives. You stop when the work is done.

I crossed to the safe built into the wall, spun the dial and opened it. I took out the small bag containing the diamonds and put it in my pocket. A million pounds' worth didn't take up a lot of space. I left the shotgun in the safe, but took out the pistol and shoulder holster, hefted the gun in my hands for a moment or two and then put it back.

"Good move," Sam said from the doorway.

"But is it?" I replied. "These guys are going to be carrying. If things turn nasty maybe we should have some backup. They nearly killed Chloe remember."

"It's Parliament Square, Dan. Anybody starts producing hardware and nobody's going to get very far. You got any idea of the amount of security down there?"

"Makes me wonder why they chose it for the exchange."

Sam shrugged. "It's a big open space in the center of London. Lots of exits, lots of entrances. They can have eyes on us from a hundred different places. We try anything and they'll know it. There's security all around the parliament buildings. We're out in the open. It's a perfect—"

I held my hand up to stop him. I had a bad feeling he was going to say *killing ground*.

Chapter 65

I HADN'T FELT the hairs on the back of my neck prickle so much since my days in Iraq.

Back then, marking out a minefield in the middle of no-man's-land was like playing Russian Roulette every day. Sam was right. Parliament Square is a big open space located at the north-west end of the Palace of Westminster, or the Houses of Parliament as they're called on the bottles of that old brown sauce.

I was standing with my back to the Robert Peel statue, as ordered. Presumably they had picked that depiction of the founder of the first metropolitan police force in the world as some kind of ironic joke.

If it was, then I wasn't laughing. I was scanning the area. The man who gave his name to the British "Bobby" was on the south-western edge of the large green that was in the middle of the square. Around it stood, among other buildings, the Collegiate Church of St. Peter at Westminster—or Westminster Abbey to you and me—the smaller Anglican church of St. Margaret, the parish church of the Houses of Parliament, and 100 Parliament Street, headquarters of Her Majesty's Revenue and Customs.

And from where I was standing I could have picked up a stone and thrown it at the Middlesex Guildhall, which is home to the Supreme Court of the United Kingdom. Like I said, I think Hannah Shapiro's abductors were tweaking our noses a little. Still, you could understand why the area was so popular with tourists.

Especially on a Sunday.

There were four major roads into the square and a Tube station right by it.

I looked at my watch. A couple of minutes or so to go.

Sam Riddel was somewhere close by, but I

couldn't see him. Not that he was going to be able to do a great deal if something bad went down. In addition we had people stationed on each of the roads into the square and by the entrances to the Tube station.

It was the second hot day in a row. Certainly breaking records for the time of year. I looked at my watch again. Showtime.

My phone went. I checked the ID: Brad Dexter. "Yes, Brad?"

"You got a big crowd marching down past me, Dan. Heading into the square. They just appeared from nowhere."

The phone beeped again, another incoming call: Suzy this time—different street, same message. And again. And again. All four watch stations saying the same thing.

All hell broke loose.

First came the noise. Megaphones and chants. Then the people. Random groups seemed to join together as hundreds started pouring in from St. Margaret Street, Broad Sanctuary, Great George Street and Bridge Street. Banners were unfurled as they all headed toward the green.

A group of black-faced Border-style Morris dancers were capering about in outlandish costumes, heading toward me as more and more banners were unfurled. The chanting grew louder.

Until the summer of last year there had been a permanent protest camp set up on the green. A ragbag assortment of tents, flags and slogan banners, with straw bales used for toilets. The camp called itself the Democracy village.

Originally the protest consisted of just one man, Brian Haw. He set up the site in 2001 to protest against the suffering caused by the sanctions imposed on the Iraqis in the 1990s. However, as events unfolded in Iraq he stayed to protest against the invasion and occupation. The more recent self-styled Democracy Village was not aligned with him and when the people had been evicted a year ago they'd vowed they would be back.

A number of smaller demonstrations had already taken place but this looked like a large-scale organized one. As this kind of protest was illegal in the square they obviously hadn't made any public announcements about it.

I looked at my watch again and my phone vibrated in my pocket. I took it out, flicked the lock off and clicked on the incoming-message icon. It read: "Don't forget to pay the piper."

I looked across the square.

The black-faced dancers in black, yellow and green rags and with feathers in their hats were about fifty yards or so away now. People were milling around them. One of them was holding out a gaudy cap as if to collect money. But it was neither the time or place for that—unless they were looking to collect big, of course.

I could see why they had picked this time and place now. It was absolute chaos. The dancers didn't seem to be in any hurry, mind. They were dancing and twirling, shouting and clattering sticks.

I've always hated Morris dancers. Now I wished I had packed some serious heat. Do the whole world a favor right there and then!

I looked at them. None of them was big enough to be Brendan Ferres. That was for sure. The guy with the collecting hat was tall but nowhere near as wide as Ferres and he was wearing black-rimmed glasses. One of the dancers in the middle didn't seem too enthusiastic. Smaller-framed than the others. Hard to tell from this distance, but my guess was that it was Hannah. She was surrounded at all times. As one dancer twirled away another jigged in. They were corralling her.

Just as well I didn't bring the shotgun. Like I said, I would have been sorely tempted to take them all down. Wasn't my call, to make though, and the instructions from Harlan Shapiro through Jack Morgan had been explicit. No heroics. No improvisation. Just pay them the agreed amount and get Hannah home safe.

I put my hand in my pocket, putting it around the bag of diamonds, clasping it tight.

And then everything went to hell in a handcart.

Chapter 66

A LARGE GROUP of uniformed police-men came running past the dancers, heading straight for me.

DI Kirsty Webb followed closely behind.

The crowd milled past the dancers who had stopped dancing and were watching me. The lead dancer pointed his finger at me like the barrel of a gun and mimed pulling the trigger. Then they were lost in the huge crowd that surged around them. I tried to give chase but at that moment the riot police arrived and a wall of perspex shields and raised batons blocked my way.

"What the hell are you doing here, Kirsty?"

"We got a call!"

"What are you talking about? Got a call from who?"

Kirsty held her warrant card up and led me past the riot police who were attempting to "kettle" the demonstrators behind us.

"Division got an anonymous call. Telling us the missing package will be delivered at the Robert Peel statue here at ten o'clock. We got here as fast as we could."

"Yeah, well, you just might have served her a death sentence."

She glared right back at me. "You got the same message, I take it? Seeing as you're here."

"Something like that."

She shook her head. "When, Dan? When did you get the message?"

I didn't answer.

"You already knew, didn't you? Last night, all the time you were fucking me, you knew! And you didn't tell me."

Kirsty slapped me across the face. Hard.

Felt like old times.

"They said they'd kill her if the police were involved." I had to shout to be heard above the noise. "What was I supposed to do?" I said.

"Maybe you could have trusted me."

"The person who called it in—man or woman?"

"Man."

"Accent?"

"I don't know, Dan. The woodentop who took the call just wrote it down and stuck it on my desk. Didn't think it was important."

" 'Woodentop' was an expression the kidnappers used."

"What, you think it was me?" she snapped sarcastically.

"Of course not—just thinking out loud."

"Seems to me you've left it a little late for thinking. We had a chance here. You should have told me."

"I would have done if I could."

"Doing the right thing isn't exactly your strong point, is it, Dan?"

"You didn't seem to have any complaints last night."

Kirsty snorted angrily. "I wondered how long it would take you to bring that up. You got me drunk on cheap brandy, is all. Doesn't change anything."

"You don't have to tell me!"

"And you have got more serious things to worry about."

"Yeah, I do know that."

"Do you, though?"

"You got a point to make, Kirsty, how about you spit it out?"

"Somebody told us where the exchange was going to take place." She looked across at Sam and Suzy as they forced their way toward us through the crowds. Brad Dexter was following behind with more of his security team trailing in their wake.

"Yeah, so what's your point?" I had to shout again. Hundreds of the protesters had produced those vuvuzela horns from last year's World Cup and were blasting away behind the perspex wall that the police had formed.

"It wasn't whoever took the girl who phoned us, was it?"

"No."

"So who else knew?"

"No one."

"Just you, Dan. You and your team of

superheroes." Kirsty did practically spit the last couple of words out. I took in what she was saying but she spelled it out for me anyway.

"Someone's rotten on your team, Dan. Someone set you up."

Chapter 67

HARLAN SHAPIRO WASN'T much to look at.

But then, what are multibillionaires supposed to look like? He was a small, quiet man. Dustin Hoffman's shy cousin, perhaps.

He had been angry, naturally, when I explained what had happened at Parliament Square but hadn't gone ballistic, which surprised me a little. One thing all billionaires have in common—they're used to getting their own way.

Del Rio was exactly as I remembered him, though: hard as nails and a man of few words. But when he spoke people listened, or they did if they knew what was good for them.

I hadn't told Harlan what Kirsty had said to me but I outlined it to Del Rio who was with me in my office drinking black coffee. Their flight had been delayed and hadn't landed until just after ten o'clock. About the same time the blacked-up Morris dancers had disappeared into the crowds. You would have thought their distinctive costumes would have made them easy to spot. But by the time the chaos had been brought under control they had long gone.

I held a hand to my cheek, remembering the slap Kirsty had given me. Maybe she cared after all.

Del Rio put his cup down. "Your ex-wife reckons we've got a rotten apple in Private?" he said.

"It makes sense."

"You got any theories?"

"No, and I can't see the point in the play. What do they get out of it?"

"How many people here knew about the drop?"

"We took a big team out there, covering all the exits."

"So it could have been pretty much anybody in your outfit?"

I nodded. "Or Stateside," I said.

"How do you figure?"

I opened a desk drawer and flipped a picture of the dark-suited American who'd been with Brendan Ferres and Ronnie Allen at his bar last night.

"I kept thinking this has nothing to do with the original kidnapping. Nothing to do with America. But now I don't know." I tapped on the photo. "Do you know this guy?"

Del Rio tilted his chin slightly and worked his jaw muscles as he looked at the picture. "Wiseguy, name of Sally Manzino. East Coast. Importer and exporter."

"I take it we're not talking coffee beans."

"He's on the payroll of the Noccia family. Not the mobile-phone people. Sally Manzino is their East Coast connection. Private has had dealings with the family before. What's the connection?"

"This man"—I pointed to a photo of Brendan Ferres—"was seen entering the university where Hannah was studying, a couple of hours before she was abducted. He works for a piece of work called Ronnie Allen."

"I've heard the name."

"He denies any connection with the kidnapping."

"You buy it?"

I shrugged. "It's not his usual line and if he knew what Harlan Shapiro was worth, then if he *had* taken the girl he'd be asking for a lot more than a million pounds' worth of pretty stones."

"It's not exactly chump change, but I take your point. So what's his story?"

"Snake Ferres reckons he was making a delivery."

"Drugs?"

"Yeah. Tertiary-educational institutions in our country are not exactly immune from drug abuse. And in the main the students at Chancellors come from money. They can afford the good stuff."

"And Ronnie Allen can provide it?"

"He certainly can."

"I'll speak to Jack. Check them out."

"If Noccia is involved in the kidnapping, is he likely to say so?"

"Depends how you ask the question," Del Rio said.

He had a point. I finished my own coffee and my mobile rang as Sam came into the office. I waved him in, looked at the caller ID and saw the number had been withheld. I answered it, clicking it to loudspeaker.

"Dan Carter."

The same mechanical voice as before boomed out.

"You were told not to talk to the police, Mister Carter."

"Hang on," I said. "You've got to listen to me..."

"No, you have to listen to me," he said. *"You were told not to speak to the police and you were told what the consequences would be if you did so."*

"It wasn't us," I said, keeping my voice level.

There was a pause. *"You get one more chance, Mister Carter."*

I sighed quietly. "Go on…"

"As is traditional in these kind of negotiations, when instructions are ignored you get penalized. The fee has gone up to five million. Same deal. Flawless stones. Five million pounds' worth."

"Where and when?"

"Two o'clock this afternoon. Eastbound plat-form for the Metropolitan Line. Finchley Road Tube station. Have Harlan Shapiro with you. Anyone else and the consequences will be termi-nal. Her father is to make the drop."

"If I can arrange—"

"He's in the country, Mister Carter. Please don't take us for fools. That's the deal. It is not negotiable."

"Okay."

"Trust us, this is your last shot. Sit on the sec-ond bench heading toward the end of the plat-form and put him on the first Metropolitan train to Baker Street. Not a Jubilee Line train."

"How do I know Hannah Shapiro isn't already dead?"

"Check your e-mail, Mister Carter. There's all the information you need."

Chapter 68

THE LINE WENT DEAD.

I walked around my desk and sat down, pulling my keyboard toward me and angling my monitor so Del Rio and Sam could see it.

I opened my mailbox and there were three new messages.

Two of them were unrelated but the third was from a similar random numbers and letters address as the first YouTube message I had received. The subject line read *Last Chance Saloon*.

I opened the e-mail and sure enough the message was the same as the first—another hyperlink to a YouTube address.

I clicked on the hyperlink and it opened

to a dark screen in the video panel. I clicked on the play icon and after a second or so it faded up on the same room as before. This time, however, Hannah Shapiro was sitting on a chair. She was still wearing the same black underwear, and her face was scrubbed clean of any makeup. She looked like the girl I had first met. Young, vulnerable and very afraid.

She had good reason to be.

What was different this time was that she had explosives strapped around her body. Wires connecting the various packages, suicide bomber-style. Rope hung again from one wrist and the other hand held a typewritten note.

She looked at the camera, her voice trembling.

"They want you to know," she said, "that this bomb I am wearing can be triggered remotely. Any attempt to do anything other than what you are instructed to do and it will be detonated. Likewise if you attempt to deliver fake diamonds. They will be examined and if they are not genuine the device will be detonated. If police are there again as they were this morning, the device will be detonated."

She let the paper fall to the floor as tears welled in her large, terrified eyes.

"Please help me," she added in a desperate whisper.

The screen faded to blackness and I rewound the video and paused it. Looking at the devices strapped to her body.

"They look genuine to you?" asked Sam.

"Yup," I replied.

"We have to tell the police, then."

"Can't do that," Del Rio said softly.

Sam held his hands up. "We can't let a walking bomb get on the London Underground."

"We go to the police and they'll kill her," I said to Sam.

"What is it they call it—collateral damage?" he persisted.

"They're not going to do anything, Sam. They want the money, is all. It's business."

Del Rio worked his jaw muscles again. "We have to protect the client," he said. "That's our job here. We save the girl."

Chapter 69

HARLAN SHAPIRO HAD barely said three words to me since our first meeting earlier that morning.

Sam and Del Rio had driven us to the Finchley Road Tube station and we had been sitting on the seat as we'd been told, for some twenty-five minutes. It was five minutes to two. I had looked at my watch seconds earlier. But I checked it again, anyway. Hard to be perfectly calm when a bomb is thundering up the Metropolitan Line on its way for a date with you.

We had been put between a rock and a very hard place. If Hannah was indeed on the train then theoretically we could have placed operatives at all stations on the Metropolitan Line between Finchly Road and the four terminuses it finished at: Uxbridge, Watford, Chesham and Amersham.

We had the manpower for that. But the Metropolitan Line intersected with other lines on the Underground at many stations and with the overland mainline services at Harrow-on-the-Hill. Meaning that the kidnappers could start their journey potentially from anywhere in London and still end up heading toward us on the eastbound train that was due in five minutes. Private had a lot of resources but we didn't have enough for that, not in the time available to us.

We could have done what Sam wanted and informed the authorities. But that would have resulted in the entire Tube network being closed down and we would have had no way of protecting Hannah Shapiro.

I didn't believe they would set the bomb off—if, indeed, it was live. But I could understand the logic of it. They had to make sure the merchandise we were using for the exchange was the genuine article. Hannah was their security. If they handed her over before they could check, they had no way of knowing whether the ransom paid was genuine.

This way they did. It would take time to disarm the explosives strapped around Hannah. Through my work with the RMP I knew a thing or two about bombs. None of it good. But in the RMP we didn't disarm them, we simply marked and secured them for the experts to get in. And we didn't stay too close when they did!

Sam and Del Rio were now waiting at Baker Street. We had received a further e-mail saying that if everything was as it should be then Hannah and her father would disembark there. The journey from Finchley Road gave the kidnappers time for their expert to get his loupe out, I guess, and examine the stones. They would find them genuine. Not easy to get five million pounds' worth of gems on a Sunday afternoon. But, like I said, Private has resources and reach.

Del Rio had also talked to Jack Morgan who had spoken to a high-ranking member of the Noccia family on the West Coast.

The word had come back that the Italian-American we had seen with Ronnie Allen, Sally Manzino, was a made man, and highly placed in the family's operation. He had nothing to do with Hannah's kidnapping and we could take that as cast-iron. Jack Morgan had some kind of deal with the Noccia family, I don't know what. Apparently he had helped them out over some turf war of their own a year or two back so there was some kind of mutual back-scratching.

Either way, Manzino was out of the frame. This was looking like a totally home-grown operation.

I looked at my watch again. Three minutes to go. Harlan Shapiro turned to me. His eyes were sunken, haunted.

"My daughter is very precious to me, Mister Carter," he said.

"I know."

"I made a very grave error of judgment some years ago, and Hannah had to pay a terrible price."

I nodded. He was right.

"My wife, of course, paid the ultimate

price. And if I could change events in time I would gladly have taken her place. Do you understand me?"

"I do, sir," I said. And I did.

"These animals who have taken my daughter. If anything goes wrong on this train journey...I want you to track them down and slaughter them."

He looked at me, his eyes animated now. "Will you do that?"

"You have my word: we won't let this lie, Mister Shapiro. But these people are businessmen. They have a perverse logic to what they are doing. The logic means that they will keep you alive, Mister Shapiro. You and your daughter."

"They are terrorists, Mister Carter. I don't believe logic is the driving force here."

"They are acting like terrorists but they're not the same thing. If they detonate any explosive device on a London Underground train they will have the full and focused attention of the national police forces bearing down on them. Together with the Home Office, the anti-terrorism squad and your own Home-land Security department. They don't want that. Believe me."

He nodded. His eyes weak, unfocused. "I guess we have to believe that."

Chapter 70

THE OVERHEAD MONITOR showed that the train would be arriving in one minute.

As I looked up at it a train clattered into the platform. Jubilee Line. False alarm.

It was very warm. One of those days you get in May which are like a glorious early summer and I was wearing polarized aviator sunglasses against the brightness of the sun.

Finchley Road is an open-air station. From there to all destinations west, the Tube is actually overground. It is at Finchley Road station heading east that the Metropolitan Line enters the tunnel network. The underground labyrinth connecting all parts of London. The

Jubilee Line train left. Thirty seconds later the Metropolitan Line train came in.

It was crowded, particularly for a Sunday. But there was a big concert on later at the O2 Arena, the re-formed Take That were headlining and thousands of people were heading east for it.

Harlan Shapiro and I stood up as the train pulled to a stop, and headed to the door which opened opposite the seat we had been told to wait at.

Harlan Shapiro stepped aboard.

I scanned the carriages and what faces I could see I didn't recognize. The doors closed and the train began to pull out.

I let the carriage go, then jogged alongside the train and leaped in between two of the carriages where there was a small gap for the guard to walk through.

The train picked up speed and as it went into the tunnel the lights dimmed and it became dark.

My feet flew from under me and I fell backward toward the gap.

Chapter 71

LUCKILY SOMEONE HAD opened the window on one of the doors.

I managed to grab its top edge before I was sucked under the train.

I pulled myself upright and opened the door. A group of middle-aged women looked at me, startled. I smiled apologetically and tried to make my way through.

It wasn't easy. I wasn't sure what I'd hoped to achieve by getting on the train but I couldn't just do nothing. I'd made a promise first to Hannah Shapiro and now to her father, and I intended to keep it. I made my way about halfway down the carriage when the train stopped briefly, as it often did on this stretch of track. I walked onto the end of the carriage and it started up again.

I looked through the windows between the carriages but there was no sign of Hannah or her father. I opened the door again, apologizing to the people who had to move out of the way. I considered flashing them my card but decided against it. Given the circumstances, it was probably best not to let people know who I was or who I was working for.

I worked my way down through the next carriage. It was just as packed as the others. Mainly women—a lot of them in their thirties or forties. Dressed a lot younger and giggling like schoolchildren on their way to their first concert.

What would happen if the kidnappers detonated the explosives didn't bear thinking about.

I had been entirely rational in my reassurances to Harlan Shapiro. But logic was one thing and human emotion another, and emotion was a far stronger force than logic. As I was just about to find out.

Chapter 72

PETER CHAPPEL WAS a forty-five-year-old ophthalmic optician with a small practice in Chesham, a quiet Buckinghamshire market town set amidst the rolling natural beauty of the Chilterns.

His premises were on the High Street and, although it was a Sunday, he had come into his shop to sort through some paperwork and receipts that he needed to send off to his accountant for the quarterly VAT return. He had an elderly female assistant who worked with him, but as often as not he would find himself coming into the shop on his day off to catch up with the admin.

He put all the receipts together into a

large white envelope, sealed and addressed it, walked through to the reception area and left it on his assistant's desk to go out in the morning post. He was ahead of schedule but Peter Chappel was a man who paid attention to detail.

He walked back to his examination room. It was windowless, with an old-fashioned roll-top desk in the corner that he used for an office. He unplugged and picked up the laptop that was sitting on the faded green leather and deliberated for a moment.

It was a few minutes past three o'clock and Peter Chappel made a decision. Pulling at an eye-test chart, he swung it out from the wall to reveal a safe behind it.

He put the laptop into the safe, closed the door and spun the dial. Then he put the eye chart back in place and bustled back out through reception.

He picked up a couple of carrier bags that he had left by the front door and then went out onto the street, putting them down again so he could lock the door behind him.

He looked at his watch again and set off

for home. He was a little late but not much and he certainly didn't want to miss any of the fun. Luckily he lived just a hundred yards or so away from his shop in Punch Bowl Lane. Quite appropriate, Peter Chappel thought to himself as he strolled quickly along Red Lion Street—there was no show without Punch, after all, as the old saying goes.

Chapter 73

TOM CHALLONER HAD worked for the Underground for thirty years.

He was a stationmaster and would be retiring in the autumn. At ten minutes past three he was sitting at his desk taking what he considered a well-earned tea break, timing himself as he finished *The Times* crossword.

The shock waves from the explosion shattered the window of his office and knocked him from his chair to lie unconscious on the floor.

Near Edgware Road Tube station, Kirsty Webb was sitting at her desk in one of the CID offices at Paddington Green. Cursing the ever-increasing bureaucratic demands that meant she and her colleagues spent more time doing paperwork than they ever did out on the street solving crimes. Or trying to.

She had given up on the paperwork an hour ago and had been working on a presentation that she would be giving in a few days' time in Manchester. She had been shortlisted as one of three final applicants for the new post in the newly created division. Each of them had to give a fifteen-minute talk. A case study of a successful murder case on which they had worked.

Kirsty had wanted to give her presentation on the "Ring-Finger Murders" as one of the red-top papers had named them—a title that had been taken up by most of the broadcast media. But she had been sidelined on the case because it had been taken over by the serial-crimes unit and she found herself relegated back to donkey work. Taking statements, filing reports, dead-end policing.

She put her pen down, picked up a sheet of paper with random thoughts and doodles on it, screwed it into a ball and was about to throw it across the room into a waste-paper bin when a call came.

She looked at the caller ID, then across the room to where a couple of male colleagues were discussing yesterday's football game. She walked out of the office, along to the steps at the end of the corridor and answered it.

"DI Webb," she said.

"Kirsty, it's Doctor Lee. I've got some news." Kirsty felt a small flutter of expectation. She could tell by the woman's voice that something significant had happened.

"What have you got for me, Wendy?"

"Dan had me run the DNA analysis for you."

"Yeah, I know," said Kirsty impatiently.

"We've got a hit."

"Hang on." Kirsty lodged the phone in the crook of her shoulder and pulled out her notepad and pen.

"Shoot."

"She's a Romanian national. A nurse—and she's got a criminal record back at home so we got lucky. You wouldn't have got a hit on your police systems and would have had to go to Interpol, which would have taken even longer."

"Thanks, Wendy."

"Thank Dan. He put me on it on my day off."

"Sorry about that."

"I'm only kidding. I was just waiting for a call at my end. We're all eyes out on the Shapiro case, anyway. Nobody's having any time off."

"I guess not."

"So you can buy Dan a beer when you see him."

"If I can get hold of him I will. He's not answering his phone."

"I know—I tried him first. Probably out of network coverage or his phone's run down."

Kirsty nodded.

"So, my Jane Doe. What's her name?"

"Adriana Kisslinger. She was twenty-seven."

"What was her offense?"

"Prostitution. She was offering executive bed baths in the hospital she was working at, apparently. The ward sister didn't approve."

"And it's illegal in Romania?"

"Prostitution is, yes. Ironic, isn't it? Romania is listed as one of the biggest sources of human trafficking in the world."

"I know. Thanks again for this, Wendy."

"Like I said—"

"Yeah, yeah. I know," Kirsty interrupted. "I will when I speak with him."

Chapter 74

HANNAH SHAPIRO LOOKED up, surprised, as I walked toward her.

She was standing, holding onto one of the poles in the doors section of the carriage. Surrounded by more excited women but, whereas their faces were bright with anticipation, hers was crumpled, her haunted eyes still free of makeup. They welled with tears as I quietly said her name. She spun round and walked straight into my enfolding arms.

I hugged her tight to me. She was wearing an oversized white raincoat and not much beneath it.

Which was good news. She might have just had her underwear on but at least she wasn't strapped around with explosives. After a moment she stepped back a little and I was glad that she did. Like I said, Hannah had grown quite a bit since I had last seen her.

"What happened?" I asked her.

"They took my dad, Mister Carter. They've taken him."

"How?"

"When the train stopped in the tunnel. There was someone outside, waiting. They went through those." She pointed at the connecting doors.

They had got off the train the same way I had got on. But it didn't make any sense— they could hardly have walked back through the tunnel. Not with the trains running.

"Did you recognize any of the men who took you?" I asked as daylight filled the train once more as it pulled into Baker Street station.

Hannah shook her head. "They were wearing masks when they jumped on us in the street. And I never saw their faces in the house they kept me in. I was in the dark the whole time."

"And today?"

"This morning they were all painted black. They painted me, too."

I nodded. "I saw you but we couldn't get to you."

"I know."

"And this afternoon they were all wearing comedy Take That face masks."

"Where did you get on the train?"

"I don't know. Out in the country."

We stepped out onto the platform and she wobbled a little, holding my arm to steady herself and then gripping it harder.

"How are Chloe and Laura?" she asked, her voice even more tremulous.

"Laura suffered a cut to her arm but she's okay."

"And Chloe?"

"Is still in hospital, Hannah. But she's going to be fine."

I figured that if I said it confidently enough it might make it so. People were still pouring out of the train, heading for the eastbound platform of the Jubilee Line. A guard was waiting for them to clear so he could whistle the train on. I went up to him and told him that I had seen an unattended bag on one of the storage racks over the seats.

It held up the train long enough for me to have a word with the driver. He had stopped in the tunnel due to signaling. It was a common enough occurrence when a train was waiting for traffic to clear ahead. There would be trains doing the very same thing now because we had backed up the system.

Fifteen minutes later and we were outside in one of Private's mobile offices. A large black van with blacked-out windows and a state-of-the-art communications system inside.

We had put a transmitting device on Harlan Shapiro, strong enough to track from above the tunnel. That section wasn't very deep, after all: it was classified as subsurface, not really underground at all. The device was disguised as a tie clip and the signal it was broadcasting translated as a flashing dot on our computer monitor displaying a map of central London. I called up the schematic of the London Underground system and superimposed it. Sure enough, the flashing light corresponded with where the train had stopped in the tunnel. The dot wasn't moving.

"He can't still be down there," said Sam who was standing beside me with Del Rio.

Hannah Shapiro was sitting huddled on one of the bench seats along the left side of the van, holding a cup of tea but not really drinking it. I guessed she was lost in dark memories and darker imaginings about what might be happening to her father. Personally, I was kicking myself. Harlan Shapiro had been the target all along. Never mind the golden egg, they had wanted the golden goddamned goose.

I moved the remote-control mouse and clicked it, this time synchronizing Google Street View with the flashing symbol.

"Son of a bitch," I said out loud.

"What is it?" asked Del Rio.

It was unlikely he would know what it was. Not a lot of people in London did, either.

We were looking at a bricked-up building. A series of arches all filled in with the same dark gray brick as the rest of it. It looked like a church or a Victorian orangery, maybe, if the arches had been filled with glass. Up until a few years ago, the building had housed a Chinese restaurant but now it was standing empty, waiting to become part of the infrastructure again as a substation. It had been built in 1868 and closed in 1939 when England was at war with Germany and the USA was still watching from the sidelines.

"It's Marlborough Road," I said.

"Which is?"

"Marlborough Road Tube Station," I explained. "One of many old Tube stations hidden throughout the Underground network. The platform for it isn't even underground—they walked up and out and could be anywhere by now."

"So where does that leave us?" asked Del Rio.

I looked over at Hannah Shapiro looking into her mug of hot tea as if the answers might be found within it. Somehow I doubted it.

"It leaves us with a job to do," I said determinedly. "And I know just where to start."

Chapter 75

DI KIRSTY WEBB was feeling the kind of excitement she got when the "tide" of a case changed.

She'd considered taking the information to her superiors but she would have had to explain where and how she had got the identification.

She didn't want to do that. It could cost her her detective-inspector status. It would certainly cost her the shot at the promotion she wanted and the move to Manchester that she'd thought she wanted—and wasn't the hell sure about now. Damn Dan Carter! Why did she have to go and jump into bed with him again like some drunken teenager!

Kirsty shook away the thought and concentrated on her computer screen. Adriana Kisslinger had come into the country over a year ago and had worked on a temporary basis at a number of hospitals. Moving around London as an agency nurse: Northwick Park Hospital, the Royal Free Hospital in Hampstead. Then, bingo, she had also worked a three-month stint at Stoke Mandeville in Buckinghamshire. After that nothing was showing for a few months. If she had been working anywhere she'd been doing it off the books. Unless she had gone back to her sideline, of course. Not every prostitute filled in a tax return.

A couple of calls later and Kirsty had Adriana Kisslinger's last known address. It was in Punch Bowl Lane in Chesham.

Chapter 76

BACK IN THE office I had assembled the troops.

The bad feeling in the air was palpable. We had brought back Hannah Shapiro. But no one was celebrating. Harlan Shapiro had known what was at stake. He had been very clear: he had lost his daughter once—he wasn't about to lose her again. Whatever the cost. And he knew full well it was not just a monetary cost.

We didn't have a clue what their next move would be. Harlan Shapiro was worth billions. His daughter had been a sprat set to catch a diamond-studded mackerel. The ransom demand had always seemed small to us. Now we knew why. Looked like it was seed money to set up the real deal. The stakes were about to go very high.

Kirsty had been as good as her word and had copied everything the Met had on the case over to me. Maybe there was something in all the data that had been missed.

Del Rio had taken Hannah back to her college rooms. She needed a shower and clean clothes. Suzy had gone with them.

I was sitting with Adrian Tuttle, working our way through the photographs that the SOCO team had collected. They were all digital, not as good as Adrian would have taken, and were displayed on his widescreen Apple monitor.

Doctor Wendy Lee, meanwhile, was looking at the other forensic reports. Sam was reading through the police interviews of the students and staff who had been in the bar, or near it, when the abduction had gone down.

On the screen Adrian Tuttle had yet another shot of the cobbled street. Close-ups of the blood which we already knew was Laura Skelton's.

He clicked his mouse and moved onto a wide-angle shot of the street. Pretty much an exact version of the same pictures that we had taken when our people had got to the scene. Except that had been later and the police had gone by then.

I moved the mouse and clicked on the next photo.

Another wide-angle shot of the scene from another perspective. But Adrian muttered something and snatched the mouse from me, clicking back to the previous shot.

I looked at the picture, puzzled. He'd seen something I hadn't. "What?" I asked.

Chapter 77

ADRIAN TUTTLE IGNORED me, clicking on a series of icons and drop-down menus. The screen split in two and he pulled down more menus.

The picture we had been looking at remained on the left-hand screen. On the right he had called up our own forensic photos that had been taken on the night of the kidnapping. Adrian hadn't been responsible for those: he had been working on the woman found in the lock-up in King's Cross.

He flicked through the images until he found a wide-angle shot that matched the one the police had taken. If it was a spot-the-difference competition I couldn't have circled one, let alone ten.

He pointed to the top left-hand corner of the first picture. "See that?"

I shrugged. "Just the differences of light," I said. "Ours were taken later, remember, and they had their lights set up in different positions."

Adrian shook his head. "It's not a trick of the light."

"What is it, then?"

"It's an object. It was here in this street when the police SOCO unit were there. And it wasn't there an hour or so later when we took our photos."

"So what is it, then?" I repeated.

"I don't know."

Adrian clicked on the mouse again, dragging a dotted line around the small area and releasing it to blow up the image. The picture became pixelated, even more blurred.

"Still none the wiser, Adrian," I said.

"We can do something about that," he replied.

He typed on his keyboard and bounced the image across to Sci in the Los Angeles headquarters.

Within minutes, a message pinged back across the Atlantic and Adrian opened the attachment. Our American associate had run the image through a powerful image-enhancement system. The kind of technology that analyzes space-telescope imagery of landscapes on Mars.

What we had was the corner and a fold or two of a blanket. Dark brown and red, in a checkered or tartan pattern. One edge of the blanket was folded across but there was part of a label visible, with the letters Q and U on it.

"Doesn't tell us much, I'm afraid, Dan," said Adrian apologetically.

See, Adrian was good with the detail. He hadn't even taken the photograph and yet he remembered the smallest discrepancy between the two images. But me? I knew a goddamned clue when I saw one!

Chapter 78

"SHIT!"

DI Kirsty Webb kicked the tire of her car. But it did little to ease her frustration.

She had thought she'd made a breakthrough in the case but now that she had arrived in Chesham it seemed extremely probable that she was looking at another dead end.

Literally.

The house she had come to had had a sizable chunk blown out of it. Debris strewn all around. The windows smashed in the small station across the road from it.

She checked the address on the open page of her notebook as she walked up to the

Police—Do Not Cross line. No mistake about it. It was the last known address of Adriana Kisslinger.

She ducked under the tape and flashed a quick, humorless smile to the young uniformed officer who approached her. "It's okay," she said, flashing her warrant card. "DI Webb. So, what have we got?"

"There's been an accident."

He would have said more but DI James appeared in the doorway. "Inspector Webb," she said, a little puzzled to see her.

"Natalie."

"Have there been some developments? On the Colin Harris case? Is that why you're here?"

"It looks that way," said Kirsty.

"What do you mean?"

"Whatever this was . . . I'm guessing it wasn't an accident," Kirsty gestured at the house.

"We were working on the assumption that it was."

DI Natalie James led Kirsty through the house into a kitchen, the far wall of which was missing. A third of the ceiling was gone, with beams and plaster hanging down and debris strewn across the floor.

Kirsty looked up a little suspiciously. "Is it safe?"

The Buckinghamshire DI smiled reassuringly. "Come through."

Kirsty followed her through what would have been a back door to the garden patio off the kitchen. A brick wall had been blown into the next-door neighbor's garden, with metal wreckage strewn around both. A number of white-suited SOCO officers were working the garden.

"They're mainly looking for the rest of his body," she explained.

"Who was it?"

"Local optician. Peter Chappel. Wasn't he who you were here to see?" she asked, puzzled.

Kirsty shook her head. "This was the last address I could find for my Jane Doe discovered on Friday night."

"With the finger missing?"

"Exactly."

"And you know who she is now?"

"A tip-off from a collar. Information to barter. Vice Squad alerted us. Her name is Adriana Kisslinger. Romanian. Busted back home for prostitution."

"And here?"

"Working as a contract nurse. Dropped off the radar some months back. She was working at Stoke Mandeville."

"So Serious Crimes aren't going away any time soon."

"They won't when they find this out, no."

"You haven't told them?"

"I didn't know, did I? Anonymous tips have to be checked out. I was just following up an old address on a possible ident. You know how it works. So what happened here, exactly?"

"Peter Chappel had a barbecue planned for this afternoon. Came home from his shop after sorting out some paperwork. Put the wine to chill in the fridge and came out here to get the grill going."

"It was a gas barbecue?"

"Range-style, three-burner. Propane gas

cylinder in the metal oven. He turned the dial, pushed the ignite button. And…Boom!"

"There was a leak?"

"Looks that way. Like I said, we thought it was accidental."

"Think again," said Kirsty Webb.

Chapter 79

CHLOE, LAURA AND Hannah all shared a three-bed apartment in a student-accommodation block.

I nodded at the security guard we'd had placed at the entrance to the building. She wasn't in uniform and I was discreet about it. The authorities still didn't know that we had Hannah back safe and we wanted to keep it that way. Time enough for explanations and recriminations later.

Priority one was getting Harlan Shapiro back. His daughter's rooms were on the ground floor. I keyed in the entrance code at the door and walked into a brightly lit warm corridor with rugs on the floor, flowers on a side table and modern artwork on either wall between the doors to the student apartments. To the right as I walked in was the students' kitchen. Far fancier than the one I remembered from my student days.

Sitting at the table was Suzy, drinking a cup of tea, and Sam Riddel doing likewise. Herbal for him, no doubt.

I threw Suzy a slightly critical look. "I thought I said to stay with Hannah?"

"She had a visitor."

"Laura?"

"No."

I knew they hadn't let Chloe out. I had the hospital on speed-dial. With Chloe things were going well. They were talking of moving her out of intensive care. Which was good. But no way were they letting her home yet. Which was bad.

I snapped back to the present. "So who?"

"Her tutor. Professor Kidman."

I smiled, briefly. Not like Suzy to be jealous. But then I realized she wasn't being jealous. It was a good call—the professor did look like the actress.

"Annabelle," I said.

"Annabelle?"

"How did she know?"

"I guess Hannah called her."

"You let her use the phone?"

"Didn't say not to," Sam joined in.

They were right. I hadn't. "Could make things complicated, word gets out," I said.

Suzy smiled, but her eyes were deadpan. "Maybe you could have a word with *Annabelle*? Buy us some time."

"Yeah," I said.

I knocked on the door and, after a pause, walked in. Hannah was dressed in a bathrobe. Her hair was wet.

She was being hugged by Professor Weston who smiled gratefully at me as I entered. Hannah didn't move for a while, her head nestled against the older woman's shoulder.

Annabelle gave her back a reassuring pat. Like a surrogate mother, which I guess she was in some ways. Apart from her age. A surrogate older sister, maybe.

"Thanks for bringing her back to us," Annabelle said.

"*De nada*," I replied. And I was right, it was nothing. All I'd achieved was to swap one hostage for another and pay the kidnappers five million pounds for the privilege.

Hannah straightened herself and moved away from the professor. "Thank you, Mister Carter," she said.

"I told you, it's Dan. And you can thank me when I get your dad back home."

Hannah nodded and, although her face had been scrubbed clean and glowed once more with the innocence of youth, there was still a deep sadness in her eyes.

"So, what brings you here, Mister Carter?" asked the professor.

"I think we have a lead."

"Really?"

"A witness."

Chapter 80

"A WITNESS?"

The professor looked surprised. "I thought there was no one there. Why hasn't he come forward before?"

"Who is it?" asked Hannah.

"We don't know yet."

"I don't understand," said the professor.

"We found something on one of the crime scene photos, Annabelle."

"What was it?"

"A scrap of material. Well, not a scrap really, just the part of it that was visible in the photograph."

"What kind of material?"

"A blanket. Belonging, we think, to some-one who was sleeping rough."

"You think he was there when I was attacked?"

"It's possible. He may have seen something. May have a number plate." I shrugged.

The professor rubbed Hannah's back and smiled hopefully.

"Well, that's good, then, isn't it?" she said.

"It's a long shot. But if someone was there when the girls were attacked, when Hannah was taken, it's something at least."

"I just want my dad back," said Hannah. Tears starting again in her eyes.

"And we're going to get him back. Get dressed, Hannah. We've got somewhere safe to take you."

"Where?" asked the professor.

"Not far."

"Give me two minutes," said Hannah.

The professor held out her arms and gave her another hug, then stroked her cheek. "I'll only be at the end of the phone if you need me. And if you want, I'll come straight back."

"Are you going somewhere...Annabelle?" Hannah was clearly not happy.

"A symposium. Up in Harrogate. Maybe I should just cancel..."

Hannah shook her head. "I'll be fine."

"We'll take good care of her, I promise," I added.

Seems I had made that promise before but the professor fixed me with a considering look and then nodded. "I guess you will," she said. She took a step toward me and held out her hand.

It was as firm a grasp as I remembered, and as warm. I realized I was holding on a tad long. Annabelle looked at me appraisingly. I held her gaze. Not easy with a psychiatrist. You always think they can see right through you. What am I saying? She's a woman. Most women can see right through me. I'm like the guy from *Chicago*. And I don't mean Walt Disney.

"You'll keep me posted, Mister Carter?"

"Of course."

Chapter 81

DI JAMES JIGGLED some keys in her hands.

They were the spare keys to the optician's, a scant hundred yards from where the shop's owner had been blown into pieces.

"I'm not sure I should be doing this," she said.

Kirsty Webb bit on her lower lip. It was a big ask and she knew that. Going outside the official channels in an investigation was not looked on kindly. The police force was like the army. You had to work together as a team. That was drummed into you every bit as hard at Hendon as it was in any army boot camp.

"Far as anyone knows, there is no connection between the body in Stoke Mandeville morgue and the recently deceased optician," Kirsty said finally.

"Except we know there is."

"You phone it in…and it's out of our hands."

"I know that, too."

"There could be some serious kudos going round with this collar if we make it."

"And some serious shit either way."

Kirsty nodded. "Risk and reward."

The Buckinghamshire-based detective tossed the keys in the air and clutched them in her fist.

"The sisterhood doing it for themselves?" she said.

Kirsty shrugged. "Something like that."

DI James stepped over to the shop's door. "Come on, then, Alice," she said. "Let's go down the rabbit hole."

She slotted the Chubb key in the lock and turned it. She depressed the door handle and opened the door.

"Just the one lock?" Kirsty asked, surprised.

"This is Chesham," said DI James. "We don't have crime in Chesham."

"I wouldn't bet on it," said Kirsty Webb.

It didn't take long to process the shop. A couple of desks, a couple of cupboards, a big filing cabinet with patients' records, duplicated no doubt in electronic form on the computer.

They had split up. DI James took the front office and reception area and Kirsty Webb checked the back office and examination room.

Half an hour later Kirsty came out to the front, still wearing latex gloves, and looked at her new colleague who was sitting behind the reception desk reading an office diary. "Anything?" she asked.

DI James looked up from the A4-sized book. "Chappel kept an office diary. He used it for personal stuff too."

"Don't tell me. He's made a confession. Death by gas barbecue. It was an elaborate suicide."

DI James flashed a brief smile and shook

her head. "If only. It would make our jobs a lot easier if people did the decent thing like that."

"People did the decent thing, we'd be out of a job, Natalie."

"And that's the truth. But what we have got here is a list of his guests for the barbecuing he was planning."

"And?"

"Among others we have one of the doctors who signed off on the brain-death certification for Colin Harris, a Dr. Sarah Wilde, and the surgeon who performed the subsequent heart transplant, Mister Alistair Lloyd."

"One of the people on that list knew that Chappel was planning a barbecue, could have tampered with the gas regulator. Set a leak so that when he switched it on it would explode? Is that what you're thinking?"

"Could be. Forensics are working on what's left of the barbecue. It may show that the regulator was tampered with." She shrugged. "It may not."

"I guess those two from the hospital are

worth checking out. See where they were prior to the arranged meeting time. See if they had opportunity."

"It's not the opportunity that I am puzzled by," said Natalie James.

Kirsty waited for her to finish the thought.

"It's the motive."

Chapter 82

POLICE CONSTABLE MARK Smith was a tall man.

Somewhat over six foot. He wasn't sure by how much any more. At one time he was six three but the years on the beat and the aging process generally meant he rode a little lower in the saddle nowadays. And he didn't have the heart to measure by how much.

He was in his early fifties and looking forward to retiring sometime in the near future. He had it all planned. Out of the city, off to the coast. He'd leave his uniform behind happily, and swap his baton for a fly-fishing rod. His wife was a history teacher in a state school in Ealing, and she was looking forward to retiring too.

Between them they had a nice pension organized and enough money to buy a small B&B on the South Coast. Community meant something there, and if a man was found lying on the street he wasn't just stepped over. Mark Smith was happy to be a plain old-fashioned beat copper, and, truth to tell, he was proud of it too. Just because he was looking forward to retirement didn't mean he thought any less of his job.

"It's like that old guy from Greek legend, you know?" he asked me as we sat by the window in a Middle Eastern café on Old Compton Street, drinking cups of coffee you could have stood up a spoon in and watching half the world throng past.

I nodded. I knew exactly who he meant—we had had this conversation many times before. He continued anyway.

"Sisyphus, the old geezer punished by the gods for killing travelers and visitors. He had to roll this huge rock up a big hill and, before he could reach the top, it would roll all the way back down and he had to start all over again."

"I know," I said.

"And you know what the ironic thing is?"

"Go on."

"It's not the travelers or the visitors who die out there on those cold streets..."

I looked out of the window at the heat shimmering off the pavement. Today might have been a preternaturally hot day. But the streets of London could certainly get cold.

Cold enough to kill.

Mark Smith knew that better than most. He was part of the Westminster Police's Safer Streets' Homeless Unit, the SSHU. They dealt with about sixteen thousand or so homeless people who slept rough on the streets each year. No matter what the weather. Up to two hundred a night sometimes.

I passed the photo across the small ridged aluminum-topped table and he picked it up and looked at it. Mark fumbled in his pocket and produced a slim spectacle case, sliding out a pair of reading glasses and setting them on the end of his nose.

He nodded almost immediately. "That'll be the Major," he said.

"Major?"

"He's certainly been in the service sometime. That's how he got the name, plus the fact that he's from an educated background."

"Which is rare on the streets."

"More common than you might think."

Mark was right, of course.

People ended up on the streets for all kinds of reasons. Mental-health issues. Children running away from abusive homes, adults fleeing from the demons they could no longer confront. Many of the homeless people on the streets of London were like the Major—ex-servicemen and women battling with alcohol and depression. A vicious circle of self-medication that spiralled out of control.

I finished my coffee and stood up. "You know where he is?"

Constable Smith looked at his watch. "I've got a good idea."

I tossed a five-pound note on the table which just about covered the tip and two coffees, and headed out into the bustle of the metropolis.

I slipped on my pair of Ray-Bans and slung my jacket over my shoulder, following the tall policeman as he led me along Charing Cross Road toward Tottenham Court Road.

Chapter 83

THERE ARE A number of soup kitchens, plus day and night drop-in centers, for the homeless in London. If you know where to go.

Part of PC Mark Smith's job was to let people know. Some people were made homeless through a change of circumstances—the breakdown of a relationship or the loss of a job, for example. Their homelessness could often be a temporary state, but for others it was a way of life. For these people there was a pattern to their lives on the street and Mark Smith got to know them pretty well.

Not all the centers were open on a Sunday, but St. Joseph's off Tottenham Court Road ran a soup kitchen on Sunday afternoons, between services.

Sure enough, the Major was where PC Smith expected him to be. A number of people, young and old, were gathered around the van which was parked outside the church.

The man was instantly recognizable. Had a dark brown tartan picnic blanket from Aquascutum draped over his shoulders, despite the heat. He was sitting on the church step, sipping on a large styrofoam cup of soup.

He looked up at us as we approached. His eyes seemed sharp, focused—he could have been forty or he could have been sixty. He had long gray curly hair and an unruly beard and, although he was ill-kempt, he looked clean. He took care of himself as best he could, that much was evident.

He nodded to PC Smith, gave me an appraising look and then saluted me. I smiled. It was a good sign. I saluted him back.

He nodded, pleased. "I thought you were military."

"Ex."

"RMP?"

"You're pretty good at this."

"You're with him." He nodded at PC Smith. "You walk like military. Hold yourself like military. Reckon you could handle yourself if push came to shove."

"It has been known."

"So what do you want with me?"

"We've got a couple of questions for you, major."

"I wasn't there," he said. Then his body convulsed in a hacking cough, soup spilling onto the step. He shuffled sideways, away from it.

"We'll get you some more," I said.

"I still wasn't there," he mumbled, looking at the floor. His eyes were slightly out of focus now.

"Weren't where?"

He looked up at me, his eyes brightening again.

"See, it's courts. Wallahs in wigs..." he said. "I see nothing, I don't have to report, see?"

I did see. "It's okay, major, you talk to us and you don't have to talk to anybody else. No courts, no police."

"Your word? Officer and gentleman?"

"My word."

"The van was there. The two girls walked up to it. They heard that other girl calling them. Then it all went mad."

"They didn't see you?"

"No one sees the major. Not if he doesn't want to be seen." He tapped his nose. "Special training, you know."

"So what did you see?"

"The first two, they were chatting with the men in hoods, then they pretended to be attacked. Screaming as the other girl came round the corner and started fighting."

I felt as though someone had punched me in the gut. I'd been played for a fool. We all had. All along.

Hannah Shapiro had set the whole thing up. I'd taken her spiel and swallowed it—hook, line and sinker.

Harlan Shapiro had been the real catch all along and she had been the perfect bait. Perfect for Jack, perfect for me and perfect for Harlan.

Guilt. It's a powerful motivator.

And a deadly one.

Chapter 84

KIRSTY WEBB AND DI Natalie James stood in front of the exposed safe.

Looking for a series of numbers that would open it, they had been through Chappel's diary and every bit of paperwork.

Nothing.

DI Webb was convinced that they would be written down somewhere. They always were. When it came to passwords or codes, the public were pretty bad like that.

It was like leaving a key under the doormat, or in a wellington boot on the back porch, or under a flowerpot as millions of people throughout the country did. Might as well just leave the door wide open and a welcome mat for burglars to wipe their feet on.

Kirsty nibbled on a thumbnail, then pulled out her mobile and tapped in some numbers.

"Dan," she said when it was answered, "I need your mate Gary's number." She listened for a moment. "I've got a safe that needs opening, that's why! It's a combination dial. And I can't find the code anywhere... okay, I'll try that and call you back if I need you."

"Who was that?" asked DI James after she hung up.

"My ex-husband."

"That wise?"

"I certainly wasn't wise marrying him."

"I meant telling him what you're up to."

"He runs a private detective agency. He's been helping me."

DI James threw her a pointed look. "Like fast-tracking DNA identification."

Kirsty nodded. "So forth and suchlike."

"And this Gary—he's a security consultant for him?"

"Something like that."

"Must be some agency to run a DNA check that fast, and with the Romanian police."

"He's with Private International."

"Yeah. They have resources," DI James said dryly. She nodded at the safe. "So what's he suggest?"

"That we try his date of birth. Most common numeric aide-memoire, apparently."

"Aide-memoire, you say?"

"Dan's been to college. Thinks he's smart."

"And is he?" DI James pulled out her notebook and flicked through a couple of pages.

"He's smart in some areas, dumb as a box of rocks in the ones that count."

DI James stepped up to the safe and spun the dial clockwise and counterclockwise a number of times. She paused and tried the handle.

Nothing.

"Try his number plate," Kirsty suggested.

DI James flicked through her notebook, spun the dial again a few times and turned the handle.

Open sesame.

Inside was the laptop that the optician had

placed there earlier. DI James reached in took it out and put it on the desk. There was nothing else in the safe.

Kirsty eased the laptop open and pressed the power button.

The computer's desktop display appeared. A coastal scene—somewhere near Dover, by the looks of it.

The desktop was remarkably uncluttered. Kirsty probably had fifty or sixty icons on her machine's desktop.

She used the track pad below the keyboard and clicked on the Windows symbol. The system was a few years old and running Vista by the looks of it. Kirsty went to the start function and clicked on recent documents. It revealed a drop-down menu of about ten jpegs. Kirsty clicked on one and a picture filled the screen.

After a moment Kirsty swallowed dryly and nodded to her colleague.

"Well, there's your motive," she said.

Chapter 85

THE SUN WAS still high in the sky that Sunday.

But it was late afternoon, almost evening now, and a light wind had picked up. The caretaker was doing his final rounds in the cemetery and it would soon be time to lock up.

He looked across at a lone figure, the only visitor left in the park. Kneeling in front of a child's plot that had a large white marble headstone. Disproportionately large compared with the tragic smallness of the plot. It was more than a headstone, it was a monument in the grand Victorian style.

Fresh flowers had been laid there every day for the last month. Some parents looked after their children in death better than others did in life, the caretaker thought to himself as he glanced at his watch. He'd give it five minutes and then he'd have to lock up. Sad world, he thought to himself for the umpteenth time, in which you have to lock a cemetery against the ravages of vandalism and mischief.

The inscription on the gravestone read: "In loving memory of Emily Jane Lloyd: she danced through our lives all too briefly, and now she dances with the angels. 14/2/2000—19/3/2009."

There was a small lidded chalice at the front of the plot among the stone angels and the vases of flowers. The surgeon leaned forward and raised the lid.

If the caretaker had been able to see what was inside the chalice, he would have had far more troubling thoughts about the state of the world than those caused by mere vandalism that he'd had earlier.

The surgeon opened a small handkerchief and removed the object inside. A scarred, burned piece of flesh. A human finger. Or part of it. The surgeon put it in the pot among the others and closed the lid, replacing the container back with the other objects adorning the shrine to the dead girl.

The voice was a soft whisper, almost a chant. "Just one more to go, my darling."

Chapter 86

HANNAH SHAPIRO WAS dressed now.

Tight jeans tucked into knee-length chocolate-brown boots, a sweater, her hair tied back, makeup on. The transformation was amazing.

She was rubbing her right wrist, still red from the rough abrasion of the rope she had been tied with. Attention to detail. You have to admire that.

"We know it was a set-up, Hannah. Tell us now what we need to know and it'll go easier for you."

"I've done nothing wrong. You've made a mistake, Mister Carter."

Mister Carter. Just like the mechanical

voice had called me on the telephone. It had been her all along, laughing at us. Laughing at me.

I remembered the younger Hannah once more, sitting next to me on the flight over, discussing F. Scott Fitzgerald and teasing me. I realized the past wasn't just another country, as another novelist once said. You can travel to another country but the past is a whole different life.

"Where have they taken your father, Hannah?" I asked.

She shrugged.

I felt like taking two steps forward and backhanding her across the face. My goddaughter had been hospitalized because of her. She'd had us dancing around like puppets while she jerked the strings and it made me angrier than I had felt for a long, long time.

She must have seen something in my eyes because she stepped back a pace.

Her eyes flickered nervously. There was still something wrong with the picture. But I couldn't work out what.

"You can talk to us, Hannah..." I said.

Her eyes flicked to Del Rio who was leaning against the wall and saying nothing.

He'd told me earlier that it was my play. He'd follow my lead. I didn't think we'd need the good cop, bad cop routine. We had her cold and she knew it. Just a matter of time.

"Or we can take you down to Paddington Green and you can talk to the cops," I continued.

"He deserved it!" she spat out finally.

"Why?"

"Why?" Hannah shouted back at me, incredulous. "Why do you think, you dumb prick!"

Her West Coast accent had come back strongly now. "He refused to pay the ransom and my mother died. She died, Mister Carter! But not before I was made to watch her being raped. And then they shot her."

She broke down in tears and I regretted the urge to slap her. I felt more like putting my arms around her. She was right in some ways. Maybe Harlan Shapiro did deserve a bit of payback. But not this.

"My god-daughter nearly died," I said instead.

"She wasn't meant to get hurt. She wasn't even meant to be there."

"Who were the others, Hannah? We know about Laura, but who were the others who were there?"

She shook her head. "I'm not going to tell you. I don't care what you do. He deserved this. So he's had a fright? Look what *I* had to go through."

"If anything happens to him, Hannah, you will be in a whole world more trouble than you're in already."

"Nothing is going to happen to him," she said. But her eyes were darting around again and she was rubbing her scraped arm, unaware that she was doing it.

Hannah didn't believe herself, either.

And that worried the hell out of me.

Chapter 87

ADRIAN TUTTLE REWOUND the video clip again.

I got him to pause it and enhance the image. It was the first video they had sent and I had to admit that Hannah did a pretty good acting job. I got Adrian to split the screen and then played the second clip. I freeze-framed it. Zoomed in on her arm.

"See that, Adrian?" I asked.

"Yes," he said. Like I said, he was good at spot-the-difference.

Wendy Lee was passing and leaned over. "Contusions on her arm in the second video. Not in the first."

"And what does that tell us?"

"That she was faking being tied up the first time round and not the second."

The memory of her rubbing her arm just a short while ago flicked into my mind. Her arm was definitely sore.

"So what changed? What was it?"

"Have you found the other girl yet?"

I shook my head. I had called Sam to meet me at the student accommodation block. Laura Skelton wasn't there. Her wardrobe was empty, clothes hangers on the floor. Empty drawers left open. It looked as though she had packed a bag and left. Hurriedly. Sam was out trying to track her down. I didn't hold out much hope.

I let the second tape play on.

Hannah looked at the camera, her voice trembling. "They want you to know," she said, "that this bomb I am wearing can be triggered remotely. Any attempt to do anything other than what you are instructed to do and it will be detonated. Likewise if you attempt to deliver fake diamonds. They will be examined and if they are not genuine the device will be detonated. If police are there again as they were this morning, the device will be detonated."

She let the paper fall to the floor as tears welled in her large, terrified eyes.

"Please help me," she added in a desperate whisper.

The screen faded to blackness again.

Hannah was begging for help—that was genuine. She believed that they had strapped explosives to her and would kill her if we didn't comply with their instructions.

Something had happened between yesterday and today.

What?

My mobile phone rang. I looked at the caller ID and answered it.

"What have you got for me, Suzy?" I listened and nodded. "Sit on him," I said. "I'll be right there."

I clicked my phone shut and stood up, grabbing my jacket.

"Something happening?" asked Wendy Lee.

"Laura Skelton just had a visitor. One of the rugby guys from Friday night."

Adrian Tuttle stood up. "You want some backup?" he said. He was being serious.

"No, you're all right," I answered. "Suzy and I should be able to handle it."

"What would you do if he turned nasty, Adrian?" asked Wendy Lee. "Distract him with some origami?"

"I've got some moves," he said. Striking a pose. He looked like an emaciated heron.

"Just work the data," I said. "Something's there. Something's not right."

Chapter 88

DETECTIVE INSPECTORS KIRSTY Webb and Natalie James jumped out of their parked car and slammed the doors behind them.

An ambulance was pulled up outside the house that they had been about to call at and a couple of police cars were parked beside it. Lights flashing. Crime-scene tape about to cordon off the area.

Kirsty Webb felt a sinking feeling in her gut again as they hurried up to the door. She always seemed to be one step behind on this case. A couple of uniformed officers were standing outside. Kirsty and DI James showed them their warrant cards.

"What's happened?"

"You here to see Alistair Lloyd? The surgeon?" asked one of the uniforms. A petite woman in her mid-twenties.

"Yes."

"You're too late, I'm afraid. He performed a..." she hesitated "...a minor procedure, then topped himself."

"What kind of procedure?"

The other officer grimaced. "He cut off one of his fingers with a samurai sword. And then fell on it. The sword, not the finger."

"Jesus."

"Yeah. There's quite a bit of blood." She nodded at DI James. "Your boss has been trying to get hold of you. He's inside."

The two DIs, walked into the house. It was a bungalow, almost open-plan. A small hall led into a large lounge-and-kitchen area. Several doors led off it. The one on the far right was open and bursts of bright light flashed from the room behind it.

A medium-sized man, balding, overweight, with a scruffy jacket and a skew-whiff tie came out as they walked over. He rubbed his hand over a chin that was dark with more than just a five o'clock shadow. It made a rasping sound and he shrugged apologetically.

"I was halfway through my Sunday lunch when I got the call. Slow-roast shoulder of pork. Dauphinoise potatoes. You must be DI Webb?" He stuck out his hand.

Kirsty shook it. "Yeah."

"Chief Inspector Holland." He turned to DI James. "Tried to get hold of you."

DI James took out her phone and looked at it, unlocking the keyboard. "Must have been out of range at the time."

Holland nodded impassively and turned to Kirsty. "And yours? Spoke to your governor at Paddington."

"It's in the car, charging."

He nodded again. "Either way it don't much amount to a hill of beans, I guess—as your man in the hat once had it."

"Sir?"

"No glory due on this one. Your serious-crime gang are on their way over. But this, as they say, is a done deal. See for yourself if you've the stomach for it." Holland rubbed his own stomach absentmindedly, probably regretting starting his lunch at all. He ushered the two DIs into the room.

There was a plain black teak table in front of a window with open venetian blinds, also in black. Matching cabinets stretched left and right along the wall in front of the desk.

A Japanese suit of armor stood in one corner of the room.

There was a chopping block on the desk and a white handkerchief was laid neatly next to it. Beyond that on the desk was a wooden holder. Ceremonial. On the handkerchief a small pool of blood had soaked through. A severed finger lay in the middle of it.

Chapter 89

ALISTAIR LLOYD WAS lying on the floor.

The samurai sword that should have been sitting in its holder was stuck through the center of his body. He had toppled sideways and there was blood pooled around him on the floor. A lot of it.

The SOCO photographer took more shots in a quick burst and left the room, leaving the forensic pathologist to go to work.

"He left a note," said Chief Inspector Holland.

"Typed?" asked Kirsty Webb, thinking back to Colin Harris's supposed suicide.

"Handwritten. And, judging by other materials here, it looks authentic to me. Signed, and fingerprints on the paper, no doubt, which I have every belief will match his own."

"Right."

The CI nodded down the hall to where more white-suited SOCOs were bagging evidence in the kitchen. "And we found human remains in his freezer. Individually bagged-up organs."

"The Jane Does'?"

"We need to check, but yeah, probably."

"What the hell did he take their organs for?"

Chief Inspector Holland spread his hands. "This guy was all kinds of nutter. For all we know, he was going to make a casserole with them."

"What did he say in the note?" asked Kirsty.

"He confesses to the four killings."

"Why did he do it?"

"He was part of a group. Exchanging photos."

Kirsty nodded. She'd seen the photos. "And what happened?"

"One of the people gathering the photos. A Romanian nurse…"

"Adriana Kisslinger?"

The CI looked puzzled. "How did you know that?"

"I didn't. I guess you just confirmed it, though. It was a line of inquiry."

Holland looked for a moment as if he might press her on the matter but shrugged it off. Not his problem. "Anyway, she started blackmailing the group—a teacher, a social worker, a surgeon. Figured the surgeon in particular could be the jackpot."

"So, what—he killed them all?"

"And then he killed himself."

"Guilt?"

"Who knows?" Holland gestured at the Japanese armor. "He was obviously a sick fantasist. Doubt we'll ever really know what was going through his head. He says he was confronted with what he really was, according to his suicide note, and couldn't deal with it any more."

"Very Japanese."

The chief inspector nodded. "Looks like he was a big fan of the culture."

"And the fingers?" asked DI James.

Holland shrugged. "No idea."

"Japanese again," said Kirsty Webb. "The Yakuza. They have a tradition of cutting off a finger if one of them does something wrong."

"You seem to know a lot about this stuff."

Kirsty shook her head. "Only from films. Robert Mitchum was in a movie about it. Cut off half his finger in it."

"Seems particularly appropriate in this case, then," said the chief inspector.

"Sir?" asked DI James.

"Kiddy-fiddlers," Holland said, anger sparking in his eyes. "It's not all I'd cut off."

Chapter 90

SUZY WAS LEANING against the wall by the door to the three girls' apartment.

Tim Graham was sitting on the couch, holding a bloodied handkerchief to his nose. He was glaring at me.

"You're not going to get away with this."

"You threatening me, Tim?" I asked.

"I'm promising you."

"Because if you want Suzy here to..."

He shrank back into the sofa.

"He didn't want to wait to meet you, Dan. I had to persuade him."

"You didn't have to break my nose."

"He took a swing." She shrugged. "What's a girl to do?"

"You want to tell us what you are doing here, Tim?" I asked.

"I don't have to tell you anything."

I sighed. "See, this isn't one of those good cop, bad cop situations. We're both bad cops."

"Right," he snorted derisively. "You're not even cops."

I took three paces across the room and hit him. Hard. Backhanded my fist to the left side of his head. He flew off the sofa and landed on the floor, whimpering. Tears starting in his eyes.

I was glad. Truth was I was tempted to bust him on the nose again—finish the job that Suzy had started. But I needed to get some answers first.

"Let me explain something to you, Mister Graham," I said, squatting down on my heels and speaking patiently. "Laura and Hannah drugged my god-daughter. She was clubbed with a baseball bat like a baby seal and was left to die in the gutter."

I bent down, grabbed him with both hands, picked him up and threw him back onto the sofa.

"Do I have your attention now?" I asked.

Graham nodded, holding a hand to his nose which was running with blood and drool.

"Because of them she is lying in intensive care, fighting for her life." That last bit wasn't strictly true any more but I had no intention of letting the maggot squirming on the sofa know that.

"I had nothing to do with any of it."

I turned to Suzy. "I'm going outside for a cigarette. Why don't you see if you can loosen his memory some?"

I headed for the door. He wasn't to know that I didn't smoke.

"Wait!" He practically shouted it.

I didn't blame him. I wouldn't want Suzy putting the hard question to me, either. And I'm a professional tough guy.

"She wasn't supposed to get hurt."

"Who wasn't?"

"Chloe. She wasn't even supposed to be there. Laura slipped something in her drink. It should have knocked her out of things for a while. Not enough to do any damage."

"Where did she get it?"

Graham shifted nervously on the sofa. "I don't know."

"Where do you live?"

He shrugged. "What's that got to do with anything?"

"Suzy, ask him again for me."

"Sure, boss." She stepped forward from the wall.

"Okay, okay. Just keep that mad bitch away from me!"

I saw Suzy's upper lip twitch a fraction and figured that young Tim would pay for that remark sooner or later.

"I live across the hall," he said.

I hauled him upright. "Lead on, MacDuff."

At the end of the corridor we entered a living room much like the one where we had just been. Only this one was littered with the kind of detritus you would expect from a bunch of male students.

Tim Graham was making a show of looking for the key to his bedroom door. Patting his pockets. I raised my right leg and kicked the door off its hinges.

"Jesus," he said. "Who are you people?"

I pushed him inside.

Suzy followed us in, wrinkling her nose. "For Christ's sake, Tim, you ever think of opening a window sometimes?" she said and crossed to do just that.

I was glad she did. If the outer room was a mess, this was a midden. I pushed the student onto his unmade bed and started going through his chest of drawers. Third drawer down I found what I was looking for.

Chapter 91

"STUDYING TO BE a pharmacist?" I asked.

"Media studies, actually," Tim Graham replied petulantly and Suzy slapped him around the head.

"What was that for?"

"If there's one thing I hate more than students," she said, "it's bloody media-studies students."

I tipped the contents of the drawer over him. Folded packets of paper. Bags of dope. Lumps of resin. Bottles of pills. I guess Tim Graham was your go-to guy on campus for recreational chemicals.

"You don't know who you're dealing with," he said angrily.

"Are you threatening me again, Tim?"

"It's not me you have to worry about."

I knew who he was talking about. I'd get to him later. I picked up a DVD that had landed on the floor and put it in my pocket.

"You got no right to take anything."

"You want to wait here with him, Suzy, while I phone this through to the police?" I said.

"No. Don't do this, man. We can work something out."

Man? Was he living in the 1960s?

"Start talking."

"It was all supposed to be a joke."

"Some joke."

"Well, not a joke. Payback for Hannah's old man. She was always ragging on about him. We were just going to wind him up. You know?"

"I haven't got the faintest idea."

"Laura asked me to get some of the guys to help."

"And you just went along with it."

"Laura said she'd make it worth my while, you know what I mean."

He gave me a conspiratorial nod. I felt like smashing my fist into his face.

"So it was all supposed to be an elaborate joke. Hannah getting back at her father. What went wrong? How did my god-daughter end up in the hospital?"

Graham stood up from the bed, holding his hands out apologetically. "Like I said, Chloe wasn't supposed to be there. Laura brought someone along. A real heavy dude."

I had a fair idea who the "dude" was and I had a fair idea who had introduced him to Laura Skelton.

"Collect that stuff up," I said to Suzy.

"Hey, come on, man."

"That's 'Mister Carter' to you."

"I told you all I know." Graham looked over nervously at his stash. "I need to move that on."

"Not going to happen."

Suzy upended a kitbag that was lying on the floor and then scooped the drugs into it.

"I got to sell that to pay for it. You know how this works. They'll kill me."

"Hopefully," I said.

"Shit," Graham said. I thought he was going to start crying again.

"Where's Laura Skelton now?" I asked him.

"I don't know. Honestly. She hasn't been seen since yesterday. Nobody knows where she is."

"Come on," I said to Suzy and walked to the door.

"They're going to hurt me bad," Graham called out to me.

"Get used to it," said Suzy and kicked him full in the nuts.

He really shouldn't have called her a bitch.

Chapter 92

"WHERE TO NOW, then, Mister Carter?" said Suzy with decidedly ironic deference.

"What?" she said then, puzzled by the look on my face.

"I've been ten kinds of idiot, Suzy."

I hurried down the corridor and back to the apartment that Chloe shared with Hannah and Laura. In Laura's bedroom I picked up from the floor the bathrobe that she had been wearing earlier. It pretty much confirmed what I had suddenly realized. I sniffed it.

"You going to tell me what this is all about, or am I just putting you down as another typical male pervert, Dan?" said Suzy.

I tossed her the bathrobe "Do you smell that?"

"Perfume?"

"Chanel No. 5."

Suzy held the robe closer and smelled again. "I think you're right," she said.

I knew I was. I'd spent enough on the stuff for my ex-wife over the years.

"I wouldn't have put Hannah down for that," said Suzy.

"She wasn't wearing it," I replied. "Look at the collar."

She looked at a faint red smudge. "Lipstick."

"Right."

I knew exactly who wore Chanel No. 5, the color of lipstick that could leave such a mark and who also insisted on calling me "Mister Carter." I remembered the hand that she had stroked Hannah Shapiro's cheek with. It hadn't been a maternal gesture as I had imagined.

It had been the caress of a lover.

Chapter 93

FIFTEEN MINUTES LATER and we were back in front of Adrian Tuttle's computer screen.

Adrian ran the kidnappers' phone message to me through an audio sequencer and displayed a section in a waveform graphic.

Below the first graphic he ran a second piece of recorded audio and displayed it. This was the time Hannah had called me without benefit of voice distortion. The exact same phrase. Adrian aligned the two and they matched perfectly.

If I was enough of a contortionist I would have kicked myself. I had been puzzling over what had changed between Saturday night and Sunday morning and realized what it was. Harlan Shapiro was making the trip over. They hadn't thought he would, given his past form. When he did, the goalposts were moved. The only person I had told that he was coming, outside of our own people, had been Professor Annabelle Weston.

I drummed my fingers on the table. Thinking. She had said she was going away on a conference. That was a lie. She was obviously moving Harlan Shapiro somewhere. And where was Laura Skelton?

I punched Del Rio's number into the phone and told him to put Hannah on. Her voice was querulous, subdued.

"I know what's been happening, Hannah," I said. "And I know you had your reasons."

"You don't know the half of it!"

"I know I don't. What happened to you was awful."

"Awful?" She laughed, but it was a far from happy sound. "You really don't know anything, do you?"

"I know about you and Professor Weston, Hannah. I know she took advantage of you."

She laughed again. It was a brittle sound.

"She didn't take advantage of me. I love her, Mister Carter."

"She was your tutor."

"She was my tutor and my counselor and my lover and my friend! And I don't expect you to ever understand."

"We need to know where she is. We need to get your father home safe."

"That's exactly what we don't need. That was what the million pounds was for. I was never going home."

"So what changed?"

Hannah hesitated. Not quite so strident now. "We figured it wasn't enough. We figured five million was more like it."

I doubted that she had done any of the figuring at all. She was just a pawn in somebody else's game. I felt sympathy for her, for that much at least.

"So where are they now, Hannah?" I asked pointedly. "And why aren't you with them?"

"Plans change."

I pictured her on the other end of the line,

cradling the phone on her shoulder, rubbing her abraded wrist. Remembering how things had changed suddenly for her.

"They hurt you, Hannah," I said softly. "They can't be allowed to get away with that. They can't be allowed to hurt your father."

"My father hurt me." The voice was almost a whisper. Under all the makeup and the clothes and the womanliness she presented to the world, she was still a small frightened girl at heart. A girl I had promised—and failed— to look after.

"I know he did," I said. "And he's sorry— he put his life on the line today for you. If he could go back to that other time he would do everything differently."

"I'm not talking about him not paying the ransom, Mister Carter. I'm not talking about him letting my mother be raped and butchered."

Hannah's voice had gone hard again and I felt the hair rise on the back of my neck.

"He used to come to my room, Mister Carter," she said. "At night. *We had to comfort each other,* he said. *There were just the two of us now*...And he hurt me."

I gripped the phone tight in my hand.

Seemed I had been wrong about pretty much everything.

Chapter 94

I GOT ADRIAN to hack into the personnel records for Chancellors.

It seemed that Annabelle Weston had done her original degree at Cambridge University but had studied for her Master's at Harvard.

I phoned Jack again. He was still holed up in a hotel and being babysat by the FBI. But he had his phone and he had his people standing by round the clock. I filled him in and ten minutes later he phoned me back. I hadn't thought that the case had anything to do with America. But I was wrong. It had everything to do with it.

"I got my contact in Homeland Security to run Annabelle Weston's name through their system," he said. "And he got a hit. She's on their watch list."

"Why?"

"She had a relationship with a guy called Jesus Ferdinand. His mother is Kareema Ferdinand, an exiled Palestinian poet and political activist. Kareema was visiting relatives in the Gaza Strip in 1987 when the First Intifada kicked off. She stayed behind to protest against armed action. Urging the Palestinians to protest peacefully. On Christmas Eve 1987 she was murdered for her pains. The masked gunmen who shot her down as she walked home were never identified."

"Israelis?"

"That's what the Palestinians claimed. But most people think she was murdered by her own people for collaborating with the Israeli forces."

"Ironic."

"Isn't it? But her son Jesus back in America puts the blame squarely on the Israelis. He converts to Islam, becomes highly radicalized. Over the years he has been the prime suspect in a number of incidents. Never been proven."

"And Professor Weston kept up her relationship with him?"

"Yes. He was killed last year when Israeli marines boarded a ship trying to break the blockade and run humanitarian aid into Gaza."

"So she's out for revenge?"

"She found out who Hannah was, who her father was and, yeah...it looks like payback time."

"She operating on her own?"

"Our intel says Jesus Ferdinand had links with Hamas and other paramilitary organizations."

"Shit."

"You need to get Harlan Shapiro back, Dan."

Chapter 95

PROFESSOR ANNABELLE WESTON lived in an expensive mews-style two-bedroomed house not far from Marylebone High Street—and she hadn't paid for it with her earnings from Chancellors.

She'd inherited a fortune when her father, an oil and steel billionaire, had died. So she certainly didn't want for money. Which was what baffled me most about the whole thing. Until Jack Morgan told me what Harlan Shapiro had been working on before he was taken.

I leaned on the doorbell again. No response.

I hadn't expected any.

I stood with Del Rio at the professor's door and looked at Hannah Shapiro who was sitting with Sam Riddel in the back of my car. She was gazing at me through the window with an expression on her face that I couldn't read.

Somewhere in there was the girl I knew. Somewhere was the woman she had become.

I thought of the consequences of these sequences of events. I thought of my lovely god-daughter Chloe. I remembered the tubes attached to her. I remembered the bandaging around her head. I remembered the beeping noises the monitors made as they checked her vital signs. I remembered her closed eyelids, the eyes flicking behind them as though she were trying to find her way home from the darkness.

I remembered the promise to her dad that I had made as he lay dying in my arms in a dust-blown wreck of a town in Iraq.

Then I picked up the police-issue battering ram and smashed Professor Annabelle Weston's front door in.

Chapter 96

DEL RIO WENT in first.

He held his gun in a two-handed grip, sweeping the room for hostile targets.

I dropped the "enforcer," as it was known, to one side. It landed with a heavy thud on the polished wooden floor, taking large chips out of it. I didn't feel guilty.

Luckily, no alarm bells had gone off. Score one for the good guys.

Expensive rugs were positioned around the room. A small TV in the corner. Matching burgundy leather sofas with tartan fabric trimming, and assorted throw cushions. The kitchen beyond was neat, pristine. Polished chrome and pale white wood.

An open door to the side led upstairs, and another ground-floor door was closed. I was about to open it when Del Rio shook his head and raised his pistol once more.

He kicked the door open. A downstairs bathroom. Empty.

Upstairs, Annabelle Weston had converted one of the two bedrooms into a small office. The venetian blind covering the window and the plain wall looked all too familiar. She had filmed Hannah's pieces to camera for us there.

Thirty minutes later and we had finished searching. Nothing. Hannah couldn't tell us where the professor had gone, either. She didn't know.

I'm not a psychiatrist but I could see how easily Hannah could have been manipulated. She must have had a very poor view of men.

A father whom she had considered had abandoned her and who then took advantage of her in the most abusive of ways. She had watched men rape and kill her mother. She had been robbed of her mother's love and had grown up in a house where she had come to hate her father. Not hard for a vibrant, charismatic and beautiful woman like Annabelle Weston to channel those feelings in other directions.

Not hard for her to turn the young woman's need for love into something more physical.

Annabelle Weston had left behind a laptop in her office. She must have been so sure that Hannah wouldn't betray her, and that we wouldn't be smart enough to put two and two together. Maybe she figured we were onto her before we were. She knew we'd found a witness and had gone to ground.

Del Rio and I hadn't been able to break the security on the laptop and access her secure files, so Adrian Tuttle had had his second evening of the weekend spoiled. Fifteen minutes after I called him from the professor's apartment he turned up with his dinner date. Five minutes later he told us he couldn't crack it either.

His dinner date, a painfully shy Australian woman in her mid-twenties, told him to stand aside. In less than sixty seconds she had cracked wide open the security systems that were in place on the professor's computer.

A blush brightened her cheeks. I could see what Adrian Tuttle saw in her. She had a nice smile, too. Adrian himself was watching her like the cat who's got the cream.

"Told you she was good," he said.

"And you were right." I smiled at her as she moved aside. "Adrian tells me you've just finished a doctorate in this kind of stuff."

"Yeah," she said blushing again.

"How would you feel about working for the private sector? So happens we have a vacancy in our computer-forensics division."

"Fair dinkum?" she asked.

"Oh, yeah," I said. "Very fair dinkum."

"I'll have a think about that, then."

I nodded. "Good."

Fifteen minutes later, after trawling through all manner of coded files, I hit the mother-lode.

"Jesus Christ!" I said out loud.

Chapter 97

HALF AN HOUR later we were sitting in the conference room.

Up on the screen Professor Annabelle Weston was in her office in mid-counseling session.

Her student and patient sat in the reclining chair. Hannah Shapiro. Her head lolled back, her mouth slightly open, her eyes closed, but a sluggish movement behind them, as the eyes move when searching for a memory. And the professor's voice: honeyed, silken, soporific. Planting seeds as carefully and deliberately as an Iraqi insurgent building a bomb.

I picked up the remote and paused the tape. I figured Hannah had seen enough.

Hannah shook her head, dragging the back of her right hand across her eyes. Tears streaming down her cheeks.

"Why would anybody do something like that?" she asked.

I didn't reply. I knew exactly why Annabelle Weston had done it. She had taken an already vulnerable young woman and made her even more emotionally wrecked. So she could build her up again and make a tool out of her.

It's what cults did, it was what oppressive regimes did. Break down a person's personality, their individuality and mold them into becoming part of a machine.

"So he never did any of those things?"

"No," I said. "You were in a heightened state of suggestion. She led you down a series of thoughts that weren't your own to a conclusion that was entirely hers."

"It was so long ago, I was thirteen. I couldn't remember exactly, because..." She trailed off.

"It's what she was counting on. You had all those bad feelings because of what had happened to your mother, parts of what had happened on that day you recall. She let you think that the abuse had occurred but you had driven them out of your memory because you couldn't face them."

"It's called False Memory Syndrome, Hannah," said Sam. "It's a form of brainwashing."

"She used me."

The sadness in Hannah's voice was heartbreaking—or it would have been had I not thought of Chloe.

"You had deep-seated issues with your father, which she exploited. Abandonment issues, betrayal issues. You had a lot of anger. In your eyes he was responsible for what happened to your mother, after all, and at thirteen years old things can seem very black and white in moral terms."

"He *was* to blame! He refused to pay the ransom. It was peanuts and he did nothing!"

"He thought he was doing the right thing, Hannah. He hired Jack Morgan," I reminded her.

"Who got there too late!"

"He saved you."

"Maybe I'd have been better off dead."

"No, you wouldn't. Jack Morgan didn't have the resources back then that we do now. He was on his own."

"Then my father should have gone to the police."

"Do you know what the statistics of surviving a kidnapping are, even if the ransom is paid?"

Hannah shook her head.

"They're not good, Hannah. Your father took the national line: you don't deal with terrorists."

"They weren't terrorists."

"They held a gun to yours and your mother's heads and threatened to kill you if he didn't pay the ransom. You got a better word for what they did?"

She looked down at the floor again. Taking it all in. Annabelle Weston had been like a second mother to her. Except that she had been betrayed all over again. She looked up, her face wet with tears once more.

"I believed her."

"I know, Hannah. And she's going to pay for it, I promise you."

"And you always keep your promises!"

"I try."

"You promised to look after me."

"And it's what I'm doing. You have the truth, Hannah. You have that, at least. What you do with it is up to you now."

Hannah nodded, straightened herself and looked at me with something like determination in her eyes.

"Okay," she said.

Chapter 98

"THE FIRST TAPE you made you were play-acting, the second time you weren't. What happened?"

"Annabelle..." Hannah caught herself, the name seemingly tasting like ash in her mouth. "She kept me at her apartment. She came back excited with the news that my father was flying over."

I nodded. It was pretty much as I had deduced.

"She made some calls. Soon after that some people came."

"Who?"

"I don't know. A woman in a burka and two men with her. But they were deferential to the burka woman. They were like body-guards."

"And what did they say?"

"I don't know. They all spoke in Arabic. At least, the women did. The men said nothing. Then they tied me up, properly this time, and left me in Annabelle's study. She didn't talk to me again."

"And there was nothing else you can remember?"

"When they arrived the women hugged. It was a long hug, not as though they had just met. It seemed more than just a greeting."

"Like lovers, you mean?"

Hannah shrugged, pink spots of color brightening her cheeks. "Maybe," she said quietly.

"And did she say a name?"

"They both said the same thing."

"Which was?"

"It sounded like 'cut min holby.'"

"Holby? Like the TV show?"

"Something like that."

"Kht Mn Qlby?" said Del Rio, speaking for the first time in a long while.

Chapter 99

HANNAH LOOKED OVER at Del Rio. "Say it again."

"Kht Mn Qlby," he repeated and Hannah nodded.

"That's it. That's what they both said."

"What does it mean?" I asked Del Rio.

He shrugged. " 'Sister of My Heart.' Something like that."

"Sounds like lovers to me," said Sam.

Del Rio grunted. I looked at Hannah. She was clearly conflicted: she had been in love with Annabelle Weston and now she was finding out that she had been betrayed in the worst possible way.

"She said we'd be together when all this

was over. She said she had to tie me up because things had changed. But she also said that she loved me, that she'd come for me."

"Believing someone loves you is not the worst crime in the world, Hannah," I said.

If Hannah heard me, then she didn't register it. "And all the time there was someone else."

"Maybe not."

I moved to the telephone console and requested a video conference with Sci. After a few moments of blank screen, the dull gray disappeared in a flurry of pixelation to be replaced with the image of Doctor Science sitting in his office.

"What can I do for you, Dan?" he asked.

"Annabelle Weston had a relationship with Jesus Ferdinand…"

"That's correct."

"Can you check your records and see if he has any surviving relatives?"

"Sure."

His hands flashed over his computer keyboards with expert speed.

After a few moments the Doctor turned

back to us. "His father died some years back and…" He turned his monitor so we could see it and pressed some keys. A woman's face filled the screen.

She was in her thirties and had almond-shaped eyes made enormous with kohl in a heart-shaped face. Her skin was the color of caramel. She wore a scarf that draped loosely around her neck and framed her face.

She was beautiful.

"His sister—Mary Angela Al-Massri."

The Doctor clicked on some more keys and the picture was replaced with biographical data. "She's living in England and she's married to a member of the Palestinian General Delegation to the UK."

Chapter 100

SCI'S HANDS FLEW over his keyboard once more. "I just mailed you the data."

"Thanks, Sci."

"*De nada*. We're here twenty-four seven till we get the scientist home."

A monkey scampered into view and jumped onto his lap. He patted its head affectionately.

He clicked on the keyboard and the screen went blank again. That's another thing about the Americans that I like. They just hang up on you. No need for good-byes. There's a job to be done. Get on with it.

I pulled up the data he had sent. Mary Angela certainly was a striking woman.

" 'Sister of her heart,' Mary Angela said.

Her brother was Annabelle's heart. It was him she loved."

I scrolled through the data on the screen. "The delegation's based in Hampstead."

"Is it an embassy?" asked Sam.

I shook my head. "Kind of. But Palestine isn't an independent state. So it has the same kind of functions but without any real clout. It basically represents the interests of the PLO and the PNA."

"No diplomatic immunity," said Del Rio, getting to the heart of the matter.

"So what do we do?" asked Suzy.

I scrolled through the data. "Mary Angela's husband—Youssef Saad Al-Massri—he's a translator working for the delegation."

"Translator?"

"Officially, anyway. Who knows? Could be Hamas."

"I don't think so," said Del Rio.

"Go on," I prompted him.

"The way this whole thing has been conducted. Opportunistic. Reactive. Shifting goalposts as the situation changed."

"Yes?"

"If Hamas is behind this or Palestine Islamic Jihad, or the Al-Aqsa Martyrs' Brigade or any of those other groups—then do you really think Hannah would still be sitting here?" said Del Rio.

I looked across at Hannah, still shell-shocked, closed in on herself, her arms wrapped around her body, and realized that Del Rio had a point. She'd never have been found. Certainly not alive.

"So we're not dealing with one of the mainstream outfits?"

Del Rio shook his head.

"Which is good, right?" asked Lucy, speaking for the first time.

I looked at her and forced a half-smile, remembering what had happened when free-lancers operating out of their area of expertise had kidnapped the girl and her mother before, and lied.

"Yeah," I said. "It's good."

Maybe it was. Maybe there was still time.

I turned back to the monitor and scrolled through the data. "Mary Angela's husband lives out of the city."

"Where?"

"Moor Park. West of London—a small estate between Northwood and Rickmansworth. One of the richest concentrations of real estate in the country." The translation game clearly paid more than I would have guessed. "They don't know we're onto them yet. But they must be figuring it's a matter of time so I suggest we take the house in Moor Park."

"What about the delegation building?" asked Sam.

"I don't see it. Like Del Rio says, this is most likely a freelance op. I'll call Brad Dexter, though, get a team of boys to stake it out. Check anyone leaving."

I snatched up the keys up from the table. "If he's not in Moor Park we'll come back and go in. They don't have immunity, remember. Not from the law and definitely not from us."

"Hang on, sir," said Lucy.

"What?"

"It's been on the news. Westway is closed and the North Circular is jammed solid because of it. Traffic heading west is at a standstill out there."

"That's okay, Lucy," said Sam. "We weren't going to drive anyway. We're in a bit of a hurry."

His face was as impassive as those on the big stone statues you see on Easter Island, but I could hear the amusement in his voice.

Bastard.

Chapter 101

I SAID BEFORE that London is a beautiful city.

And it is. But it's designed to be viewed from the ground, looking up at the gloriously eclectic mix of Georgian architecture and futuristic high-rise buildings. As it was now, though, it was looking more like a scene from *Blade Runner* as the helicopter banked and headed west.

Private has its own helicopter pad on the roof of its building. Civilians weren't supposed to have them in the metropolis. Al-Fayed had notoriously tried for years to get one on the roof of Harrods and had failed. But we were under contract to the police and the military and had special dispensation.

Sam Riddel held a full pilot's license, enabling him to fly a number of aircraft including the one we were in. He looked across at me and grinned.

I was assuming that he wouldn't be able to read my expression. I had blacked my face, as had Suzy and Del Rio behind me. Like them, I was also wearing black military fatigues. It was dark now and the cloud cover ahead thankfully blocked the light of a full moon.

I had decided that a small team was the best option. Stealth rather than a show of force. Get it wrong and we could pay the price. Or Harlan Shapiro would pay the price. And that was not an option. Lucy had come with us to retrieve the rope and Hannah had been left behind at the offices. A couple of security guards with her in case she decided to switch sides again.

I ignored Sam's taunting grin and kept my gaze fixed ahead. Below me the traffic was as snarled as Lucy had said it would be. Above us the chopper's rotor blade thwopped and spun, but the ride was incredibly smooth. Thankfully there was very little wind.

In very little time we had made the twenty-six mile journey and were flying over Moor Park.

Normally a helicopter flying over a residential area might have caused some interest. But a huge military base, much of it underground, was half a mile away. HMS *Warrior* where Western Allied Fleet Command was based. The command center for the Falklands War and also home to the USAF which had a base there. Helicopters in the air thereabouts were a very common occurrence.

As we flew over the target house I pointed the thermal-image device I was holding at it and put the lens to my eyes. The house went the familiar murky green you get through night-vision goggles, but little dots of color appeared. Glowing red and indicating the heat signatures of human beings. Live ones, anyway. I counted six. Four moving downstairs and two static ones upstairs. I figured those to be Harlan Shapiro and whoever was guarding him. I hoped that was the case, anyway—it meant he was alive, at least.

The helicopter banked again. I hated when it did that and was sure that Sam did it deliberately. The Palestinian translator's house was set apart from the others in a small private road that led to Moor Park Golf Course. Famous for hosting the Bob Hope Classic for a number of years, but most notable for the current clubhouse having once been the residence, along with Hampton Court Palace, of one Cardinal Thomas Wolsey, ill-fated adviser to Henry the Eighth and the man who had given his name to the university where Harlan Shapiro had sent his daughter to be safe.

The irony was not lost on me.

Sam maneuverd the helicopter to a hovering standstill. Lucy opened the door and threw out the long black rope, one end fixed securely inside. At least, I damn well hoped it was securely fixed.

Del Rio checked that his pistol was firm in its holster and went out first, grabbing the rope and sliding down it as easily as if it were a fireman's pole.

I was next. I clipped the harness ring round the rope, checked it and took a deep breath. I was earning my pay check this weekend, no doubt about that. But I had trained to abseil. Just because I didn't like it didn't mean I couldn't do it. I didn't say "Geronimo." I said something entirely less gleeful and stepped out, dropping down the rope in short sequences. The rope was still some eight feet from the ground when I released fully and dropped.

We had picked a soft target. The seventeenth green on the West Course. A short par four, surrounded on three sides by trees.

Not long afterward Suzy thudded to the ground a few yards from me. Less than thirty seconds after that and all three of us were thankfully back on terra firma.

I looked at the damage that we had done to the soft ground and guessed that the greenkeeper would be none too happy come the morning.

I signaled to the others and we headed off. The house was some hundred yards away behind the trees. As we moved into the cover of them no alarm sounded—no sirens, no shouting.

So far, so good.

A movement behind me. I turned too late.

I dropped like a felled tree.

Chapter 102

SOME TIME LATER I came to and tried to move.

I couldn't. My hands had been tied behind my back to a wooden chair. Suzy and Del Rio sat beside me, similarly trussed.

My head felt like I'd landed on it when I'd dropped from the helicopter. But I was alive and I was conscious. I guess my skull was a bit thicker than Chloe's, which would be unusual. Female skulls are usually a little thicker than men's. Maybe whoever had hit me hadn't been as good as Chloe's attacker.

We were in the lounge of a very expensively decorated house. There was color everywhere. Golds and reds and greens. On the expensive rugs that dotted the floor, on the wallpaper that covered the walls, on the drapes that were curled back from the French windows that led out to an extensive lawn, and on the exquisitely upholstered furniture.

I lifted my head and looked across at Suzy and Del Rio, wincing as the pain nailed through the back of my head.

"What happened?" I asked.

"You were hit with a golf club."

"A driver," added Suzy. "Titleist, I think."

"And you guys?"

"People stepped out with semi-automatic weapons. A few of them. We considered it politic to comply with their instructions."

"Hard to argue with an AK-47"

Del Rio nodded. "That is a fact."

"So what's the plan?"

"Not formulated one as such."

At that moment Harlan Shapiro walked into the room.

Chapter 103

HARLAN SHAPIRO'S MOUTH was bound with duct tape and he held his hands high in the air.

He was followed in by Annabelle Weston holding a gun, and by a woman wearing the full burka.

"So it was the professor in the drawing room with the revolver all along," I said.

"Sit over there," Annabelle said to Harlan, ignoring me and gesturing with her gun to a high-backed red leather chair.

Harlan Shapiro crossed over and sat down. Outside, a large man in black fatigues and with a scarf wrapped round his head walked past the French windows.

Mujahedin as security guards. Nice neighborhood.

"And you must be Mary Angela," I said, addressing the woman in the burka. "Shame to cover yourself up—you have beautiful eyes."

The woman swept her hand up, removing the part of her garment covering her head, and swinging her lustrous hair behind her. She looked at me and smiled.

"That's very courteous of you to say so."

I must have registered some surprise because her smile deepened. "Oh, I only wear it when it suits."

"Nice house you have, too. Mister Burka must be paid a pretty penny for his translation skills."

"*I* own the house, Mister Carter," said Annabelle Weston.

Of course she did. "Please call me Dan," I said. "I feel we're bonding, Annabelle."

"I am sure you are a very charming man, Dan. You're handsome, clearly very resourceful, more intelligent than you pretend to be." Annabelle shrugged. "I don't know, in another life."

I didn't like the sound of that. "I quite like this life," I said, hoping that my voice was sounding steady.

"I have no intention of harming you. Nobody needs to get hurt here."

"Tell that to the guy who used the back of my head as a tee peg," I said.

Annabelle frowned. "I'm sorry about that. That wasn't supposed to happen. One of my team with a personal grudge against you. He has been reprimanded."

"Seems to have happened once before. Once too often," I said.

"Again, that was never our intention."

"So what *is* your intention?" asked Del Rio. I could see his jaw working harder than usual. His hands behind the chair flexing and unflexing, trying to loosen the rope.

"Like I said. Nobody is going to be hurt as long as you cooperate"

"So what's the figure? Five million was just for openers, we get that. So what's the number?" Del Rio said.

"It was never about money."

"So what is it about, you mad bitch?" said Suzy coolly, possibly not helping matters.

"It's about justice," said Mary Angela Al-Massri.

"For your brother?"

"No, Mister Carter. For Palestine."

"And your husband thinks this will achieve it?"

"My husband has nothing to do with this. Right now he is at a conference in Brussels."

"So the pair of you figured that you'd solve the problems of Palestine by kidnapping an American millionaire and demanding what for his release? That Israel allow you to set up a nation state just like that?"

"We have no intention of releasing him. Not yet, at least."

"What's the point, then?"

"Our homeland for over a thousand years was taken from us to create the state of Israel. A crime in which the governments of both America and the United Kingdom were complicit."

I noticed the guard pass again. Clearly he

had a regular patrol around the grounds of the house.

"I am familiar with the arguments. Terrorism isn't the solution."

The professor snorted derisively. "You know nothing about it. People resort to what you call terrorism when they have no other choice. Israel has a nuclear capability and Palestinians have slingshots."

Mary Angela came over and took the gun from the professor, keeping it pointed at Harlan Shapiro. She was clearly the one in charge here. "Do you know what Gandhi said of the situation, Mister Carter?" she asked.

I shrugged, as best I could, given that I was tied up pretty tightly. "You say tomato, I say tomato . . . let's call the whole thing off?"

Mary Angela didn't smile. Tough crowd.

"He said *'Palestine belongs to the Arabs in the same sense that England belongs to the English or France to the French. Nothing can be said against the Arab resistance in the face of overwhelming odds.'* And this is not an act of religion. It is an act of peace."

"You lost me there, princess," I said. "Seems to me that's a gun you are holding, not an olive branch or a banana."

I wanted to keep her talking. By my reckoning the guard should have passed by again and he hadn't.

"The only way peace can be brought about in that part of the Middle East is by parity," Annabelle Weston said, the passion sparking in her turquoise eyes.

"All the Palestinians can do by way of retaliation against the fact that a part of their country has been made a concentration camp is to fire small rockets over the border from Gaza."

"And kidnapping Harlan Shapiro does what, exactly?"

Mary Angela looked at me and smiled. I took no comfort from it.

"It will guide those rockets, Mister Carter."

Chapter 104

THE PENNY DROPPED.

Jack had told me that Harlan Shapiro had been working on localized missile-guidance systems.

"And not just over the borders into Israel. Our people have had to resort to the use of suicide bombers to target areas. People prepared to sacrifice themselves to the cause because there was no way of guiding small missiles to a specific target."

The professor smiled at me. It didn't make me feel a whole lot better.

"Hannah's father here has been developing a system that can track to a mobile phone. It means that the missile can be dialed in.

The suicide bomber doesn't even have to be present."

She was right. The implications were enormous. Anywhere could be targeted. If you didn't have to take the explosives through security, you wouldn't need car bombs and bombers could just, as she said, dial destruction right in.

And it wouldn't end there. If this technology got into the hands of Al Qaida who knew what could happen? Their aim wasn't just to drive Israel out of the Middle East, it was to make the whole world Muslim. Jihad didn't do conference tables.

I looked out of the window. The guard had seemingly grown an inch or two taller. About Sam Riddel's height.

I needed to create a distraction. I stood up as best I could, my knees bent.

Mary Angela Al-Massri pointed the gun at me. There was no humor in her eyes, no matter how beautiful they were. "Just sit down, Mister Carter. Like I said, nobody needs to get hurt here. Trust me—I am well trained."

Hamas-trained, I was guessing, just like her brother. Which did not bode well.

I hopped backward and smashed myself into the wall, shattering the chair and loosening the ropes. I stumbled up to my knees.

"I am quite prepared to shoot you."

"Believe her, Dan. You wouldn't be the first," said Annabelle Weston.

The guard came in through the French windows and turned to me.

"If he moves again, shoot him," Mary Angela shouted, her voice ugly now. That's the thing with some of these peace activists: they are so damn keen on killing people.

I stood up and Sam Riddel tossed me the gun and stood aside. I pointed the gun at an astonished Mary Angela and grinned. "Mexican stand-off," I said.

She moved closer to put the gun against Harlan Shapiro's head.

"He'll be the first to die," she said.

I put a single round in her forehead. Turned out she was wrong about that.

Chapter 105

OUTSIDE I COULD just about feel the cold night air on my face.

I was vaguely aware of uniformed men running past me, weapons raised. United States Air Force by the looks of them. They were shouting but I couldn't hear them. I was in a bubble.

I was remembering the unblemished beauty of Mary Angela Al-Massri's face. Her wide, brown, mesmerizing eyes. I remembered the sound that the pistol made, and I remembered the beauty of that face I'd wrecked. The life behind it snuffed out in an instant.

And then I leaned against a tree in the garden and threw up.

I felt a hand on my shoulder. I dragged my hand across my lips and looked up. It was Del Rio.

"You okay?"

"I will be."

He nodded, working his jaw.

"Something I need to take care of first," I said. "Close this case."

He nodded again. "You need some backup?"

I shook my head. "Things are going to get complicated here. I need to make a move."

Del Rio shook his head. "It's all taken care of. We can sort out the details later."

"How so?"

"Jack Morgan has reach."

I nodded gratefully. It was true.

"So. Like I said, you need some backup?"

I shook my head again. "I'll be good."

Del Rio slapped me on the shoulder. "You got some, anyway. And your man who don't handle guns wouldn't be much use in this, I'm guessing."

I nodded gratefully. He was guessing right.

Chapter 106

BRENDAN "SNAKE" FERRES lived in the downstairs maisonette of a converted Victorian town house in Lady Margaret Road on the border of Kentish Town and Tufnell Park.

Del Rio and I had parked the car further down the street and we approached on foot. The curtains were drawn at the front of the house but there was some light spilling from a small gap between them. A television was playing loudly.

I gestured to Del Rio and we made our way around the side of the maisonette into the back garden. The bottom half belonged to the apartment above Ferres: it was neat, well ordered. The top part belonged to Ferres and was the opposite. I stepped over an upturned milk crate in the long grass of what should have been his lawn and walked up to the side door that led into his kitchen.

I had the enforcer gripped in both hands. Del Rio positioned himself to the right-hand side of the door and took his weapon from his holster, holding it two-handed.

The door looked flimsy enough to be simply kicked in but I wasn't taking any chances. I swung the heavy metal ram against the lock.

I stepped back as Del Rio rushed into the house, sweeping his gun from side to side in front of him. I followed behind as he ran forward through the short hallway toward the lounge. I stayed back, dropping the enforcer and taking out the gun I had got from Gary Webster.

A scream rang out from the other room.

Chapter 107

HOLDING THE GUN, I kicked the first door open.

Behind it was an empty bedroom. I waited a moment or two and then did the same with the second door. Another bedroom. No one in it. I let out a sigh of relief, realizing I had been holding my breath, and walked into the lounge.

Del Rio was leaning against the wall, working his jaw muscles and pointing his weapon at Laura Skelton who was cowering against the corner of the sofa, her eyes wide with terror.

If any of the neighbors had heard her scream there was no sign of it. Unless someone was calling the police, of course. But if they were it didn't matter.

I'd already done the same.

I slipped the rucksack off my shoulder and threw it at her.

"What's this?" Her eyes darted back and forth between me and Del Rio.

"Brendan's supplier at Chancellors has gone out of business. We thought your boyfriend might like his gear back."

Laura looked in the bag. "I don't understand."

"You don't have to understand, darling," said Del Rio. "You're not in the game any more."

"Give me your mobile phone," I said.

"I don't have a mobile."

"You want to give him the phone?" Del Rio raised his pistol slightly. "Or you want to be a hero like your fat fuck of a boyfriend?"

She pulled her phone out of her pocket and threw it over to me. I slipped it in my jacket pocket, then bent down and ripped the house phone out of its socket, kicked the junction box off and smashed the connections with my heel.

"You don't know what you're dealing with." Laura crossed her arms and a petulant look appeared on her face.

She was an attractive young woman, no denying that. But there was a hardness in her eyes every bit as ugly as the slap mark bruising her cheek. Brendan Ferres was a hero, all right.

"Where is he, Laura?" I asked.

"You want to shoot me, shoot me. But I'm not putting myself between you and Brendan."

I didn't blame her. And I didn't much care. I knew exactly where he was.

"We're going to the bar now, Laura. You tip him off that we're coming and we'll come back for you and do more than smash your phone in."

If she was cowed by that remark you couldn't have told by the smirk on her face.

"You go up against Brendan Ferres in Ronnie Allen's bar and you won't be going anywhere, tough guy! Except in a hearse."

"You'll be glad to know that Chloe Smith

is out of intensive care—they reckon she'll make a full recovery."

A look flicked through Laura's eyes then. Sure enough, a flicker of fear.

"That wasn't my fault. That wasn't supposed to happen. How were we supposed to know she was going to turn into some kung-fu bloody madwoman?"

"You saying she deserved it?"

The look flashed through her eyes again. "I'm just saying it wasn't my fault. Brendan wasn't supposed to hurt anyone."

I looked at her coldly. "Well, he did. And now he's going to pay for it."

"You got any sense, mister, you'll walk away from him now and keep on walking."

I looked over at Del Rio. "What do you reckon, Del? We should walk away?"

He worked his jaw muscles a little. "Nah," he said. "I don't do walking away."

I looked at my watch. Just over forty-eight hours since it had begun and it was way past time to finish it.

Chapter 108

I PULLED UP the zipper on my jacket.

"Why'd you do it, Laura? You're a bright kid. You're at a top university."

"You got any idea what it costs to go to university nowadays? The sort of debt you leave with?"

"A lot of people deal with it."

Anger danced in her eyes. She had the kind of beauty that made it easy for her to get what she wanted in life. Easy for her to justify her actions to herself. She wore her sense of self-entitlement as easily as she wore her designer jeans.

"Yeah, well, I was dealing with it too," she said. "A little dealing. A little video work.

Then Hannah offered me the big score. Even if her father didn't ante up—and she didn't expect him to—then she was going to pay me big time anyway."

"Never mind who got hurt along the way."

"No one was supposed to get hurt!" Laura shouted at me. "My dad's a plumber, for chrissake! I didn't have money like Hannah and Chloe or most of them at college. I didn't have privilege. All I had was debt. And she had the power to take that away."

She shrugged. "It wasn't a hard call to make. Besides, you know..." She shrugged again, collecting herself, a cruel smile curving her lips. "It was supposed to be fun."

I nodded to Del Rio and we walked out the front door. She'd learn soon enough what fun was.

Five minutes later and we watched from the front seats of my car, parked back a bit and across the road from her house.

Laura came out wearing a black parka, with the rucksack slung over her shoulder. She walked away from us without even looking around. Already high on whatever she had sampled from the media student's stash, no doubt.

She got about twenty yards before DI Kirsty Webb stepped out of an unmarked police car, followed by a uniformed officer, and put her under arrest.

As busts went, it wasn't the high-profile case that Kirsty had been looking to solve this weekend. But it probably gave her a degree of personal satisfaction as she cuffed Laura none too kindly and shoved her head down as she maneuverd her into the back of the car. Like I said, Kirsty was fond of Chloe too.

And also like I said, I had made a call earlier. Laura Skelton might not have made it to a phone box but I had given my ex the heads-up. I had made one other phone call, too.

Del Rio looked at me from the passenger seat. "Ready?" he asked.

I nodded, resisting the impulse to say I was born ready.

"Let's finish it," I said instead.

Chapter 109

THE ENFORCER COULD open triple-locked and bolted doors. The trunk of a BMW was no match. The lid flew open and an alarm started shrieking.

We were in the car park at the back of the Turk's Head, up the road a half-mile or so from where we had watched Laura Skelton being driven away into a whole new world of misery.

Del Rio was leaning, in his normal casual style, against the brick wall of the bar, his gun held alongside his leg, watching the back exit.

A short while later a stocky man came

through the door, some five foot nine inches tall, barrel-chested and with a neck about twice the size of mine. He was carrying a set of car keys in his hand.

"The fuck you think you're doing?" he said to me, not quite believing what he was seeing. His eyes bulging like a pug's on steroids. He pushed the key fob to turn the alarm off.

"He said it was okay," I said and pointed to Del Rio who was now pointing his gun at the bull-necked man.

"You know whose car that is?"

I nodded. "We were invited."

The man looked at Del Rio, his hand twitching. The bulge under his jacket showed he was carrying. I guess he was weighing up the odds.

"I wouldn't," said Del Rio.

The man held his hands up and let Del Rio take his gun off him.

"No one's going to spank you for this," I said to the heavy. "We take full responsibility."

He glared back at me and then smiled. It

was not a pretty sight. "Fuck you," he said. "It's your fucking funeral."

I reached into the boot of Brendan Ferres's BMW and pulled out the baseball bat that I was pretty sure I would find there.

Showtime.

Chapter 110

THE HEAVY WALKED into the bar, hands held high.

There were no customers as such. Ronnie Allen sat at his usual table with Brendan Ferres, the East Coast Mafiosi Sally Manzino and his glamorous companion.

Sitting next to Brendan Ferres was Rebecca Allen, Ronnie Allen's daughter who was engaged to be married to the man whose baseball bat I was holding. She was every bit as large as life as I remembered her. She was dressed to kill in tight jeans, a low-cut peasant blouse, her full lips were painted blood-red and her big blue eyes sparkled beneath the mass of blonde hair that tumbled around her heart-shaped face. I think she rather liked the look of Del Rio. I was probably too much the urban sophisticate for her. She smiled and sat back to watch.

Brendan Ferres turned round to see what she was smiling at and nearly spat out the beer he was drinking. He put his pint down and pulled out a gun. He was fast, I'll give him that much.

"Tell the prick to drop the piece, Carter," he said. "Or I'm going to put one in you."

I flashed a quick smile back at him. "I don't think so, Brendan. You and me, we're going to have a little dance."

"The fuck you talking about?"

Ronnie Allen tapped Brendan on the shoulder. "Give me the gun, Brendan."

Ferres looked at him puzzled for a moment, and then shrugged. "Sure, boss. But shoot him in the gut—I'd like to see him wriggle a while before he dies."

Ronnie Allen held the gun secure on the table. "I believe the gentleman asked you for a dance."

Now Ferres looked really perplexed. "What's going on, Ronnie?"

Rebecca Allen turned her gaze back on me. "Did you bring the item you mentioned on the phone?" Her voice was low but sultry. She reminded me of the young Diana Dors. Marilyn Monroe on steroids, maybe.

I walked across to the table and tossed the DVD I had taken from the media student down in front of her.

Chapter 111

THE DVD WAS titled *Snake Charmer* and the cover featured a naked Brendan Ferres and Laura Skelton.

They were engaging in an act not taught on the media-studies course.

Ferres looked across at it, the color draining from his face. "What the fuck is that?"

"Your contact at Chancellors, Brendan. Laura and the media student. Little sideline for him. He likes to make films. Specialist nature. Mail order." I smiled at him again. "Sometimes people don't even know they are being filmed."

Ferres shook his head. "There's been some kind of mistake," he said to Ronnie Allen. His tongue darting nervously to lick his suddenly dry lips.

"You told me you had nothing to do with his god-daughter being hurt," said Ronnie Allen, his voice soft.

"It was an accident."

"Yeah, her head got in the way, scumbag," I said. "And you were just practicing for a try-out with the New York Yankees."

"Shut the fuck up!" Ferres turned to Ronnie Allen. "Why is this fuck even still here?"

"Because I invited him," said Rebecca Allen. Her voice was warm, friendly, but her eyes had gone arctic cold.

"That's not me." Brendan gestured at the damning evidence.

"You know anyone else who's enough of a dipshit to get a tattoo of a snake doodled on his wing-wang?" I asked.

Brendan Ferres looked at me. The color had come back into his face now. He was flushed with it. A dark angry red.

"Fuck this!" he said and charged at me.

Like I said, he was quick.

I swung the baseball bat, but he got to me

before I could finish the swing. Grabbing me in a bear hug and pushing me backward to smash against the wall.

He locked his arms around me and I held back just as tightly. He was grunting with fury and I couldn't shake him loose.

"You sure you want to do this?" Del Rio asked me, gesturing with his gun to let me know he could put an end to things.

I couldn't speak. Damn it, I couldn't breathe, let alone speak. I shook my head and rammed my knee upward into Ferres's crotch. He moved sideways as I did, grunted but didn't loosen his grip. I dipped my head and then butted upward, catching him under the chin. His grip loosened. I stepped back and drove the end of the baseball bat hard into his solar plexus.

He doubled over, making a painful gurgling sound. I stepped back to take a breath or two into my own pained chest, then swung the baseball bat as hard as I could into his left knee.

Ferres crashed to the floor. His face purple now as he sucked in air, trying to hold his hands to his shattered knee as if he could piece the fractured pieces back together. He looked up at me, a squealing sound issuing from between his clenched teeth.

"Why don't you finish him?"

I turned round. Rebecca Allen was standing behind me, watching her fiancé writhe on the floor in agony.

"I'm done here," I said.

"You don't finish him, he's going to come find you and kill you," said Del Rio.

He was right. I had killed before, God knew. I had killed that very night. Put a round of high-velocity ammunition into the forehead of a beautiful woman. There was nothing beautiful about Brendan Ferres. Nothing redeemable about him as a human being. The world would be a far better place without his breath in it. I pictured him swinging the same bat that I was now holding into Chloe's head. And I pictured myself doing the same to his. Cracking it open like a coconut.

Instead I let my arm go limp, resting the head of the baseball bat on the floor.

I turned to Del Rio. "I'm done here," I said.

"I'm not," said Rebecca Allen, and took the baseball bat from me.

I looked over at her father. "We good?" I asked.

"We're good," he said.

I nodded to Del Rio who touched his fingers to his forehead, tipped them as a kind of salute to Rebecca, and then followed me out of the door.

The door closed mercifully before the screaming started up in earnest again.

I didn't think we would be seeing Brendan Ferres any more. I didn't think I'd lose much sleep over it, either.

An hour and half later I was having three broken ribs checked over in the hospital.

As the doctor stepped away Chloe came into the treatment room and into my arms.

If there were tears in my eyes it was probably because she hugged me a little too hard.

Chapter 112

Morning. One week later.

DETECTIVE INSPECTOR KIRSTY Webb closed her car door behind her.

She ducked under the police-cordon tape that had once again been put up to keep the public away from the lock-up in King's Cross. The same lock-up where the gruesome discovery had been made by the hapless Jason Kendrick just a week before.

Two lock-ups were open now. The one that Kirsty had already seen and the one beside it. The serious-crime squad had worked through the numerous files and boxes of paper that the deceased surgeon Alistair Lloyd had kept in his garage and had made a connection between him and Edward Morrison, the owner of the original lock-up.

Morrison had been part of the ring with the surgeon and a few others, it transpired. They were still compiling a list. Adriana Kisslinger only knew some of the contacts the surgeon had.

Kirsty nodded to Adrian Tuttle as he came out of the building, his camera bag slung over his shoulder.

The inside of the lock-up had been turned into a child's bedroom. A young child's, with a cartoon bedspread on the adult-sized bed, stuffed toys everywhere, including an enormous giant panda. There was a video camera mounted on a tripod facing the bed.

Doctor Wendy Lee was handing some paperwork to Kirsty's boss, DSI Andrew Harrington, for him to sign. She nodded briefly to Kirsty as she passed, clearly in a hurry to get out of the place. Kirsty didn't blame her. Just being there made her skin itch, made her want to turn around and stand in a hot shower for thirty minutes.

Instead, she reached into her pocket and drew out an envelope with her letter of resignation inside and looked across at her boss.

DSI Harrington was a slightly built man in his mid-forties. He was of average height with a sallow complexion and a receding hairline. His teeth were slightly nicotine-stained and his eyes could not hold her gaze for long. She had never liked the man.

"I'm sorry you didn't get the job, Kirsty," he said.

"Most likely the better man did."

"You're a field operative. It's what you're good at. Do you really see yourself behind a desk, juggling phones and computer files?"

"No, I don't, sir. Which is why, as I said, I'm resigning."

She held out the envelope.

"You absolutely sure about this?"

"Yeah, I am."

"I'll keep it in my drawer for a week or so. You're due the leave anyway."

"Won't make any difference."

"Still."

Kirsty nodded, then looked around the

"set" that had been constructed in the lock-up. She didn't care to think about what had taken place there and was heartily glad she didn't have to view the DVDs they had found, or try to identify the victims.

"So this just about wraps it up?" she said.

"I guess it does."

Kirsty knew that her failure to get the job was partly down to Harrington and the testimonial he had written. She wasn't supposed to have seen it but she had. She had access to resources of her own. Maybe it was flattering that he had been careful enough to praise her, but Harrington had left enough between the lines to edge her out. He wanted to keep her on his team. Keep her on his terms. And she'd had enough of that.

Which was why she walked out of the lock-up and didn't tell him how wrong he had been.

Wrong about everything.

This didn't wrap it up at all.

Chapter 113

THE SURGEON KNELT down and removed the wilted flowers from the vases on the left and right of the small plot.

She laid them neatly to one side. Replaced them with fresh flowers as a shadow fell across the white pea shingle.

"Can I help you?" she asked without looking around. The surgeon was of medium height and dressed in a dark gray trouser suit. Her hair was silver, the color of brushed aluminum. Her eyes were alert, intelligent but filled with sadness.

"My name's Kirsty Webb, Doctor Lloyd. I'm a detective inspector from the Metropolitan Police."

"I thought you might be." Doctor Lloyd gathered the flowers she had collected, put them in a plastic shopping bag and stood up.

"I'm here to talk about your husband."

"Ex-husband. We were divorced over a year ago. Attention to details, detective. I should imagine it is just as vital in your line of work as it is in mine."

"The devil is in the detail?"

"Gods and devils. I guess your job is finding out which."

"We get there in the end. Sometimes."

The surgeon nodded. "So what led you to me?"

"Everything was a little too neat." Kirsty shrugged. "Something about it all seemed hinky to me."

"Hinky?"

"Something not quite right. An American expression. My husband is over-fond of using them, I'm afraid."

"You're not wearing a ring."

"Ex-husband, I should have said."

The older woman tilted her head slightly, as if approving.

"I went to the pubs near to the area where Colin Harris's body was found. He had alcohol in his system. Sleeping medication. We were supposed to think it was suicide—but things didn't add up."

"I see."

"One of the barmen in a local bar recognized his picture. Remembered him drinking a short while before the incident. He was with a woman. The woman he described matched you, Doctor Lloyd, when I looked into it. I showed the barman your photo from the hospital records and he confirmed it."

"Female intuition?"

Kirsty shook her head. "Police intuition."

Doctor Lloyd gazed down at the grave of her daughter. "Female intuition isn't all it's cracked up to be, is it?" she said.

Chapter 114

"WHEN DID YOU find out about him?" Kirsty asked.

Doctor Lloyd looked up at her for a moment or two, then sighed. Her whole body relaxed, as if an intolerable burden that she had been carrying for some time had been lifted from her. Her eyes were still desolate, however. Filled with the kind of pain that can never go away.

"About the sort of monster he was?"

Kirsty waited for her to continue.

"You'd think a wife would know. It's the sort of detail, after all, that..." Doctor Lloyd shook her head, letting the words trail off. The enormity of what she had discovered seemingly beyond her power to articulate it. "She came to me. The whore…"

"Andrea Kisslinger?"

Anger sparked in the surgeon's eyes. "Alistair was paying her. But not enough. It never is enough for people like her, is it? She figured the shame and the scandal. But she didn't realize…"

The older woman bent over and straightened the new flowers, not speaking for nearly a minute. Kirsty waited, letting her compose her thoughts, find the words she needed to say.

"She was nine years old, inspector, and she hanged herself."

Kirsty nodded—she already knew. "I'm sorry."

"Have you any idea what it is like for a mother to walk in to her child's bedroom and discover that?"

"I can't even imagine."

"I watch people die every day, Inspector Webb. It's my job. As much as I…as we try to save them. We can't. We can't save them all."

"I know."

"Some people don't deserve to live, it's as simple as that. You see a cancer, you cut it out, you stop the infection spreading if you can. People say we doctors play God, and in some ways we do. Once you have had the power of life and death...well, it wasn't hard to do what I did. At least they gave something to others in the end. One of them even saved a life. A deserving life. Shame it couldn't have worked like that with the others."

"Why take the organs, then?"

"Evidence, inspector. Just enough, no more. The final nail, if you like, in his coffin." Doctor Lloyd smiled humorlessly, her lips thin with more than the chill in the air. "I know the police like things tied up as neatly as we surgeons do."

Kirsty Webb looked at the older woman's eyes. To her, she seemed perfectly sane. Sounded perfectly rational. Who knew... maybe she was. Compared with her husband and people like him—maybe she wasn't mad at all.

"You confronted Alistair?"

"I gave him a choice, inspector." She looked down at the small grave. "Which was more than Emily had."

"You should have come to us."

"You'd think it would be hard for this kind of people to find each other, wouldn't you? But it isn't. And do you know why, Inspector Webb?"

Kirsty shook her head.

"Because there are so damn many of them. And you all know that."

Kirsty didn't reply. She didn't need to. The woman was right. Doctor Lloyd straightened herself. A half-smile played on her lips for a moment and she squared her shoulders.

"So are you going to place me under arrest?" she said. "You have no proof, I take it, other than that a woman who looked like me was seen in a bar with Colin Harris?"

"You seem quite confident of that."

"You're on your own, inspector. I know how these things work. You'd have squad cars, lights flashing, sirens. There'd be a news crew filming you making the arrest of your career. All you have, after all, is a barman's vague recollection prompted by yourself. I think it's called leading the witness. And your *instincts*, of course. But I don't think you'll find that they are recognized as evidence in a court of law."

"My instincts aren't important now."

"And why's that?"

"Because I resigned from the force this morning. I'm not in the police any more."

"So why are you here?"

"Because I needed to know."

"Either way, it's over now." But the surgeon's shoulders sagged again, contradicting her words. It could never be over for her.

"Turn yourself in, Doctor Lloyd."

"And who is that going to help?"

Kirsty looked at her sympathetically as tears welled in the older woman's eyes. "You," she said softly.

"And who would bring Emily flowers? Who would look after her then?"

The woman couldn't hold the tears back now and Kirsty put her arms around her. Doctor Lloyd's heart was pounding, her fragile form fluttering within the younger woman's embrace. She felt as though her bones were hollow.

In some ways, ex-Detective Inspector Kirsty Webb was glad she had resigned earlier that day. Justice as far as the law was concerned was a matter of science. But people weren't machines. She didn't know what the other woman, even now crumpling in on herself, deserved. That was way beyond Kirsty's area of expertise. Police didn't get to make that call. Their job was to unearth the facts, and Kirsty didn't believe she had the moral compass to put these facts in order and make a judgment. She was glad she didn't have to.

She'd made a call to Detective Inspector Natalie James just before she had handed in her notice.

She figured things would fall as they did.

Chapter 115

I STOOD BY the window, watching Alison Chambers walk to her car once more.

A week had passed. She still swung her hips, still flipped the bird at me over her shoulder as she got into the driver's seat. Nothing had changed, it seemed, but everything had.

Like I say, some cases you win, some you lose—and some you win but it doesn't feel like it.

I had killed a woman and that wasn't something you just shake off like the rain from your hair.

I remembered the noise, the shouting, the mayhem. At the time I had let it wash past me. But it still visited me in my dreams at night. I knew how that worked, though. In time it would pass. My hands might have been bloody but my conscience was clean. I had done the job I had been paid to do.

When I hadn't made contact as agreed, Sam had called the contact in the USAF based at HMS *Warrior* a mile away that Jack Morgan had given us and had come in ahead of them. They weren't far behind him. The Palestinians took two more casualties before they were overrun. Score three for democracy, nil for terrorism, I figured. Only, like I say, it didn't feel like that.

Men in black suits arrived. In the old days they would have been CIA and MI5. Nowadays it was Homeland Security for the U.S. of A and some unknown quasi-military unit sanctioned by the Home Office for us. Either way, it was like a Mafia clean-up crew sent in to eradicate evidence, dispose of the bodies.

The professor and the remaining members of her team who were still alive—including Ashleigh Roughton, the CUL rugby captain— were spirited away. Turned out that Roughton thought the professor was in love with him as well.

As far as the suits were concerned—officially, we were never there. Del Rio and I left to settle matters with Brendan Ferres. Harlan Shapiro was taken to be reunited with his daughter and they were booked on a hastily scheduled jet to fly them straight back to the States first thing in the morning.

I never saw either of them again.

Part of me felt that Hannah should have stayed behind to face some sort of music for the sequence of events that she had set in motion. Mostly, though, I felt glad that it was all over. Hannah and her father were back under the watchful eye of Jack Morgan. They were his concern now.

I turned and looked at Bogart and Bacall. Marlowe looked like he was judging me, as ever. I didn't care. It was Friday evening, I had the weekend ahead of me and once again Dan Carter had a date lined up. I smiled at Bacall. "Here's looking at you, kid."

Chapter 116

IF THE COOL blonde at reception was pleased to see me back at the restaurant once more there was no clue to it in her perfectly made-up face.

I was wearing my blue tie again, with a black linen suit this time. It gave me an air of casual sophistication, I thought. I didn't want to send out the wrong signals. After all, it was just a dinner. Not a dinner date. We had both been clear about that. Very clear.

Blondie ran her finger down the list of bookings again, her left eyebrow raised a minuscule amount once more, enough to make a point.

"Ah yes, Mister Cotter. I remember you

couldn't stay very long with us on your last visit."

"It's Carter," I said. "Dan Carter. And no, I am afraid something came up. Work. You know how it is?"

"Might I recommend you turn off your mobile phone?" she said. "You were very lucky we were able to fit you in again at such short notice. I'd hate for another evening to be spoiled for you."

Frankly, it looked like that was exactly what she would have liked. And she was right. I should have turned my phone off. But doing so then, after being practically told to do so by a jumped-up waitress, was never going to happen.

"I can't do that, I am afraid," I said. "I'm a surgeon. Heart surgeon. Pediatric heart surgeon."

See, that's the trouble with lies—they can run away with you. My companion snorted but said nothing, and the receptionist inched her eyebrow a scintilla further heavenwards.

"Follow me, then, please, Doctor Carter," she said.

"That's Mister Carter," I replied. I guess she'd thought she'd catch me out. She'd have to get up a lot earlier in the morning to do that.

"That a new suit, Dan?" asked Kirsty as we were led to my table.

I laughed. "Hardly. Why do you ask?"

"Because you've got a label still on the back of your trousers."

The receptionist chuckled and held out a chair for Kirsty. I swept my hand around the back of my trousers. There was nothing there.

"You're too easy," said Kirsty as she sat down.

I joined her and picked up the wine list. "So why were you running late?"

"I had to see someone."

"So are we celebrating?"

"Did I get the job, you're asking?"

I nodded.

"As far as that goes, no, we are not celebrating."

"I'm sorry to hear that."

"Sorry that I'm not moving to Manchester?"

I looked at her. Her emerald green eyes still the kind that a man fell into and drowned. "Sorry that you didn't get what you wanted," I said.

"Are we still talking about the job?"

"What are you going to do now?"

Kirsty picked up the menu. "I'm going to consider my options"

"I've heard the prawn cocktail is very good," I said.

She laughed. I liked the sound of it. Gave me an idea I'd probably regret.

Twenty minutes later and our starter arrived. I was having creamed truffled goat's cheese, with asparagus and pickled beetroot. My partner, as they say, plumped for the twice-baked Norfolk dapple soufflé with a mixed-leaf salad and a herb vinaigrette. No drop scones and fish eggs for us.

I took a sip of my lager, picked up my fork and was about to spear a beetroot when my mobile phone rang. Noisily. I smiled apologetically at the diners at the neighboring table and fished it out of my pocket.

Even as I looked at the caller ID Kirsty

snatched it out of my hand. She saw who was calling too and switched the phone off, throwing me a withering look as she did so.

"I cannot believe that woman."

Alison Chambers, of course.

Moments later her own phone trilled—a lot more quietly than mine had. I shrugged at the neighboring diners again. What could you do?

"Kirsty Webb?" she answered. A degree of coldness that would have chilled an Inuit creeping into her voice.

She listened for a moment or two and then nodded. "Okay. I'll tell him." She hung up without waiting for a reply and served me a cool look.

"That was Alison," she said.

I had gathered that much.

"She's down at Paddington Green nick."

"And...?"

"And she's there representing one of your clients."

"Good for her, but I'm sure it's nothing that can't wait until morning."

"Sean Chester has just been murdered."

I put my fork down, the uneaten beetroot still speared on its tines. Sean Chester had been one of our clients. The ex-producer on one of the biggest *continuing dramas* as they called them nowadays.

"What happened?"

"He was shot dead two hours ago, Dan. And they've arrested your favorite star Melinda Hamilton for it."

Another one of our clients. "They booked her?"

"No. She's not been charged yet, but your hotshot lawyer girlfriend reckons it's a matter of hours, not days."

I sighed, finished my beer and reached for my jacket.

"Well, are you coming or not?" I said.

"I'm off the job," Kirsty replied.

"Not any more," I said, standing up and giving her the full Dan Carter wattage.

"Welcome to Private."

About the Authors

JAMES PATTERSON has created more enduring fictional characters than any other novelist writing today. He is the author of the Alex Cross novels, the most popular detective series of the past twenty-five years. He also writes the bestselling Women's Murder Club novels, set in San Francisco, and the top-selling New York detective series of all time, featuring Detective Michael Bennett. James Patterson has had more *New York Times* bestsellers than any other writer, ever, according to *Guinness World Records*. Since his first novel won the Edgar Award in 1977, James Patterson's books have sold more than 240 million copies. For previews of his upcoming books and more

information about the author, visit www
.JamesPatterson.com.

MARK PEARSON is the author of Britain's
bestselling Jack Delaney crime series. In
addition to his novel writing, he is a multi-
award-nominated television scriptwriter and
has worked on a variety of shows for the BBC
and ITV.

JAMES PATTERSON PRESENTS
A THRILLING NEW NOVEL IN HIS
SIZZLING PRIVATE SERIES…

The world's best investigators from
Private search for a missing agent
whose secrets can plunge Berlin
into a new darkness.

Please turn this page
for an exciting preview of

Private Berlin.

One

AT TEN O'CLOCK on a moonless September evening, Chris Schneider slipped toward a long abandoned building on the eastern outskirts of Berlin, his mind whirling with dark images and old vows.

Late-thirties, and dressed in dark clothes, Schneider drew out a .40 Glock pistol and eased forward, alert to the dry rustle of the thorn bushes and goldenrod and the vines that engulfed the place.

He hesitated, staring at the silhouette of the building, recalling some of the horror that he'd felt coming here for the first time, and realizing that he'd been waiting almost three decades for this moment.

Indeed, for ten years he'd trained his mind and body.

For ten years after that he'd actively sought revenge, but to no avail.

In the past decade, Schneider had come to believe it might never happen, that his past had not only disappeared, it had died; and with it the chance to exact true payback for himself and the others.

But here was his chance to be the avenging angel they'd all believed in.

Schneider heard voices in his mind, all shrieking at him to go forward and put a just ending to their story.

At their calling, Schneider felt himself harden inside. They deserved a just ending. He intended to give it to them.

By now he'd reached the steps of the building. The chain hung from the barn doors, which stood ajar. He stared at the darkness, feeling his gut hollow and his knees weaken.

You've waited a lifetime, Schneider told himself. Finish it. Now.

For all of us.

Schneider toed open the door. He stepped inside, smelling traces of stale urine, burnt copper, and something dead.

His mind flashed with the image of a door swinging shut and locking, and for a moment that alone threatened to cripple him completely.

But then Schneider felt righteous vengeance ignite inside him. He pressed the safety lever on the trigger, readying it to fire. He flicked on the flashlight taped to the gun, giving him a soft red beam with which to dissect the place.

Boot prints marred the dust.

Schneider's heart pounded as he followed them. Cement rooms, more like stalls really, stood to either side of the passage. Even though the footprints went straight ahead, he searched the rooms one by one. In the last, he stopped and stared, seeing a horror film playing behind his eyes.

He tore his attention away, but noticed his gun hand was trembling.

The hallway met a second set of barn

doors. The lock hung loose in the hasp. The doors were parted a foot, leading into a cavernous space.

He heard fluttering, stepped inside, and aimed his light and pistol into the rafters, seeing pigeons blinking in their roost.

The smell of death was worse here. Schneider swung his light all around, looking for the source. Rusted bolts jutted from the floor. Girders and trusses overhead supported a track that ran the length of the space.

Corroded hooks hung on chains from the track.

The footprints cut diagonally left away from the doorway. He followed, aware of those bolts in the floor, and not wanting to trip.

Schneider meant to look into the girders again, but was distracted by something scampering ahead of him. He crouched, aiming the gun and light toward the noise.

A line of rats scurried toward a gaping hole in the floor on the far side of the room. The boot prints went straight to the hole and disappeared. He heard rats squealing and hissing the closer he got.

To the left of the hole stood a metal tube of a slightly smaller diameter than the hole. Atop it lay a sewer grate. On the right of the hole was a small gas blower, the kind used to get clippings off walkways.

Schneider stepped to the hole and shined the light into a shaft of corrugated steel. Ten feet down, the shaft ended in space. Four feet below that lay a gravel floor.

A female corpse sprawled on the gravel. Rats were swarming her.

Schneider knew her nonetheless.

He'd been searching for her all over Berlin and Germany, hoping against hope that she was alive.

But he was far, far too late.

The desire for vengeance that had been a low flame inside Schneider fueled and exploded through him now. He wanted to shoot at anything that moved. He wanted to scream into the hole and call out her killer to receive his just due.

But then Schneider's colder, rational side took over.

This was bigger than him now, bigger than all of us. It wasn't about revenge anymore. It was about bringing someone heinous into the harsh light, exposing him for what he was and what he had been.

Go outside, he thought. Call the KriPo. Get them involved. Now.

Schneider turned and, sweeping the room behind him with the light, started back toward the hallway. He had taken six or seven steps when he heard what sounded like a very large bird fluttering.

He tried to react, tried to get his gun moving up toward the sound.

But the dark figure was already dropping from his hiding spot in the deep shadows above the rusted overhead track.

Boots struck Schneider's collarbones. He collapsed backward and landed on one of those bolts sticking up out of the floor.

The bolt impaled him, broke his spine, and paralyzed him.

The Glock clattered away.

There was so much fiery pain Schneider could not speak, let alone scream. The silhouette of a man appeared above him. He aimed his flashlight at his own upper body, revealing a man wearing a black mask that covered his nose, cheeks, and forehead.

The masked man began to speak, and Schneider knew him instantly, as if twenty-eight years had passed in a day.

"You thought you were prepared for this, Chris, hmmm?" the masked man asked, amused. He made a clicking noise in his throat. "You were never prepared for this, no matter what you may have told yourself all those years ago."

A knife appeared in the masked man's other hand. He squatted by Rolf, and touched the blade to his throat.

"My friends will come quicker if I bleed you," he said. "A few hours in their care, and your mask will be gone, Chris. No one would ever recognize you then, not even your own dear, sweet mother, hmmm?"

Books by James Patterson

FEATURING ALEX CROSS

Merry Christmas, Alex Cross

Kill Alex Cross

Cross Fire

I, Alex Cross

Alex Cross's TRIAL (with Richard DiLallo)

Cross Country

Double Cross

Cross (also published as *Alex Cross*)

Mary, Mary

London Bridges

The Big Bad Wolf

Four Blind Mice

Violets Are Blue

Roses Are Red

Pop Goes the Weasel

Cat & Mouse

Jack & Jill

Kiss the Girls

Along Came a Spider

THE WOMEN'S MURDER CLUB

11th Hour (with Maxine Paetro)

10th Anniversary (with Maxine Paetro)

The 9th Judgment (with Maxine Paetro)

The 8th Confession (with Maxine Paetro)

7th Heaven (with Maxine Paetro)

The 6th Target (with Maxine Paetro)

The 5th Horseman (with Maxine Paetro)

4th of July (with Maxine Paetro)

3rd Degree (with Andrew Gross)

2nd Chance (with Andrew Gross)

1st to Die

FEATURING MICHAEL BENNETT

I, Michael Bennett (with Michael Ledwidge)

Tick Tock (with Michael Ledwidge)

Worst Case (with Michael Ledwidge)

Run for Your Life (with Michael Ledwidge)

Step on a Crack (with Michael Ledwidge)

THE PRIVATE NOVELS

Private Games (with Mark Sullivan)

Private: #1 Suspect (with Maxine Paetro)

Private (with Maxine Paetro)

STANDALONE BOOKS

NYPD Red

Zoo

Guilty Wives (with David Ellis)

The Christmas Wedding (with Richard DiLallo)

Kill Me If You Can (with Marshall Karp)

Now You See Her (with Michael Ledwidge)

Toys (with Neil McMahon)

Don't Blink (with Howard Roughan)

The Postcard Killers (with Liza Marklund)

The Murder of King Tut (with Martin Dugard)

Swimsuit (with Maxine Paetro)

Against Medical Advice (with Hal Friedman)

Sail (with Howard Roughan)

Sundays at Tiffany's (with Gabrielle Charbonnet)

You've Been Warned (with Howard Roughan)

The Quickie (with Michael Ledwidge)

Judge & Jury (with Andrew Gross)

Beach Road (with Peter de Jonge)

Lifeguard (with Andrew Gross)

Honeymoon (with Howard Roughan)

Sam's Letters to Jennifer

The Lake House

The Jester (with Andrew Gross)

The Beach House (with Peter de Jonge)

Suzanne's Diary for Nicholas

Cradle and All

When the Wind Blows

Miracle on the 17th Green (with Peter de Jonge)

Hide & Seek

The Midnight Club

Black Friday (originally published as *Black Market*)

See How They Run

Season of the Machete

The Thomas Berryman Number

santaKid

FOR READERS OF ALL AGES

MAXIMUM RIDE

ANGEL: A Maximum Ride Novel

FANG: A Maximum Ride Novel

MAX: A Maximum Ride Novel

Maximum Ride: The Final Warning

Maximum Ride: Saving the World and Other Extreme Sports

Maximum Ride: School's Out—Forever

Maximum Ride: The Angel Experiment

DANIEL X

Daniel X: Game Over (with Ned Rust)

Daniel X: Demons and Druids (with Adam Sadler)

Daniel X: Watch the Skies (with Ned Rust)

The Dangerous Days of Daniel X (with Michael Ledwidge)

WITCH & WIZARD

Witch & Wizard: The Fire (with Jill Dembowski)

Witch & Wizard: The Gift (with Ned Rust)

Witch & Wizard (with Gabrielle Charbonnet)

MIDDLE SCHOOL

Middle School: Get Me Out of Here (with Chris Tebbetts, illustrated by Laura Park)

Middle School: The Worst Years of My Life (with Chris Tebbetts, illustrated by Laura Park)

For previews and information about the author, visit JamesPatterson.com or find him on Facebook or at your app store.

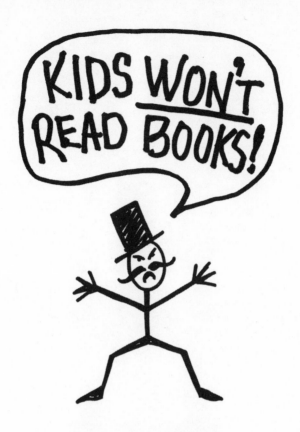